It had been dislike at first sight.

Oh, Andrew Addison was too Ivy League, stick-in-the-mud well-mannered to actually have said the words, but Daisy had seen the disapproval written across her brother-in-law's icy patrician face.

They had been forced to stand next to one another at the baptismal font while the priest murmured over Jeremy Channing Addison's little head. Animosity had hummed between them.

Each had come away that day with a definite impression of the other. Drew thought Daisy was a mindless idiot. Daisy thought Drew was a pompous jackass.

That had been four years ago. Today their orphaned nephew had become Daisy's responsibility. And Drew was pulling up in the driveway.

"Show time," Daisy muttered as the big car came to a halt.

Dear Reader,

Last year, I requested that you send me your opinions on the books that we publish—and on romances in general. Thank you so much for the many thoughtful comments. For the next couple of months, I'd like to share with you quotes from those letters. This seems very appropriate now, while we are in the midst of the THAT SPECIAL WOMAN! promotion. Each one of our readers is a special woman, as heroic as the heroines in our books.

This August has some wonderful books coming your way. *More Than He Bargained For* by Carole Halston, a warm, poignant story, is the THAT SPECIAL WOMAN! selection. Debbie Macomber also brings us the first book in her FROM THIS DAY FORWARD series—*Groom Wanted*. MORGAN'S MERCENARIES, Lindsay McKenna's action-packed trio concludes this month with *Commando*. And don't miss books from other favorite authors: Marie Ferrarella, Susan Mallery and Christine Rimmer.

I hope you enjoy this book, and all of the stories to come! Have a wonderful August!

Sincerely,

Tara Gavin
Senior Editor
Silhouette Books

Quote of the Month: "Romance books provide the escape that is needed from the sometimes crazy and hard-to-live-in world. It takes me away for that three or four hours a day to a place no one else can come into. That is why I read romances. Because sometimes there is not a happy ending, and going to a place where there is can uplift the spirit that really needs it."

—J. Majeski
New Jersey

MARIE FERRARELLA

FAMILY MATTERS

SPECIAL EDITION®

Published by Silhouette Books New York
America's Publisher of Contemporary Romance

To Valerie Hayward
With Love,
For Understanding
And Having Faith

SILHOUETTE BOOKS
300 East 42nd St., New York, N.Y. 10017

FAMILY MATTERS

Copyright © 1993 by Marie Rydzynski-Ferrarella

ISBN: 0-373-09832-4

First Silhouette Books printing August 1993

All the characters in this book have no existence outside the
imagination of the author and have no relation whatsoever to
anyone bearing the same name or names. They are not even
distantly inspired by any individual known or unknown to the
author, and all incidents are pure invention.

®: Trademark used under license and registered in the United States
Patent and Trademark Office and in other countries.

Printed in the U.S.A.

Books by Marie Ferrarella

Silhouette Special Edition

It Happened One Night #597
A Girl's Best Friend #652
Blessing in Disguise #675
Someone To Talk To #703
World's Greatest Dad #767
Family Matters #832

Silhouette Intimate Moments

Holding Out for a Hero #496
Heroes Great and Small #501

Silhouette Books

Silhouette Christmas Stories 1992
"The Night Santa Claus Returned"

Silhouette Romance

The Gift #588
Five-Alarm Affair #613
Heart to Heart #632
Mother for Hire #686
Borrowed Baby #730
Her Special Angel #744
*The Undoing of
   Justin Starbuck* #766
Man Trouble #815
The Taming of the Teen #839
Father Goose #869
Babies on His Mind #920
The Right Man #932
In Her Own Backyard #947

Books by Marie Ferrarella writing as Marie Nicole

Silhouette Desire

Tried and True #112
Buyer Beware #142
Through Laughter and Tears #161
Grand Theft: Heart #182
A Woman of Integrity #197
Country Blue #224
Last Year's Hunk #274
Foxy Lady #315
Chocolate Dreams #346
No Laughing Matter #382

Silhouette Romance

Man Undercover #373
Please Stand By #394
Mine by Write #411
Getting Physical #440

MARIE FERRARELLA

was born in Europe, raised in New York City and now lives in Southern California. She describes herself as the tired mother of two overenergetic children and the contented wife of one wonderful man. She is thrilled to be following her dream of writing full-time.

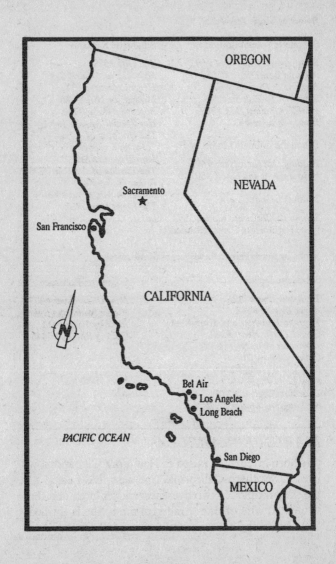

Chapter One

Anastasia "Daisy" Channing sat on the window seat of the nursery she had helped her brother-in-law and older sister wallpaper five years ago. Five years ago, when Jonathan and Alyce had been so full of life, so vital, and the future had looked wonderfully promising.

A lifetime ago.

Cartoon-faced yellow suns played hide-and-seek with pink and blue lambs across green meadows. The wallpaper had been Jonathan's choice. Jonathan, who was light-years from the Jonathan he had been the day he had stepped into Alyce's life. Or more accurately, the day she had rushed into his. With the Mustang.

An accident had brought them together and now an accident had taken them away.

But at least they're together.

Daisy hugged herself as she struggled to contain tears, listening to their only child breathe peacefully in his bed as he slept. She leaned her head against the windowpane, the cool glass soothing her aching head. But what would soothe the ache she felt in her heart?

She watched the rain fall at a steady pace. Drops slid down the multi-paned window just the way tears slid down inside of her soul.

Why?

Why did it have to be them? Why not two other people? *Anyone* else. Even her and...and Jonathan's brother, Drew, she thought hopelessly as she knotted her fingers together. Alyce and Jonathan had had so much to live for, so much love to give.

And they had Jeremy.

She looked over toward the bunk bed. Jeremy had been so proud of selecting it. It had been his first "big boy" decision and Alyce and Jonathan had applauded it.

Daisy brushed the heel of her hand against her cheek, angry at the tears, angry at the world, angry at the waste.

Now she was the one who was responsible for Jeremy. Six months ago, Alyce and Jonathan had asked her to become Jeremy's legal guardian in the event that something unforeseen ever happened. She had felt spooked just signing the papers. They had said it was only a formality and not to let it bother her.

But the unforeseen had happened and Daisy hadn't the slightest idea about how to go on, how to relieve this awful emptiness inside that was gnawing away at every fiber of her being

Alyce had been her big sister, her rock. Her best friend. Alyce and Jonathan and then Jeremy had been her family. Now there was just Jeremy. Jeremy and her.

Oh, God.

Daisy dragged her hand through her long black hair and squeezed her eyes shut. The haunting words echoed in her head. The words she had heard three days ago that had shattered life as she knew it. She had been standing in the kitchen, singing along with the radio as she prepared lunch for Jeremy. The news came on and a deep-voiced newscaster stated that a single-engine Cessna had gone down on the western side of the Rockies. The man had no idea that he was forever changing her life, hers and Jeremy's, as he said that there appeared to be no survivors.

She had dropped the pot of soup all over the floor. Over and over again, Daisy had told herself not to panic. Alyce and Jonathan weren't the only ones with a single-engine Cessna. Southern California was full of them. The planes almost littered the grounds of every airport between LAX and John Wayne Airport. Damn, the whole country was full of them.

But she had known.

Even as she dialed the radio station to get any shred of information she could, Daisy had known. All four of them were supposed to have been on that plane, on their way to a vacation in the cabin in the Rockies. Jonathan had given the cabin to Alyce as a fifth wedding anniversary present. This was to be a celebration. But Jeremy had woken up with a cold and Daisy had volunteered to stay with him, urging Alyce and Jonathan to get away and have a second honeymoon.

New tears came, hot and stinging. She rubbed those angrily away, as well. Now her anger, fueled by guilt, was aimed at herself.

If I had kept my big mouth shut, they'd both still be here.

But they weren't here. Not any longer. And because of a twist of fate, she had a little soul to watch over. She pressed her lips together, digging deep for control. She couldn't think of herself now, couldn't dwell on her own grief. She had Jeremy to think of and he made all the difference in the world. From now on, she would have to be both mother and father to him.

She wasn't going to think, she told herself, just do. She had already taken care of all the funeral arrangements, seen to everything that needed handling. She'd even notified Drew.

She shifted uncomfortably, unconsciously bracing her shoulders as she remembered him.

She had first called his home, then his office as soon as she had gotten back from the site of the wreckage. As soon as she had gotten back the use of her voice. Drew couldn't be reached, so she had finally left a lengthy message with a secretary who sounded as if her last job had been with the British prime minister. The woman had softened considerably as she had listened to Daisy recount the details, her voice catching at times, making it difficult to go on.

Drew never returned her call. Instead his secretary had called, stating that he was catching the first flight out and would be there to take care of things.

As if he thought she couldn't. That was Drew for you, she thought.

It had been dislike at first sight.

At least, she was certain it was for him. Andrew Addison was too Ivy League, stick-in-the-mud, well-mannered to actually have said the words, but Daisy had seen it in his eyes, in the set of his jaw. It was as if it was written across his icy patrician face.

By the way Drew looked at Alyce it was easy to tell that he disapproved of her sister, disapproved of the way Alyce had turned his straitlaced brother Jonathan into someone who no longer lived and breathed Dow Jones, into someone who appreciated the world outside of the *Wall Street Journal* and corporate stocks.

Drew's censure had been there the moment he had murmured a subdued hello to Alyce when he had arrived at the house for Jeremy's christening. Having missed the wedding a year earlier, this had been Drew's first meeting with his brother's new wife. His displeasure was instantly evident to Daisy.

There was nothing that aroused Daisy's ire faster than someone being critical of Alyce. And so, though Daisy and Drew had been forced to stand next to one another at the baptismal font while the kindly looking priest had murmured the appropriate words over Jeremy Channing Addison's little head, there had been nothing but the hum of animosity between them.

Alyce and her obvious effect on Jonathan hadn't been the only thing Daisy and Drew disagreed upon. As the party wore on, each time they were within the confines of the same conversation—no matter how else or how many other people were involved—Daisy and Drew wound up being at loggerheads. There didn't seem to be a single thing that they saw in the same light.

Each had come away that day with a definite impression of the other. Drew thought she was a mindless, happy idiot who took maddening delight in arguing with him about everything under the sun. Daisy thought Drew was an opinionated, pompous jackass who had missed all of life while being trapped inside the glass of his forty-story building. He was like a fly captured in amber, well preserved, but not alive.

In Drew's case, Daisy doubted that he had ever *been* alive. It was with great relief that she saw him board the plane bound for New York the next day.

That had been four years ago last June. The handful of times Drew had come to Southern California for a visit, Daisy had tried her best, for the sake of family harmony, to crack the six-inch-thick wall of ice the man seemed to have around him. To no avail. Though he was Jonathan's younger brother, he lacked Jonathan's soul.

They probably forgot to issue him one at the corporation, she thought now, miserably.

Daisy pulled her knees up to her chest, wishing she was six again and didn't have to deal with anything. Life after that age had gotten complicated. But she had always had Alyce. Wonderful, sunny Alyce. No one could ever be unhappy around her. Jonathan had discovered that. Reserved and almost humorless when they'd first met, Jonathan had thawed out to become a warm, giving human being once Alyce got to work on him.

It was something Drew probably never forgave Alyce for.

Drew reminded Daisy of Uncle Warren. Uncle Warren had been her mother's older brother. Part of a rock band, her parents left Alyce and her in Warren's care under the pretext of giving the girls a stable home while they were on the road with their band. They were away three hundred out of three hundred sixty-five days almost every year. It would have been a lonely life for the girls if they hadn't had each other. Warren Baxter was not unkind, just never actually kind, either. He treated Alyce and Daisy as he treated everything in his life—fairly but without feeling. They had called him Warren the Warden behind his back.

And now there was no Alyce. Daisy looked over at the sleeping child again and silently swore to Jeremy that he would never lack for love, not even for a moment. Even if she didn't love the boy to distraction, she owed it to Alyce's memory.

Andrew Addison's hands tightened on the steering wheel of the full-size car he had rented at the airport less than half an hour ago. LAX was always difficult to negotiate out of. The fact that Drew wanted to accomplish that feat quickly made it next to impossible.

Nerves frayed and on edge because of the reason for his being here, Drew felt like ramming the cars in his way. For one insane moment, he wanted to maneuver the maroon

Lincoln onto the sidewalk and drive up to Bel Air at eighty miles an hour.

He wanted to outrace his feelings.

Drew felt his emotions churning within him, churning so violently, he felt sick. He hadn't had a moment's peace since his secretary had given him the message. Jonathan was dead. It seemed absolutely impossible. Drew had wanted to call back, to talk to Anastasia and demand that she admit this was all a hideous joke. Part of the macabre thing she called humor.

But he hadn't called back. He hadn't had the courage at that moment to hear the words. He knew it wasn't a joke; in his heart, he knew. It was that odd sixth sense he had about Jonathan, just as he had known, six years ago, that Jonathan wasn't returning from the coast. Though Drew's need to deny the situation was strong, he hadn't been able to talk to Anastasia. If he heard her voice, he was afraid that all his own well-restrained emotions would break down. Control was all he had to hang on to.

Impatient, Drew glared at his speedometer. The needle hovered jerkily around eleven. They were moving at little more than eleven miles an hour. A crawl away from absolute gridlock he thought, biting off a curse as he ran a hand through his dark blond hair. He should have followed through on his impulse to have a helicopter meet him at the airport. There was a large open field behind Jonathan's house that could accommodate a helicopter—

The image of a helicopter had him swallowing and remembering the message that had been so delicately relayed to him. His brother and sister-in-law had been killed. In a plane accident. A single-engine Cessna for God's sake. Jonathan hated flying. He had come out to the west coast via a cross-country train the first time.

It had been his last time, Drew thought ruefully. Because he had fallen in love with a pair of soft brown eyes. Alyce had a face like an angel. Poor Jonathan never knew what hit him. He had been in unfamiliar territory in Alyce's world and had never had a chance against her. It had been a business trip that had ended up in pleasure. And made Jonathan forsake all business.

No, that was unfair, Drew thought. Jonathan hadn't forsaken all business. He had started up a branch of the corporation out here in Bel Air. It had been just the tiniest of grains when the actual silo was back in New York. Jonathan had done it purely to placate him, to try to keep the peace. Drew knew that. And he knew why Jonathan had fallen so hard for Alyce. After Drew had set his initial animosity aside, he saw all the qualities that Jonathan had found so dear. If truth be known, perhaps Drew even envied his older brother a little because he seemed so happy. It wouldn't have been the kind of life Drew would have chosen for himself. To Drew it seemed like an irresponsible madness. But it seemed to make Jonathan happy and he loved his brother enough to want him to be happy.

Now he wasn't anything.

Damn, why had Jonathan ever come out here? If Jonathan had stayed in his office on the fortieth floor, he would still be alive today.

Drew leaned on his horn as a taxi advertising a local radio station in bold magenta letters cut in front of him, making him lose precious feet of space. He swore under his breath and punched the buttons on the dashboard to turn on the air conditioner.

Lukewarm air came in with a great deal of sound and fury, but did nothing to lower the unseasonably warm temperature that pervaded the car. The air conditioner was obviously in need of repair.

So was his life.

Drew scanned through the radio stations, searching for something that would help calm his inner turmoil, knowing there was nothing that could.

He was going to miss Jonathan. God, he was going to miss him. It was one thing not to see him, knowing that Jonathan was somewhere else. Alive, vital, happy. A little crazy maybe, but alive. It was another thing knowing that he would never see his brother again.

Grief was an unfamiliar emotion for Drew. He had never allowed himself to experience it or to give in to its overwhelming, engulfing grip before, though there might have been occasion when his parents had each passed on. He had eluded it then, but he hadn't managed to elude heartbreak's scratchy, grasping fingers today.

He sought refuge in planning his next steps. He'd handle whatever needed to be done with Jonathan's estate. That scatterbrained sister-in-law of his undoubtedly wasn't up to doing anything. He had her pegged as the kind who fell apart easily, unable to deal with the real world. Why else would she always be so maddeningly cheerful each time he had the misfortune to be with her? He felt that people just shouldn't be cheerful as a general rule, not without concrete cause, and then only fleetingly. Lovely though she was, she had the IQ of a pair of shoes. Definitely not the type to shoulder responsibility.

After the funeral, he was going to take Jeremy back to New York with him. Jeremy needed a proper home. Drew hadn't the slightest idea of what to do with a four-year-old, but he could hire people for that. The best that money could buy for Jonathan's son. There would be nothing too good for the boy.

Damn it, Jonathan, why'd you have to come out here? Why'd you have to die?

Drew signaled his intent to change lanes. Surprisingly, the driver in the next lane slowed down to let him in. He had anticipated a battle, was actually hoping for one to release some of the tension he was experiencing. This simple kind action depleted his sails. Another sudden rush of sadness filled the void.

It had just begun to sprinkle. At the next corner, a young boy stood, hawking carnations, waving bouquets at each car that inched past him.

Hell of a way to make a few pennies, Drew thought absently, his mind desperately searching for diversions of any sort.

His thoughts returned to Anastasia. Why hadn't she called him as soon as the accident had happened? Why had she waited almost three days?

His full mouth tightened, thinking of her. The woman looked like some misplaced Gypsy. Her dark, exotic coloring was like Alyce's, but on Anastasia, it was somehow wilder. With her torrent of black hair and wide mouth, forever moving, forever spouting nonsense, she had struck him as the craziest woman on the face of the earth.

A crazy woman, and she had his nephew. That Jeremy was also her nephew didn't enter into the picture. She was probably eager to get rid of him and go back to doing whatever it was that she was currently doing.

A space opened up to his left and Drew aimed the hood of his car toward it. A second later he was stomping on the brake to keep from colliding with a beat-up, black 4×4 entering the same space from the other lane. Drew swore again and carefully maneuvered back into his space, now made smaller by the red sports car behind him that had inched up. A horn blared as he wedged back in.

Drew fervently wished for the helicopter again.

More than that, he wished for his brother.

It was after ten o'clock that night when Drew finally drove up his brother's driveway.

Daisy watched the big car come to a halt from Jeremy's room, adrenaline suddenly pumping madly through her veins.

"Showtime," she murmured, uncurling her body. She wasn't looking forward to this by any means.

Barefoot, a flowing caftan billowing about her as it caught a draft, Daisy tiptoed out of Jeremy's room, carefully easing the door closed behind her. The doorbell was ringing by the time she got to the stairs. Long and loud. That had to be Drew all right. It was his type of ring. Impatient. She pressed her lips together.

Be kind, Daisy. He's lost somebody, too.

"I'll get it, Irene," she called out in case the housekeeper was still up. The doorbell pealed again.

Irene, her blue eyes still red-rimmed from three days of intermittent crying, bobbed her head as the two women met in the hallway. "I've been answering this door for six years, Miss Daisy, I'd feel better doing it now, if you don't mind."

Though the doorbell sounded for the third time in sharp staccato peals, Daisy placed her hand on the white-haired woman's slightly rounded shoulder. "You'd feel better with a nice hot cup of tea, in bed. Go ahead, now." She nodded toward the back bedroom. "I'll show Mr. Addison to his room."

Irene sighed and withdrew a frail, blue-veined hand from the doorknob. Since the news, she had aged a decade, her normally abundant supply of energy deserting her almost completely. She had no idea what she would have done if Daisy hadn't taken everything over. "If you say so."

"I say so." A frequent guest at the house, Daisy knew that the woman retired early, usually around eight. Irene was just waiting up for Drew to arrive. It was taking duty beyond its call, Daisy thought.

She watched the woman walk toward the rear of the house before she turned toward the door. "Geronimo," Daisy said under her breath, pulling it open. She was totally unprepared for the sight that greeted her.

Drew looked like a wet rat. A tall, handsome, angry wet rat in a near-ruined gray suit.

Words of condolence had been on the tip of Drew's tongue. He had meant to offer them as soon as he saw Daisy. After all, even though he didn't care for her, she had suffered a loss, as well.

But good manners had been nudged rudely aside while he had stood on the steps, jabbing relentlessly at the doorbell, enduring the rain and getting completely soaked.

Distraught, upset, Drew cloaked himself in a sharp retort. "It's raining out here," he snapped when she just stood in the doorway, a barefoot Gypsy in a vibrant caftan, looking at him with eyes that were too wide, too green. Too beautiful.

A whoosh of wind sent rain in through the opened door around Drew, sprinkling her toes. Daisy let out a little noise of surprise. "So I noticed."

Drew shifted his weight forward onto the balls of his feet. Was she just going to stand there all night? "Are you going to study the weather, or let me in?"

Well, grief apparently didn't change his disposition for the better. The sympathy she was feeling toward him was on shaky ground.

"Sorry, come on in." She stepped aside to let him pass.

As soon as the funeral was over and loose ends tied up, he and Jeremy would be gone, Drew promised himself. Setting down his overnight case close to the door, he began planning his escape.

Daisy looked at the small case. Good, he wasn't going to stay long. "You certainly didn't bring much," she said for lack of anything better to say.

He took off his jacket, then looked around the wide foyer for somewhere to hang it. He settled on an antique brass hat rack near the hall closet. A small puddle formed directly under it as the jacket dripped onto the light gray tile. "I don't need much."

Her mouth twisted into a smile. Stoic to the end.

He ran his hand through his hair, pushing it away from his face. He was waiting for her to offer him a towel. He should have known better.

"Look," he began tartly in a voice his subordinates recognized and cringed before, "Anastasia—"

She heard the edge in his voice and refused to rise to the bait. He might be ill-tempered, but she didn't have to be. Besides, he might be one of those people who didn't know how to handle grief except to bluster through it. She had cried an ocean in the past three days. It had helped, a little. Drew, she instinctively knew, didn't have that kind of an option open to him.

"Please call me Daisy," she said as she ducked into the powder room and returned with a mauve towel. "It's easier."

Nothing about this woman would ever be termed as easier, he thought darkly. The towel was only large enough to wipe his face, but he took it. He sidestepped the issue of her name altogether, not wanting to be any more familiar with her than was absolutely necessary.

He pulled off his tie and stuffed it into the pocket of his trousers. Because his collar suddenly irritated him, he opened the top two buttons of his custom-made shirt.

Now that he was here, he needed to know more. "The details my secretary gave me were rather sketchy."

She shrugged, looking incredibly frail for a moment. "I don't have much to add to what I told her." She walked into the family room. "Would you like a drink?"

What I'd like is my brother back. It was much too personal a thought to share with her. "Please. I'll have whiskey. Neat."

She nodded, reaching for the bottle behind the bar Jonathan had always kept stocked for company. After pouring Drew a glass, she mixed a gin and tonic for herself. She suddenly needed something to do with her hands, somewhere to look with her eyes. She didn't want to talk about what had happened three days ago, not ever again, yet she knew Drew deserved to hear. She settled down on the sofa, aware that Drew was still standing stiffly over her. "He was taking Alyce to the cabin—"

"What cabin?"

She backtracked, losing her momentum. "Their cabin. The one he bought her for their fifth anniversary."

Were they talking about the same person? "Jonathan hates the outdoors. Hated the outdoors," he corrected himself. Would he ever get used to talking about his brother in the past tense?

"He changed his mind. I heard about the plane crash over the radio. I called the station. They put me in touch with a ranger. As soon as I could, I made them take me up there. I identified them." Her voice hoarse, Daisy took a deep gulp of air as she pulled her hand through her hair. "I told Jeremy as gently as possible. I don't think he really understands yet."

She wet her lips and plunged ahead, jumping from one topic to the next. "Look, I know we've never exactly gotten along, but I want you to know that you can come and visit him here anytime you want to."

What the hell was she talking about now? She wasn't through giving him the details he wanted, needed, to put Jonathan to rest properly in his mind.

"Visit?"

He made it sound like a foreign word. Didn't he care about Jeremy at all? Daisy wondered, suddenly impatient with this man. She tried to put it in terms he would understand. "You know, whenever your schedule lets you."

She had completely lost him. ''Why would I visit him here?''

For an intelligent man, he certainly was dense. Maybe it was the shock. ''Because Jeremy's going to be living here, with me.''

Drew stared at her, stunned. ''The hell he is.'' The words fell from his lips, tense, harsh.

What did he think, that Jeremy was going to be shipped off to a foster home or some orphanage? ''Where else would he live? I'm his legal guardian.''

Drew held the chunky glass with both hands as he took a healthy-sized swallow. It didn't help. Daisy was still sitting there when he opened his eyes.

Chapter Two

The Scotch warmed him physically, but that was all. Mentally, if anything, it made him more melancholy. It heightened his feelings of sadness and made him acutely aware of his loss. Drew glanced around the room. The last time he'd been here, he had begun to get a slight inkling of what it was his brother had found. There had been warmth, life, here. Now it was bleak and barren.

His mood and then her comment about taking his brother's son had finally opened the floodgates of reality for Drew. Even so, he didn't want to be here. Didn't want to be discussing anything with this woman. The idea of her taking custody was so ludicrous, so patently ridiculous, that for a moment, it didn't fully register. Was this her idea of a joke? The child was an Addison and as such, belonged with him.

Drew refocused his thoughts and looked—really looked—at her. Looked into her eyes. And then the horror struck him. She was serious.

"And just whose idea was this?" he asked.

The room was dark except for the lamp on the table next to the sofa where they were sitting. He carefully placed his glass on the coaster. Her reflection shimmered on the surface of the liquid within the glass, winking and blinking at him. Mocking him like some sort of fairy sprite mocked reality.

Drew waited, anticipating an incongruous reply. There was no way on God's green earth that he was about to leave that innocent child in her careless hands. Jonathan had told him all about her over the years. She'd turned her back on being a lawyer to do something with flowers, for God's sake. He owed it to Jonathan to take Jeremy with him. Besides, Jeremy was his only tie to Jonathan, and though Drew couldn't verbally express it, that connection was very, very important to him.

Their eyes held. She refused to be intimidated by his tone. Couldn't be intimidated, not after what she'd been through. "It was Jonathan's and Alyce's decision."

He didn't believe it for a minute. It was one thing for his brother to be in love with Alyce. She had turned out to be bright and funny, and most important, she had loved his brother dearly. A blind man wouldn't have been able to miss that. But it was quite another to entrust the welfare of Jonathan's only child to a whimsical bohemian who believed her flowers grew because she talked to them.

Drew looked at her, refusing to be taken in by that innocent expression that hovered so close to sensuality it should have been outlawed. "Jonathan would never have done that."

You didn't know him at all, did you? "Alyce told me it was originally his idea." Daisy pushed her own glass aside.

The drink tasted bitter on her tongue, just like this conversation. She didn't have the energy to continue it.

But there was a funeral to be faced together tomorrow and Daisy searched for some sort of middle ground for them, at least for now. Later they could draw swords; right now she hadn't the heart for it.

"Look, I can tell by your expression that you're not happy about this—"

Not happy? He thought her assessment didn't begin to do justice to the situation. "I had no idea that understatement was within your grasp."

She had an angle, he thought, she had to. What did some untethered soul who flittered from job to job possibly want with the responsibility of raising his brother's child? The first thing Drew thought of was money. She was after the money that Jeremy would inherit.

Daisy blew out a breath between teeth that were clenched to prevent her from saying something she might regret. She felt she couldn't cope with anything further tonight. She was exhausted from having maintained a good facade for Jeremy's sake. The boy had clung to her when she had returned from the site of the crash as if he silently knew that he'd never see his parents again. She'd been brave and smiled as she spoke to him. And held her own tears in check until she was alone in her room. It had been a horrible, horrible day and she wasn't about to be pushed to the wall by this neanderthal in a designer suit and fifty-dollar haircut.

She looked at him, trying to remember that Jonathan cared about this man, although for the life of her she didn't know why. "I'm not really up to hashing this out with you tonight. Could we please wait until after the funeral is over?"

He was right, she was fishing for money. She wanted him to think it over carefully, give the idea time to play in his mind. Well, if it took money to buy her off, so be it. Jeremy was worth every cent he might have to pay out. His nephew was going to have a good home. With him.

"Fair enough," Drew agreed. "After the funeral."

For a moment, sparring with Anastasia had taken his mind away from Jonathan's funeral. The realization hit him like a fist to the solar plexus. He still couldn't get himself to actually accept it. It felt like a nightmare. Any minute now, he'd wake up and realize that it was just that, an awful nightmare. He would be in his room, alone—

He sighed, rising. What good did it do to pretend? Jonathan was gone. He'd have to face it. "I'll take care of the arrangements—"

"They've been taken care of," she said dully, trying not to dwell on what had transpired in the past twelve hours. The caskets would be closed. No wake. Only she and the rescue team had seen the condition of the bodies within them. It was going to take a while before she could really sleep again.

"By you."

Drew's voice brought Daisy back to the present. She looked at him, astonished and annoyed at his words and condescending tone.

"By me." For the barest second, her voice had an edge to it.

"I see." Drew was tired and overwrought and just wanted to be alone with his pain. He'd never experienced feelings as intense as these before. His entire life had been mapped out. He always knew what he wanted to do. All the details were planned. He was always somewhat remote, removed, and analytical of a given situation. He had to be, to make a rational decision. This was different. For the first time in his life, he didn't feel in control. He felt lost, unsettled, confused and angry. Especially angry. Anger hummed within his soul, like a ricocheting ball searching for the one opening that would set it free. He turned on the likeliest candidate. "Why didn't you call me three days ago?" he demanded.

The vibrating anger she heard startled Daisy. "Excuse me?"

Was she purposely trying to play dumb? "When you first found out that the plane had gone down, why didn't you call?" he demanded. He had gone on with his life for all that time, not knowing his brother lay dead or dying. "Why didn't you tell me?"

For two cents, she would have hit him, right there, in the family room. It would have felt good, releasing the frustration that was eating away at her. But it wouldn't have done any real good and she knew it. Venting her anger by hitting Drew wouldn't have brought either Alyce or Jonathan back to her.

She dragged a ragged breath into her lungs and told him the truth. "Because I was hoping there wasn't anything to call you about." She stared at the liquid in his glass, watched it catch the light and scatter it. Just like her life, she thought. "I was hoping, praying, that somehow they were alive."

He rose, too restless to sit. "I had a right to know," he insisted.

Tears shone in her eyes as she raised her head to look at him. "Look at it this way," she told him, her voice growing hoarse, "you had three more days than I did to think everything was fine."

"I—"

Drew clenched his hands at his sides. She was going to cry. Damn it, he couldn't handle a woman's tears. He had no words, no recourse, faced with that. Tears completely undid him, leaving him feeling even more frustrated, even more helpless. For a moment, he even wanted to take her into his arms and offer some sort of words of comfort.

Except he didn't know how.

Instead, Drew shoved his hands into his damp pockets and kept them clenched there. "Look, I—I'm sorry."

She nodded numbly. Maybe he was human after all. "So am I," Daisy whispered. "So am I." *About everything.*

Drew was about to say something, what he wasn't certain, when the noise stopped him. He turned his listen. A high-pitched, eerie wail was echoing from the recesses of the house. He looked at Daisy, his brow furrowed in confusion. "What's that?"

She shed her grief and was halfway toward the stairs. Jeremy needed her. How could Drew not recognize that? "It's called crying."

He followed her, not fully realizing that he was doing so. "Jeremy?"

Of course, Jeremy. "Unless Irene's found an old Bette Davis movie to watch," she tossed over her shoulder as she hurried up the stairs.

She hoped her wisecrack would make him forget what had happened in the family room just a moment ago. She hadn't meant to cry just then, not in front of him. He would point to it as a sign of weakness and somehow twist it to his advantage when it came to Jeremy. She didn't want him thinking she was the type of woman who crumbled, no matter what the situation.

He shouldn't have had the drink, not even one sip. It only compounded his physical and emotional exhaustion. His legs felt like lead. Drew gripped the banister. He thought of his jacket and suitcase, but was too tired to retrace his steps and retrieve them. The hell with it. He'd sleep nude. "You're going to him?"

He sounded surprised. She had been right. The man had no love, no concept of what it took to raise a child. There was no way he was getting his hands on Jeremy, if that was his actual aim. "Yes, I'm going to him. He's probably frightened."

"I figured that part out." What he hadn't figured out was why she was rushing to the boy. He'd had nightmares as a child and had been informed by his governess that he had to bear up to them. Facing his fears helped to build his character. Although he did recall how grateful he had been when Jonathan had offered to sleep in his bed. Until the governess had caught him and ordered him back to his own room.

Daisy resisted the temptation to say "bravo." Biting her tongue, she continued up the stairs.

Jeremy's door was ajar, just the way she had left it. Daisy pushed it opened and found Jeremy sitting up in the bunk bed, shaking, sobbing. Putting on a bright smile, she crossed to him.

"Hey, Tiger, what's the matter?" Sitting down on the boy's bed, Daisy gathered him close and stroked his hair. "Bad dream?"

Jeremy gulped sobs, nodding his head. He looked up at Drew and then back toward his aunt with huge questions in his eyes.

Daisy settled Jeremy against her as she turned her head toward Drew. Feeling somewhat awkward, Drew ran his hand along the bedpost. The boy was the spitting image of Jonathan as a child. A lump formed in Drew's throat. The lump dissipated with the sound of Daisy's next words to Jeremy.

"Sweetheart, I'd like you to meet your uncle." She leveled a gaze at Drew and thought of his intentions to take the boy away from the only home he knew. Away from her. *The grinch who stole Christmas,* she thought.

Drew scowled at her. He moved forward toward Jeremy. "He knows who I am."

The blank look on Jeremy's face testified otherwise. "I do?"

Drew smiled down at the small face. "Of course you do. I was here just last..." Drew searched his mind for a time and then remembered. "Year," he concluded quietly.

A year was a quarter of a lifetime to a child of four. "I rest my case," Daisy said simply, straightening Jeremy's light blanket. Cartoon characters from a popular Saturday morning program romped all over it in a barrage of colors.

He wanted to tell her that she *was* a case, but refrained from what he knew was a childish display. There was no denying his emotions were in a state of upheaval that he was completely unaccustomed to. He couldn't seem get a hold of them. Irrational thoughts and reactions kept bouncing through his mind. Such as the fact that he had been here a total of fifteen minutes and was vacillating between wanting to comfort Anastasia and wanting to strangle her. Strangling was quickly edging out the former.

Daisy rose and then tucked Jeremy in properly. "Uncle Drew's going to be staying with us for a while, honey. Would you like that?"

Drew noticed that she used the word "us." He pressed his lips together grimly. She had spun a tight, secure web around Jeremy. Poor little boy, at four he didn't have a chance against her. But that was where he came in, Drew thought. He might not have been around very much before, but he was here for Jeremy now and would find away to take the boy back home. There was no doubt in Drew's mind that Daisy would quickly tire of her little charade of playing the concerned aunt and direct her fleeting attention span to something else. It seemed a safe enough assumption to make about a woman who, in Jonathan's words, shed careers and relationships with the ease that other people shed an old pair of shoes.

Jeremy struggled manfully to come to terms with all the changes in his young life, changes he didn't understand or like very much. He was almost five and hurrying to be on his way to six. He looked down at his ever-present teddy bear, as if it was the bear and not the man standing near him that he was addressing. "I guess so."

The little face was still sad, still bewildered. Daisy's heart ached for him. She had done her best to explain to Jeremy that his mommy and daddy had gone to heaven together, but she knew that he was hurt because he couldn't see them any more. What hurt most was that they had left without him.

"Not by choice," she had whispered to him at the time, holding him to her. If she lived to be a hundred, she knew that there would never be anything more difficult for her to do than to tell Jeremy that his parents were gone.

"They won't come back, even for a visit?" he had asked, struggling to understand.

She had fought back tears, telling herself she had to stay strong for Jeremy. "Perhaps in your dreams. But they're watching out for you, sweetheart. And they still love you very, very much. And I'll always be here for you."

It had been a pitifully small thing to offer the boy, but it was all she had.

Daisy looked at Drew now. She knew that he was going to try to argue with her about Jeremy's legal guardianship. It didn't matter what he said or thought. She had the law on her side. And more important, at least to her, she had Jonathan's and Alyce's wishes backing her. "Your mommy and daddy would have wanted Uncle Drew to stay with us for a while, honey," she told Jeremy.

A small smile flittered over Jeremy's lips at the mention of his parents. "Then I guess it's okay." He settled back on his pillow and sighed, one hand tightly wound around the worn bear. "I'm sleepy now."

She patted his head. "Good."

Jeremy's other hand darted out quickly as he grabbed at her wrist. His dark eyes were wide with fear. "Will you stay with me?"

Daisy understood this. Jeremy was afraid of the dark, afraid of being alone. She'd been there herself once, when she and Alyce had first come to stay with Uncle Warren. Daisy ruffled his hair. "I'm not planning on going anywhere, Tiger."

Drew regarded them both in silence for a moment. When it became evident that Daisy was really going to stay with Jeremy until the boy fell asleep, Drew quietly left the room.

He could feel her watching him all the way to the door.

How did you figure a woman like that? he wondered. She apparently got diabolical pleasure out of disputing everything he said, yet she seemed to be putty around a small child. Up to a point, he supposed that meant she had some redeeming qualities.

That wouldn't, of course, keep him from gaining custody of Jeremy and taking him back east with him. Even if he had to take her to court, and he doubted that it would come to that.

He heard her humming as he closed the door behind him, a strange, melodic song without words that wafted through the air, seeping under his very skin, reminding him of a siren's song.

What an absurd notion. Absurd.

And that, he knew, was the word for Anastasia Channing as well. Absurd.

Concentrating on that and only that, Drew managed to stave off the bottomless depression he felt and had felt ever since eleven o'clock this morning.

He went to the room where he always stayed when he visited. The first time he had arrived after the christening, he had made reservations at a hotel, but Alyce had insisted that he stay with them. It seemed that Alyce always got her way, he thought as he entered the room. She had been a subtly persuasive woman, never asking outright, just somehow bending the corners, turning things in her direction. She had a knack for making the other person think that it was their idea.

She would have made a hell of a corporate executive, or corporate raider for that matter. Drew eventually came to understand why his brother had fallen in love with her. But it still didn't stop Drew from resenting the fact that it had happened, that Jonathan had met and married Alyce. For it had taken Jonathan out of his life. Permanently.

And now there was a void within him that would never be filled.

They had been as close as brothers could be. Eighteen months apart, they had done everything together, with Jonathan always paving the way. Jonathan had been ahead of him in school, in clubs, breaking ground for him, making the painful shyness that had racked Drew as a boy easier to deal with. Words had never really been necessary between them. They understood one another without ever having to express anything, although there were times when they had talked until dawn, laying plans, dreaming of what was waiting for them. They shared the same feelings, the same reactions and, until Alyce had come into Jonathan's life, the same goals.

Drew sighed as he crossed to the double bed. He didn't bother turning on the light. It would have been a harsh intruder on his grief. Somehow, he felt better in the dark. It matched the hollowness inside.

He needed sleep, he thought, toeing off his shoes, though he doubted it would come. He felt exhausted, restless, on edge. But he needed sleep to help him cope with tomorrow, with the funeral and the fight with Anastasia that he knew lay ahead of him. He meant to have Jeremy with him when he boarded the plane for the east coast. He would do whatever it took to have him. Jeremy had a heritage waiting for him in New York. He was an Addison. Addisons went to Bently Private School for Boys and, eventually, to Harvard. Taking Jeremy's strengths into consideration when the time came, Drew would map out his nephew's life for him in a beneficial, orderly manner. There'd be no chaos for the boy the way there'd be, Drew imagined, if Jeremy lived with Anastasia.

Drew's thoughts shifted to Anastasia. At the same time, something warm and odd shifted within him that he ignored. He didn't want to go exploring any more emotions right now. He felt too drained. Order was probably not a word Anastasia was familiar with, he thought, stripping off his shirt. He let it fall to the floor. For once he didn't bother to hang up his clothing. He was just too tired to care. The shirt was joined by his pants and finally, his briefs.

There was a slight chill in the room, but he welcomed it. He'd always preferred cool weather. Sitting on the edge of the bed, Drew had just begun to take off his socks when the door opened and light flooded the room from the hall, temporarily blinding him. But not before he saw the outline of a green caftan.

"Oh!"

Daisy looked quickly down to the floor, the suitcase she had brought up from the foyer dangling from her fingers. Amused, flustered, she felt a blush rising up from her neck to her cheeks.

"I, um, didn't think you were in here," she murmured. Which was the truth. Making sure the front door was locked, she'd seen the suitcase and had only meant to leave it in his room. She hadn't wanted to run into him again tonight. And definitely not like this.

Startled, Drew had the presence of mind to yank the edge of the bedspread over himself. The multicolored velvet cover pooled strategically onto his lap. She was doing this on purpose. The woman was utterly impossible. "Where the hell would I be?"

She shrugged, purposely staring at a pattern in the powder blue Oriental rug in front of the bed. She didn't like his tone. It had been an honest mistake on her part, but she supposed he was entitled to his reaction. "There was no light in the room, I thought that maybe you'd gone outside on the patio."

Was she out of her mind? "In the rain?"

"Some people like to watch the rain falling." But he wasn't like some people. Actually, she had wondered where he had gotten to. It was too soon for him to have gone to bed so quickly, but she didn't give it too much thought. "I wasn't thinking clearly."

He felt like an idiot, sitting here completely naked except for one sock. "Another understatement."

Her head jerked up. She was tired of finding excuses for his behavior. "I came to bring this up to your room." She gave the suitcase a slight shake, wishing it was his head instead. "You forgot it downstairs. I thought you might need something in it." Kindly inclinations vanished in the face of his reaction. "Now I realize what you need is a muzzle and a book on manners."

"Manners?" he echoed incredulously. His eyes opened wide and he nearly rose before he remembered that he couldn't. "I'm not the one who came barging into your room unannounced with you stark naked."

"Sorry, next time I'll have the housekeeper announce me. Besides, you're not naked. You're wearing a sock." She bit back the giddy desire to laugh. And to stare. For a corporate executive, he had an incredibly toned and muscular build. "And I already told you it was an honest mistake." She lifted the suitcase higher. "Where do you want this?" *I know where I'd like to put it.*

He was the most ill-mannered man she had ever met. Sure he'd been through a lot, but so had she. At least he hadn't had to explain the tragedy to a four-year-old boy. Or identify the bodies.

''On the floor,'' he said coldly, ''on your way out would be nice.''

She let the suitcase slip from her fingers and it dropped to the floor with a thud. She hoped there was something inside that was breakable. It would have served him right. Just to irritate him, she let her eyes drift over him in a slow, appraising glance.

''No problem.'' She grasped the doorknob, then turned to give him one final look. ''Oh, and Drew?''

''Andrew,'' he corrected shortly, wishing she'd leave. ''What?''

''For an ill-mannered, stuffed shirt, you have nice legs. Good night, Drew.''

Daisy closed the door, feeling just a tad better than when she had opened it. For just the briefest of moments, she'd managed to get away from the sad, lonely feeling that surrounded her.

But as she walked to her room, on the other side of Jeremy's, her smile faded. The feeling was back. Daisy searched vainly for the humor, the optimism, the childlike faith in tomorrow that had always sustained her before and had seen her through the years.

It wasn't there.

It was too soon, she told herself, too soon. But it would return. After tomorrow was over, it would return. Slowly, perhaps, but it would be there. It had to be. She'd be no good to Jeremy any other way. Or to herself.

She looked in on him one last time to make sure he was still sleeping. He had held on to her hand so tightly until he had dropped off to sleep, as if afraid that she would disappear, too, just like his parents.

"Never happen, Jeremy," she whispered. "I'm yours forever."

She planned to be there for him for as long as he needed her. And no humorless, straitlaced uncle was going to change that, she thought, glancing over her shoulder toward Drew's room. No matter how good he looked wrapped in a bedspread. She and Jeremy belonged together. She was just going to have to find a way to convince Drew of that. The man *had* to have a heart somewhere. It was her job to find it and make it work.

Chapter Three

The rain gradually subsided the next morning until it was just a light, occasional sprinkle, wetting the land. But the clouds remained, ominously hovering over the area. It seemed somehow appropriate.

Daisy managed to get through the ordeal of the funeral by placing one foot in front of the other. And tightly holding on to Jeremy's hand. She had initially debated leaving the boy home with Irene. Weighing everything carefully, Daisy decided that it was important for Jeremy to attend the service. He had to be able to say goodbye in his own way.

She also thought it important that he feel the outpouring of love for his parents, which came from all directions as people who had known Jonathan and Alyce attended the services and offered their condolences.

Daisy smiled and nodded and talked. And cried silently inside. It hurt like hell, being there.

She was vaguely aware that Drew remained at her side throughout it all. That it had been his hand on her elbow, helping her into the limousine. That he had been there during that moment in the church when things had gotten just the slightest bit dark and she thought she was going to faint.

Drew felt rather than saw her sway slightly against him. His hand went around her shoulders automatically. "Are you all right?"

Because she wasn't, she didn't know if that was concern or irritation in his voice. Probably the latter. She took in two deep gulps of air, leaning against him though she hated being weak. "Yes, it's just hot in here," she muttered.

"There are a lot of people here," he commented. She saw that Drew didn't really believe her excuse, but for once, he didn't pursue it. She was grateful to him. It was a kindness she hadn't expected.

His expression was so stoic throughout the morning, Daisy didn't know what he was feeling or *if* he was feeling at all. In her heart, she chose to believe that everyone was susceptible to the same emotions. Everyone felt love, hate, grief and joy. But the expression of these emotions took on different forms with different people.

Some people, she thought, glancing at Drew's face, were embarrassed by their feelings, though she couldn't for the life of her fathom why. She ascribed the latter behavior to Drew. He reminded her a lot of Jonathan when they had first met. It was inconceivable to her that he wasn't saddened by his brother's death, that he wasn't silently grieving along with everyone else in the church.

But she wished he could show it. It would have made her feel that he was human and heartened her about the duel that was just ahead.

It was finally over. The ceremony, the people crowding Jonathan and Alyce's house—now her house she thought ruefully, for that had been part of the agreement, that she raise Jeremy in familiar surroundings—it was all over. Everyone had gone to his or her home to continue with their lives.

Now it was time for her to pick up the pieces of hers and attempt to place them into some kind of order. They had to fit together somehow, she thought, although she didn't know how. At least Jeremy was taken care of for the time being. She had made it a point to invite some of his friends over for the afternoon. They were all now playing in his room, under Irene's watchful eye. It gave them both, Daisy mused, a slight diversion. Something to do.

She watched as the rain began to fall heavily again, beating against the window. If only she knew what to do with herself.

Drew walked into the den looking for Anastasia. He found her standing by the window, just staring out. Pausing, he studied her, the set of her shoulders, the delicate profile. She looked lost, he thought, and for the first time, he knew what she was feeling. There was a small feeling of empathy, but it was gone in the next minute.

Daisy saw his reflection in the window and turned. Well, here they were, she thought. Now what? "It was a nice funeral, wasn't it?" she murmured vaguely.

He crossed the threshold, trying to banish the awkward feeling permeating through him. "Funerals are never nice."

"No," she agreed, combing her fingers through the fringe on the window shade, "they're not. But it gives the living something to cling to, I suppose."

Not me. He shrugged, not wanting her to launch into something chipper and cheerful and totally inane. He just wasn't in the mood to listen to anything like that. "We need to talk."

Here it comes. Daisy gestured to the sofa. "All right, about what?"

She felt a tenseness setting in her shoulders. She knew what he had in mind. He was taking her at her word, when she had said they'd discuss Jeremy's situation after the funeral. She had hoped that he'd give her more than an hour to pull herself together. She should have known better, she thought, sitting on the sofa. All business, that was Drew.

Was that Drew? Wasn't there a glimmer of something else, something more inside? Something she could work with? There *had* to be.

Why was she playing dumb? "It's Jeremy." Drew sat down, although he would have preferred to stand. "I want to take him home with me."

She knotted her hands together over her knee. "I already told you, I'm his legal guardian."

Which proves that justice really is blind. "All right, we'll play it your way for a minute." He proceeded to explain the matter as if he was talking to a very young, very naive person. "As his legal guardian, you can see that I have the most to offer the boy."

This emotionless robot? The hell he had. Her promise to herself to stay calm flew out the window. "The most to offer? You must be joking."

Unlike you, I'm not a happy idiot. "I never joke."

And there, she was certain, he was being honest with her. More's the pity. She looked almost sad as she said, "No, I don't suppose you do. Which is just another reason why I wouldn't let Jeremy live with you."

He expected this sort of reasoning from her. It made absolutely no sense at all. But then, neither did she. "Because I don't tell jokes?"

Missing the forest for the trees, she thought. "Because you don't know how to laugh."

She was babbling. "Since when is laughter a prerequisite for raising a child?" Annoyed, he rose and stood looking down at her.

She let out a long sigh. He sounded just like Uncle Warren had. In all those years with him, she didn't remember one instance when he had really laughed. "You really mean that, don't you? Laughter's right up there next to love and understanding." She saw that Drew didn't see her point at all. "Or don't you think those are prerequisites, either?"

He tried to figure out what exactly she was driving at. He said the only thing he thought she might remotely understand. "I love Jeremy."

She smiled. Deep down, she had always hoped that. It gave her an ace card. Maybe. "Then you'll leave him with me?" she asked hopefully.

For a moment the look on her face made him lose his train of thought. He had already acknowledged that she was a very physically attractive woman. When she smiled that way, there was something magnetic about her, something almost innocent and sweet, and though he knew it had to be an act, it was dangerously appealing.

It took him a second to pull himself free. His thoughts were becoming jumbled. It wasn't like him. "I have no intentions of letting my nephew be raised by the prototype for Auntie Mame."

It was becoming increasingly clear that the man didn't understand *anything*. "As I recall, Patrick turned out pretty well in that story."

"A fortunate accident," he concluded. "No thanks to Mame's bohemian ways. The woman was an unorthodox lunatic." He turned to look at her, his meaning clear in his eyes.

She wasn't going to get angry. She wasn't. It wouldn't help the situation one bit.

"You do know how to make the most of your words, don't you?" She set her mouth firmly as she rose to face him. It was only a little better than sitting. The man was too tall. "Jeremy's staying with me." Daisy saw the stubborn look enter his eyes. They'd be nice eyes if it weren't for that, she thought. Maybe not unduly kind, but gorgeous none-theless. What a waste. "You'll fight me on this, won't you?"

She wasn't quite as scatterbrained as he'd first thought. "Only if I have to." Maybe she'd be open to reason. "I'd rather just take Jeremy quietly. He's obviously been through enough."

She nodded. "My thoughts exactly."

Success? It felt too easy. "Then you'll give up custody?"

"No."

He nearly threw up his hands, but that would have been too emotional a gesture. Too much like her, he realized. "You are an infuriating woman."

He did frazzle easily, she thought. That would work to her advantage. She licked her lips and plunged ahead hope-fully. "But I'll make a deal with you."

Drew lifted his brow. Here it comes, he thought. The money part. "Yes?"

Good, he almost sounded reasonable. "I don't want to drag Jeremy through a court fight. He deserves better than that."

Drew began to write out the check mentally. He won-dered how much she'd settle for. "I agree."

So far, so good. "Here's my proposition. You stay here with us at the house for...say, three months. Until New Year's Day." On a roll, she began to talk faster, afraid that he would interrupt. "Let me see what kind of a guardian you'd make for him. If he takes to you, if I see that he's re-ally better off with you than me, and that's a big 'if'—" she drew a breath before finishing "—I won't stop you from taking him."

Drew stared at her. This was the last thing he would have expected her to say. "What?"

He looked at her as if she were speaking in tongues, she thought. "What part would you like me to explain?" she asked patiently.

"All of it," he muttered, then to his horror realized that she was going to launch into another explanation. "No, wait."

He held up his hand, stalling for time while he regrouped mentally. She sat quietly, waiting. How could someone who looked so innocent one moment, be such a source of trouble the next? he wondered. "Let me get this straight," he began slowly. "We're both supposed to live here."

"Yes." It would never work, she thought gleefully. He'd be gone, happily, within two weeks. Three, tops. He wasn't cut out to be a parent. It was what she was banking on. But if all else failed, she had no intentions of living up to her part of the bargain. She couldn't. Jeremy would be devastated. What she was really praying for was a miracle, a transformation on Drew's part just as there had been on Jonathan's. He'd realize that Jeremy belonged with her.

"Together." The word was etched in disbelief. She had to be crazier than even he had thought if she imagined that this had a prayer of working.

The smile she gave him could have been termed as sweet, he thought, if he didn't know any better. "It's nice to see your Harvard education paid off so well." Daisy took a deep breath, her smile fading. "Don't you see? This is the only way that will give Jeremy the opportunity to decide—"

Drew cut her short. "He's four years old. He can't possibly decide something of this magnitude for himself. Which toy to play with, yes," he conceded. "But not which relative to live with." She had to be insane to even think so.

Daisy held on to her temper, her voice deceptively soft. "He knows who he loves."

Finally. Drew had had a feeling that Anastasia would fight dirty. It was just a matter of time. "That's only because you've always been around."

She held up a finger, victorious. "My point exactly. Now you have to be around so he can learn to be comfortable with you. There's no way in the world I'm just going to hand him over to you now, when you're almost a stranger to him."

"I am not a stranger."

"He didn't recognize you," she reminded him.

Daisy dragged a hand through her tangled black hair and roamed to the window. That was the term for it, he thought, not walked, not crossed, but roamed. Like some wild, fascinating animal someone had had the good sense not to imprison yet. Not that they'd be able to, he realized. Unless she wanted them to.

She turned around to look at him, deadly serious. "It's the only way I won't fight you for custody. And I warn you, I fight to win."

He didn't doubt it for a minute. She might look small and frail, but he knew that was just her deceptive camouflage. He'd probably have his hands full in court, fighting her. Looking the way she did, she might just turn the judge in her favor. Then where would he be? And throughout it all, Jeremy would be the one to suffer.

Daisy wanted to tell Drew to pack up and go, but if she did, as sure as the sun rose in the morning, she knew that there would be papers served. Above all, she had to think of what all this would do to Jeremy. If Drew agreed to the bargain, she knew she could get him to see things her way. The possibility of anything else resulting was inconceivable to her.

She smiled at him sweetly, laying a gentling hand on his arm. "Look, just because we disagree about every topic under the sun doesn't mean we can't live under the same roof for three months."

He didn't trust her or her smile. "Prisoners do it all the time. Speaking of doing time..." He moved toward the doorway, signaling an end to the ridiculous discussion. "My staying here is unacceptable."

This was easier than she thought. He was giving in already. For the first time in three days, happiness began to bud within her. "Then you're giving up?"

Whatever gave her that idea? "No, of course not. I want you to."

So much for tidy, happy endings. She shook her head, dark hair sweeping along her shoulders like storm clouds. "No way. Over my dead body."

There was something almost stirring, he realized, about the way her eyes flashed just then. It was the kind of look that sent poets to their desks and artists to their easels. And corporate men to their antacids. He refused to be intimidated by it. Or aroused. He had less control over the latter than he would have liked. "You're only sweetening the pot."

All right, the gloves were off, she thought. She jabbed a finger at his chest and met with a good deal more physical resistance than she would have thought. A flash of the way he had looked last night when she had walked in on him crossed her mind. And warmed her even though she was braced for battle. There was an electricity here she would have liked to explore if the stakes weren't so high.

"Now listen to this. Alyce and I were raised by someone exactly like you. Our Uncle Warren. He was a topflight corporate lawyer who had blue chips instead of blood running through his veins. Our parents were always away on some road tour or other. We had about as much love passed on to us as a pair of lepers in a vacation colony. And I won't have the same thing happening to Jeremy!"

She poked his chest again for emphasis. This time, Drew grabbed her finger in his hand and pushed it firmly aside, his eyes warning her that he was not about to be backed into a corner. She dropped her hand to her side, but the look on her face remained unchanged.

God she was beautiful, he thought completely against his will. "Are you possibly suggesting that I'd be that way toward him?"

She wasn't about to back off. "No, I'm not suggesting it. I'm flat out saying it." She gave him a knowing look. "You'd send him to boarding school, wouldn't you?"

He didn't answer her directly. "And what's wrong with that?"

She answered with a question of her own. "How much time do you have?"

She was maddening, utterly maddening. Even more maddening was the fact that, in the midst of all this, he kept finding himself reacting to her in a completely emotional as well as physical manner. And he didn't like it. It wasn't like him at all. Part witch. The Channing women were all part witch, he decided, thinking of the spell Alyce had woven over his brother.

And just who the hell did Anastasia think she was, judging him? He felt his normally cool manner hovering uncomfortably close to meltdown. "So, Jeremy'd be better off living with a woman who talks to flowers and drifts aimlessly through life than going to boarding school?"

He seemed to know just enough details to cloud the issue and not enough to clear it, she thought angrily. She had her own business now and talking to flowers had turned out very well for her, thank you very much. But she wasn't going to get into an argument over his opinion of her. If he thought of her as some flighty, flaky creature with unorthodox views, that was his problem, not hers.

For the first time in her life, she wished she was taller. She didn't like the way he loomed over her. "Yes, because with me he'd have the kind of love and nurturing support that he both needs and deserves."

She was spouting emotional gibberish, but he had expected as much. What he hadn't expected was to lose his temper. But it was getting dangerously frayed around the edges. "I want to see him raised properly."

Like a little wind-up soldier, she thought bitterly. She had heard sentiments such as Drew's voiced before. In her childhood. Then they had been applied to Alyce and her. She could feel her blood run cold at the very thought of it. "I want to see him well adjusted."

He saw the impassioned look on her face and thought, quite against his will, that it made her look beautiful. "Why does it sound like we want the same thing for him when it's really not?"

Daisy let out a long breath. It helped take some of the edge off her animosity. She was willing to give the Ivy League jerk the benefit of the doubt for Jonathan's sake. "Because we both love him." She squared her shoulders. "Now, I gave you my offer. My only offer. Take it or leave it."

Drew frowned. To the untrained ear, she sounded noble, but Drew was well acquainted with deviousness. The corporate world was full of it. He wasn't fooled by her words. He trusted this woman as far as he could throw her. Less. Besides, she was only making this proposition because she knew remaining here was impossible for him.

"You can afford to play all the games you want. You're not tied down by a career."

"I own a business," she informed him, her pride wounded even though she told herself that what he thought of her didn't count. If she had gone from one thing to another, it was because she hadn't found her proper place in life before and had no problem with abandoning something that made her miserable.

She had found her niche last year.

"Doing what?" Drew asked. He couldn't quiet help the condescending tone that came into his voice.

"I own a nursery."

He thought of the boy on the corner he had seen yesterday, hawking flowers. He could see her doing the same with ease. She'd probably enjoy it, he thought, unconsciously smiling.

She had no idea why he looked so amused. She did know that she had a sudden urge to plant the heel of her shoe somewhere on his muscular torso.

"We do landscape consulting." Her anger dissipated at her next words, because of the memory that was attached to them. "I just finished redoing Alyce and Jonathan's backyard."

Drew let out a little huff, unable to picture anything that had to do with his brother without feeling pain. "Be that as it may, you're still located here. My headquarters, as you know," he said pointedly, "is on the other side of the continent."

That, too, was his problem, not hers. "They have telephones now. Work pretty well, they tell me."

Drew opened his mouth to respond, but she went on. It was what he was afraid of. The woman had a rapid-fire delivery second only to a discharging machine gun. He'd hardly formed the first syllable of the first word and she was already completing a full sentence.

"And you've heard of flying, I assume, for the business you can't conduct from here." She looked at him innocently, her eyes open wide.

Sexy. Standing there that way, he had to admit that the woman looked definitely sexy. And was a definite royal pain. "Don't patronize me."

Her eyes darkened. "Then don't be so stuffy. It's not as if you were a factory worker with a time card to punch every day. According to Jonathan, you're the boss of a major conglomerate that's spread out throughout the world. With telecommunication and fax machines that can bring the board meeting right into your living room, you're all set. You can work anywhere you want to." A smile lifted the corners of her mouth as she raised herself upon her toes to be closer to him. "What's the matter? Afraid of spending three months with me?"

He caught the faintest whiff of a cologne that brought an image of white lace and old-fashioned porch swings to his mind. How absolutely incongruous with the woman who was standing in front of him, challenging every fiber of his being. "Terrified out of my mind. But someone has to save Jeremy from your influence. And there's no one else but me."

Her smile softened, making her mouth look tempting. He bent his head, almost giving in to the sudden surge of desire before he caught himself. Drew decided that the stress of the funeral had him practically hallucinating.

Daisy's heart was hammering. My God, he had almost kissed her. In the middle of an argument? There was hope for the man yet.

She dropped onto the arm of the sofa and looked up at Drew, studying him.

From the set of his jaw, she guessed that he at least thought he was in for the duration, hoping, no doubt, to somehow outsmart her and outlast her. He had a surprise coming, she mused. She wasn't about to be outsmarted. But if they were going to be under one roof for a total of ninety days, the air had to be cleared. She knew he didn't like her. But his antagonism toward Alyce was a different matter. Alyce had been sweet, loving, kind. It irked Daisy that this man held anything but the greatest regard for a woman whose shoes he wasn't fit to clean.

"Tell me something. Why were you so horribly hostile toward my sister? She made your brother very happy." There were a thousand and one different instances Daisy could have cited for him to substantiate her statement.

He thought back to his initial feelings about Alyce. They had changed, but there was no reason to tell Anastasia that. He would have sounded as if he was backing off. So he gave her the bottom line.

"Your sister changed Jonathan. She took a highly motivated businessman and turned him into a laid-back individual who puttered in the garden."

Which was true. The last time he had been here, Jonathan had tried to get him involved in his roses. *Roses*. Though he had tried his best to be understanding, he drew the line there. There were gardeners for things such as that. Jonathan hadn't graduated at the top of his class with a degree in business from Harvard to spread mulch and manure around.

Daisy shook her head. "Horrible thing, making living things grow and thrive."

He closed his eyes. Trust her to miss the point. "That's not what I meant. He was wasting talent."

She shrugged carelessly, her silk blouse rustling against her shoulders. She didn't think Drew would understand. Absently, she ran the tip of her finger along a petal of one of the roses in the vase. The petal fell to the oak desk. The flowers she had picked at the beginning of the week, just before she had heard the news, were dying. Soon, they'd be gone, too.

Daisy roused herself. "Your idea of talent might not have been his."

It had been once, he thought. "You know, you have a way of twisting words."

She raised her eyes to his. Green eyes met gray for a moment and held. Was he totally dead behind those eyes? She refused to believe that. "I have a way of seeing the truth."

He let out a long breath. "You haven't changed any."

She struggled to hold on to her temper. She was just about out of patience and endurance. Even a saint had a breaking point and she had never considered herself particularly saintly.

"From when? You only met me a handful of times. You don't know me."

"I know all I need to know." More than enough, he added silently.

Daisy scowled at Drew. With a huff, she pushed away her hair with the back of her hand.

"Made up your steel-trap little mind, didn't you? Just like that." She snapped her fingers. "Without all the facts. Just some sort of emotional response. No, excuse me—" she held up her hand to forestall any words of correction that might be coming "—mechanical response. You don't have any emotions." Her eyes narrowed. "I really do think I frighten you."

He caught a whiff of cologne again, or maybe it was the flowers this time. It was strange that something so nebulous, so feminine, should snare his attention just now. He wished he could stop winking in and out this way and just concentrate on the fact that she was the most annoying woman God ever created. It helped to hang on to his anger at a time such as this. If he didn't, then he'd have to face the wrenching fire of emptiness that hovered, threatening to tear at his insides. And something else, equally as powerfully, waiting just beyond. Something he refused to give substance to.

"Yes, you do. I'm always afraid of crazy people, especially those in vivid colors." He waved a hand at her. "Why did you wear that to the funeral, for God's sake?'' Didn't she know how to show respect?

She was wearing a lavender suit. "It was Jonathan's favorite color," she answered quietly. "And you're not afraid of me because you think I'm crazy. You're afraid because you think I'm right and you're wrong."

That would be the day. "See, crazy, completely crazy." A beat passed and she said nothing. It was like waiting for the other shoe to fall. "All right, right and wrong about what?"

"Life. My approach to it."

Her approach. "Like a bull in a china shop?" he asked archly.

She turned her eyes toward him. The vividness of her clothes paled in comparison to the brightness of her eyes. They seemed almost electrifying as she gazed at him.

"No. Like someone who wants to savor every damn last minute." *Before there was no more life left to savor,* she thought sadly. "Who wants to try everything." He obviously wanted to try nothing, she thought. Nothing that had a risk attached to it. She wondered if he knew that.

"That's a euphemism for unstable in my book."

"Your book," she echoed, then nodded her head knowingly. "Ah, yes, that would be the 1955 YMCA version of 'The Facts of Life.'"

He had no idea why he was even trying to reason with her. Emotionally, he was about as drained as any man could be. Arguing with her wasn't helping matters any. "I'm not going to go on talking to you when you're babbling."

She watched him cross back to the doorway. He was a fairly good-looking man, she thought. What a shame he was so pigheaded.

She crossed her arms in front of her. "So, where does that leave us?"

"At each other's throats?" he guessed archly. At least, it looked that way to him.

"It doesn't have to be that way." There was a child's happiness at stake. She had to give this her best shot.

"Why? Having a personality transplant?"

Maybe the shot should be aimed at him. "No, investing in a silver bullet." *Down, Daisy. The man can't help being a jerk. It's probably something genetic.* She touched his arm, surprising him. She could tell by the way he looked at her. "All this bickering isn't going to help, or be good for Jeremy. Now we're both agreed that he's what's important here, right?" She dared him to dispute that.

He hated conceding a point to her, even if it was the truth. "Right."

She found it fascinating that he could talk through clenched teeth. "Neither one of us wants to drag him through court, right?"

"Right."

Two for two, not bad. "Yet neither one of us wants the other to raise him."

"Right," he agreed emphatically.

Then it was simple. Couldn't he see that? She smiled beatifically, tossing her hair over her shoulder, a sultry dark wave. "Then we have to try it my way. There is no other way."

There was one. He hesitated just a fraction of a second before he tried it. "Could you be bought off?"

Drew couldn't remember ever seeing eyes turn so dark so fast before. Dark and dangerous. The word magnificent whispered around the perimeters of his mind.

She couldn't tell if he was serious or not, but by his own admission, he didn't joke. That made what he suggested reprehensible. She chalked it off to stupidity. "Don't even suggest it," she said quietly, her tone all the more underscored because of it. "I don't want to have a reason to hate you."

So, she really wasn't doing this for the money. "Maybe I did misjudge you."

She arched a brow. "Maybe?"

"All right," he relented. "I misjudged you."

Daisy shook her head. He was difficult, no two ways about it. But she could handle difficult if it meant keeping Jeremy. "Like pulling teeth, Drew, but I guess you'll come around."

He didn't know just how she meant that, but he was taking no chances. "Don't hold your breath."

"So—" she stuck out her hand "—we have a bargain?"

He looked at her hand for a long moment. It was true, what she had said earlier. If necessary, he could arrange things so that he could work out of the L.A. office temporarily. And he could fly to New York for meetings that were unavoidable and couldn't be attended through the miracle of a visual hook-up. If Jeremy's welfare really depended on it, then he would have to stay.

Reluctantly, Drew took her hand. It felt small and delicate in his. Delicate. And the moon was made of green cheese. "We have a bargain."

He had the distinct image of Daniel Webster shaking hands with the devil just before the trial began. But Daniel had won that case, he reminded himself. And Drew fully intended to win this one.

Chapter Four

Margaret Reilly looked over the tops of her reading glasses as Daisy tossed her sweater carelessly in the direction of the chair. The back office of the nursery was small and crammed full of books, reports, a desk and a computer. But the morning sun filled it and made it appear somehow homey.

"Are you sure you should be back, Daisy?" She tucked away her morning newspaper, but not the box of doughnuts that was in front of her. She swallowed the bite in her mouth. "The funeral was just yesterday."

Daisy broke off a piece of the doughnut in Margaret's hand and realized that she had struck pay dirt, or raspberry jelly as it was. She quickly licked it from her fingers, savoring the sweet taste. She was fighting her way back among the living, she thought, and recovery involved all her senses.

"I've been away for four days, Margaret. I'm sure." Daisy popped the rest of the piece into her mouth. "Besides, I can't have you doing everything."

Margaret dusted the sugar from her fingers with a napkin, then took off her glasses. "Normally, I'd heartily agree. But this isn't exactly normal." She gave Daisy a huge hug. "How are you holding up?"

Daisy was grateful for the concern. It helped. "I need to work."

"Well, God knows you have it." Margaret ran a hand through her tangled blond hair. Hair that made her resemble, Daisy had affectionately pointed out, a mature Orphan Annie. "It seems like everyone in creation has been calling since you've been gone."

Margaret gestured toward a stack of order forms in the In box on the scarred desk. The desk had been a gift from Alyce, rescued from a thrift shop. It had turned out to be an unappreciated antique. Everywhere she looked, Daisy thought, there were going to be reminders of Alyce. For the rest of her life, there would be reminders. She'd have to find a way to deal with that.

"Word about us has gotten around." Margaret picked up the top two forms as she reached for another doughnut with her other hand. "I've had calls for everything from African violets to full-grown palm trees."

Daisy took the forms from Margaret. Friends since college, Margaret was more her partner than her assistant, though the mortgage papers only contained Daisy's name. The company, begun on a whim, had evolved from a simple florist shop to a landscaping consultant service with a small nursery in the back. The shop was a potpourri, like Daisy herself.

Daisy perused the first form. Indigo Company. Big time. "Palm trees?"

Margaret nodded. "The Indigo Company said they need instant landscaping for a mall they're putting up in Bedford. Seems the man in charge knew Jonathan and..." Margaret's voice trailed off. She looked at Daisy hesitantly. "Sorry."

"No reason to be," Daisy assured her, forcing her voice to sound bright. "Jonathan lent me the money to get started in this business and his connections have always brought us a lot of clients." She replaced the order forms on top of the stack. "Did you call Keeline?" she asked, referring to the largest wholesale nursery they dealt with.

"Not yet." Margaret eyed another doughnut. That would make three this morning. "The call came in yesterday afternoon."

Daisy took the order forms and secured them on her clipboard. She'd have to go over them today to make sure the proper calls were made. And check the delivery forms, as well. It wasn't that she didn't trust Margaret, it was just that Margaret tended to be easily distracted. Food or a good-looking man did it every time. "But you told them yes."

Margaret took out a third doughnut from the box and plopped it on the white napkin. A deep red stain oozed onto it.

"I told them yes. No order too large, no order too small, right?" She parroted the slogan beneath the Showers of Flowers... and Things logo outside the door and on their business card.

Daisy glanced at an invoice. Good, the five-gallon cypresses she had ordered had been delivered. Daisy checked off the form, making a note to take a look at them before having them delivered to her customer. "Right."

Margaret sighed contentedly as the doughnut plugged up the remaining space in her stomach. She fixed her attention on Daisy. "So, who was that hunk I saw standing next to you at the service?'' She flashed an apologetic grin. ''I didn't think it was right to ask yesterday.''

Daisy had to stop and think for a minute before she realized that Margaret was referring to Drew. ''That was Jonathan's brother.'' She thought of the way he had corrected her the night of his arrival. '''Andrew.'''

Margaret sighed deeply. ''What is he?''

''Annoying.'' Daisy reached for the pot of coffee Margaret had made. It was weak, but it was better than nothing. At least it was hot and she needed something to get her engine started.

Margaret shook her head. Her tight curls bobbed up and down like tiny blond springs. ''No, I mean, what does he do?''

Daisy took a sip of the coffee and then frowned. She could have gotten the same results, tastewise, if she had stuck a brown crayon into boiled water. At that moment, she would have paid a king's ransom for some old-fashioned, strong caffeine.

''I told you, annoy me.'' At least it felt as if that was his principle occupation in life since he had driven up her driveway two days ago. ''He's in the same company Jonathan was in. Heads it, actually.''

Margaret cocked her head, peering at Daisy's face. ''Sounds like the beginnings of a wonderful relationship.''

Margaret, Daisy thought, had to stop going to those old movie revivals. She downed the rest of the coffee and frowned again. Hot and terrible, no question about it. ''No relationship. More like a war.''

''Want to clarify that?'' Margaret took the cup from Daisy and replaced it with a doughnut. To Margaret, Daisy knew, sugar solved everything.

Daisy carefully turned up the side filled with jelly so that it wouldn't leak out. ''Drew *thinks* he's come to take Jeremy back with him to New York.''

Daisy had Margaret's undivided attention. "Uh-oh. Does he know that you've got legal guardianship?"

Daisy nodded and set her mouth grimly.

"And?" It seemed to Margaret that that would be the end of the matter.

Daisy's eyes darkened again, just as they had yesterday when it had happened. "He tried to buy me off."

Margaret groped behind her for a clear spot on the desk and leaned against it. "How many stitches did they have to give him in the emergency room?"

The image tickled Daisy and she laughed. "None. He remained unscarred, but it wasn't easy for me."

"I'll bet. On behalf of the female population, we thank you." The teasing grin faded as Margaret momentarily became serious. "You're not giving Jeremy to him, are you?" It was actually a rhetorical question. Daisy loved Jeremy as much as she had loved her sister and brother-in-law. If there was anything the woman was, it was fiercely loyal. Jeremy was going nowhere.

Daisy thought of the discussion they had had last night and Drew's reaction. "We have an arrangement."

Margaret leaned forward. "Sounds interesting." The grin had returned. "And he's without stitches. Hmm."

Daisy gave her a warning look. Margaret thought that everyone should be paired up. "Don't 'hmm' me. The arrangement is that he has to stay at the house for three months—"

"Better and better."

"—And in that time," Daisy pressed on doggedly, "if Jeremy grows to really love him, then I'll give Drew custody."

Margaret's grin faded and her jaw sagged in surprise. She was staring at her as if she had just declared that the world was really flat, Daisy thought. "You'd give him up?" Margaret finally said.

"In a pig's eye I will," Daisy declared firmly. "What I'm banking on is melting Mr. Ice-Water-For-Blood Addison so that he understands that Jeremy is better off staying with me. All I need," she concluded with a sigh, "is a blow torch."

"Alyce did it with Jonathan," Margaret reminded her. "As I recall, he was pretty stiff upper lipped when she first met him."

"I know, but I'm not Alyce," Daisy said wistfully.

"True." Margaret patted Daisy's hand. "But you work a lot quicker than anyone else I ever met. My money's on you, kid."

Daisy frowned as she toyed with a doughnut. "I don't know. I keep hoping that I'll find a way to make him come around, but what if I'm wrong? Right now, the man seems like an utter cold fish."

Except, Daisy amended silently, for that one moment when he looked as if he wanted to kiss her. But that could have just been her imagination.

Margaret scooted some crumbs off the desk and into the doughnut box. "If he's such a cold fish, what does he want with Jeremy?"

Daisy lifted a shoulder and let it drop. "I don't know." She would have liked to believe it was because Drew loved the boy, but she sincerely doubted that love came into the matter. Or, if it did, that Drew even realized it. She had her work cut out for her all right. "It has something to do with heritage and last names and things like that." She didn't want to waste any more time thinking about Andrew Addison and his motives. She had work to catch up on. "Come on, let's tackle these orders that came in." She gave her clipboard a little shake for emphasis. "I have a date for lunch this afternoon."

"With Mr. Wall Street?"

"Don't be silly. With my favorite short person." Daisy smiled. She hated leaving Jeremy this morning, but she assuaged the guilt by promising lunch at his favorite place. "I'm taking Jeremy to Hamburger Delight. They've just remodeled their play area and I know he's dying to break it in."

Daisy settled in behind the desk and began to divide the forms according to which wholesale nursery she would have to deal with to fill the request.

Margaret poured another cup of coffee and placed it within Daisy's reach. Daisy pointedly ignored it. "How's he taking it? Jeremy, I mean."

"Remarkably well for a four-year-old." Daisy stopped sorting to consider. "Almost too well. There seems to be a lot more of his father in him than I thought." Maybe that was for the best after all, she thought. She looked at Margaret, who was puttering around by the coffee machine. She knew procrastination when she saw it. "Come on, less talk, more work," she prodded affectionately.

Margaret pulled up a chair next to Daisy's desk. "Nice to know you haven't changed." Impulsively, Margaret gave Daisy's hand a squeeze. "Welcome back, Boss."

Daisy smiled her thanks, then looked at the forms again. There was a lot of planting here. Showers of Flowers... and Things wasn't just contracted to deliver the small orders, but to plant them, as well. And one-third of their crew on the premises had quit to go back to school full time last week. That put them in a bind. "Have we filled Eric's position, yet?"

Margaret sucked on her lower lip, suddenly chagrined. "Oh."

Daisy sighed as she looked at Margaret. She was afraid of what was coming. "What's 'oh'?"

Margaret made a comical face. "I forgot to place the ad in the newspaper."

Terrific. Daisy turned in her swivel chair and studied the bulletin board on the wall behind her desk. All the specifics of what went where and when were detailed on the spread sheet posted on it. "The Samuelsons are expecting to have three *Ligustrum* delivered and planted in their front yard today."

Margaret shook her head. "Doesn't look likely. Simon's got a bad back and Pablo's out with the flu. That just leaves you and me. The job's too small to call in a contracting crew," she pointed out.

When it rained, it poured. But, as everything else, it could be handled. Daisy squared her shoulders. "All right." She rose. "Help me load the shrubs and some bags of leaf mold and manure on the back of the truck."

"Me?"

Margaret was as sturdy-looking as Daisy was fragile. "You don't think I hired you just for your looks, do you?" Affectionately, Daisy patted Margaret's forearm. Despite Margaret's love affair with food, the woman never gained an ounce. "I knew I needed strong peasant stock to help me load things."

"Tote that barge, lift that bale."

"Now you've got the picture." Daisy laughed. She had been right about getting back to work. Being around Margaret always made her feel better. "I'll drop the shrubs off at the Samuelsons and start digging the holes myself after I have lunch with Jeremy." She paused. "Maybe I'll swing by Keeline and pick out the palm trees, too." She glanced at the form to see how many. Eight. Thank God she wasn't going to handle planting those. Keeline did its own delivering and planting. She just did the contracting. "Jeremy might get a kick out of helping me select them. It makes him feel important."

"You're not really planning on planting the Samuelson's shrubs yourself, are you?" Margaret asked as she followed Daisy out the door.

"You have a better idea?"

"Sure." She walked out to the back of the nursery with Daisy. "Stall them."

She was going to need several bags of leaf mold and manure, Daisy thought as she made her way to the rear of the yard where she had the shrubs set aside.

"That's not how a reputation gets built." Daisy began to mentally reshuffle her day, making certain that Jeremy wouldn't feel short-changed. "When I leave, you stay here in the shop and handle the walk-ins. Simon can help. I'll take care of the shrubs." She went to back their truck up to the delivery area of the nursery. "And make sure the ad for a nurseryman is in tomorrow's paper, okay?"

Margaret saluted. *"Oui, mon capitaine."*

Drew glanced at his watch as he entered the neatly tiled kitchen. Eight o'clock and no sign of her. She was probably sleeping in, he thought. It figured.

He had no patience with laid-back people. He'd been up for more than an hour already. He had showered, shaved and dressed, then called New York and informed them that he would be staying in Bel Air for a while. He didn't specify the exact length of time he would be gone. He hoped that it would ultimately be considerably less than the three months Anastasia had irrationally insisted on. With luck, he would get her to come to her senses and realize that Jeremy was better off with him before the month was out.

The CEOs hadn't been very happy about the news. He could tell by the response he had received during the three-way conversation. But he was head of the company and that put an end to the matter. At least, he had thought, hanging up, for now.

His father had inherited Addison Corporation from his father, but it had taken Drew and Jonathan to turn it into the vast conglomerate it was today. Initially begun in the 1940s as a simple electronics company, Addison Corporation had diversified to include a whole range of technology. They were now a holding company for several companies in a number of major fields. The array spanned the spectrum from television monitors to sophisticated optical imaging and sensing devices used on the latest space shuttles. And ever since Jonathan had eased away, Drew had been in charge of it all. The corporation occupied most of his waking hours, but it provided him with an enormous sense of accomplishment. It wasn't even the money. He lived basically a simple life. It was seeing something so large and diverse prospering because of him.

Consequently, Drew had no idea how to relax, how to function in a home with time on his hands. But he didn't see that as a liability. For him home was a place where he brought his work if he didn't get a chance to finish it in the office. A place where his live-in valet prepared his meals and where he slept when he wasn't on a business trip in Europe or parts of the U.S.

Without work, he felt restless, at loose ends. To just sit back and do nothing productive wasn't in his nature, even for a day. There were things he could be accomplishing. Why waste precious time?

Because he couldn't operate without a detailed daily schedule, Drew had made mental plans while he'd showered. He was going to see about creating a temporary headquarters at the small research operation Jonathan had begun in Bel Air. It was more of a scientific think tank than an actual branch office. They paid top-notch scientists to work free-form, developing ideas that might someday fuel an entire new technological field, the way PCs and VCRs once had.

Addison Corporation's actual west coast building was located in San Francisco, but Jonathan had set up an annex in Southern California because he hadn't wanted to move. Undoubtedly, it had been Alyce's idea, but Jonathan had remained adamant when discussing the matter with Drew. It was Bel Air or nothing. And so, Bel Air it was.

Drew had just begun to address the problem of the coffeemaker and how it worked when Irene walked in, followed by Jeremy.

"Good morning, Mr. Addison," Irene said crisply. "Breakfast?"

"Good morning." Drew searched his memory, trying to remember the woman's name. "Irene," he added belatedly. "Coffee."

The white head nodded once without bothering to make a confirming reply. Drew turned his attention toward Jeremy. Though he wanted the boy to live with him and knew that he loved the boy as much as he was capable of loving anyone, Drew still felt ill-at-ease in Jeremy's presence. He had little to no idea how to make idle conversation with adults, much less a child.

Drew forced a smile to his lips. "Hi, Jeremy, how are you today?"

"I'm okay." Jeremy pulled out a kitchen chair and scrambled onto it. Seated slightly askew, he stretched his feet out in front of him. The sneakers were new and almost scuff free, with large, bright blue, droopy laces. Jeremy surveyed them proudly. He was learning how to tie them himself.

Abruptly, he looked up at Drew. "Are you gonna come, too?"

Behind him, Irene was busy doing whatever she normally did. Drew decided to join Jeremy at the table for a minute while he waited for his coffee. "Come? Come where?"

"To Hamburger Delight." The "of course" was silent but implied nonetheless. The word "precocious" presented itself to Drew. "Aunt Daisy's taking me."

It sounded like the kind of establishment she would be partial to, Drew thought. "I wasn't invited." Thank God for small favors. He could just imagine the kind of food served there. Besides, he wasn't going to have time for any outings today. There was just too much to do. He was already behind by two days.

Drew half turned in his seat as Irene approached, ready to take his coffee from her. He saw that she was holding a bowl of cereal and a container of milk. Self-consciously, he let his empty hand drop as she placed both items in front of Jeremy.

The boy grasped the milk container in both hands and doused his cereal liberally. A white stream came pouring out. Drops of milk ricocheted off round, colored balls and then fell on the tablecloth. Drew squelched the impulse to brush them off with his napkin.

"You can come if you like," Jeremy said as he tried to sink pink, yellow and purple tiny balls beneath his milk. He looked up hopefully at his uncle.

Drew didn't like the way Jeremy's expectant expression made him feel. An unfamiliar tinge of guilt sliced through him, almost making him squirm. "I don't think your aunt would like me tagging along."

"Sure she would." Jeremy grinned at him, his lips already outlined in milk after one sampling. "Aunt Daisy likes everybody."

Well, he had his suspicions that the woman didn't like him and that made him a member of a very exclusive club, according to Jeremy.

"No, I really don't think that I can make—"

Drew stopped, aware that Irene was watching him and there was just the slightest frown of disapproval on her lips.

Was he going to have to contend with her while he was here as well? He wasn't used to living in a house with women. His mother had divorced his father and left when he was ten, not that she had been much of an influence in his life before then. He had spent most of his youth in all-boys boarding schools. Reckoning with the female sensibility was something completely foreign to Drew.

Still, the disapproving, maternal look made him uncomfortable. He looked at Jeremy and relented ever so slightly.

"Well, maybe. I have some things to take care of first." The boy would probably forget all about having him come along as soon as he was out of sight. Children weren't known for their lengthy attention spans, or so he had been told.

Jeremy wriggled happily. "We're going at 'leban-thirty. That's when Aunt Daisy told me she'd be back."

"Back?" Drew echoed, surprised. He glanced unconsciously toward the ceiling. She wasn't in bed? "Back from where?"

Jeremy was finally winning his battle against the cereal balls. Growing soggy, they were beginning to sink. "The flower place."

Drew glanced at his watch. No, it hadn't stopped. It was only eight-fifteen. "You mean that she's at work now?" That didn't fit the irresponsible image he had of her.

Jeremy bobbed his head up as he gleefully shoved another colorful spoonful into his mouth. The cereal still crunched.

"It smells good there. Sometimes she takes me and lets me play hide-and-seek," Jeremy confided, lowering his voice just a fraction. He smiled proudly. "She even let me help pick flowers for the backyard." Some of the exuberance left his eyes as his expression grew solemn. "Mama's backyard."

Oh, God, Drew thought, the boy was going to cry. Now what? He was as lost with a child's tears as he was with a woman's. Not relishing the prospect, Drew sought to divert Jeremy's mind. "Where is Hamburger Delight? I'd like to come."

The small shoulders rose and fell as Jeremy searched his memory. "I dunno. Over there." He pointed vaguely past Drew's head.

East. That didn't exactly narrow things down.

Irene finally brought him his coffee, freshly brewed. It smelled like heaven. "Third and Rosencrans. On the corner. Can't miss it. Unless you're not looking." She placed the cup down near his elbow, then set a creamer next to it. There was a small ceramic bowl of sugar cubes in the middle of the table. Irene moved it toward Drew.

"Not you," she warned Jeremy when his hand darted out to take one.

Drew took his coffee black and eye opening. Irene's was. He waited a beat until the hot fluid burned its way through his system, jarring everything to attention as it went.

"Thank you," he murmured in Irene's general direction. He remembered that he didn't really know his way around the area that well. "Do you have a map of the city somewhere?" he asked Irene. "I have to get to the office and set up some things."

"Are you going to eat with me?" Jeremy asked suddenly before Irene could reply.

"Sure, at Hamburger Delight." Just as he thought, no attention span whatsoever. Boarding school would quickly cure that.

The brown hair fanned out as Jeremy shook his head fiercely. "No, I mean now." Jeremy looked at the empty space on Drew's place mat. "Daddy always ate breakfast with me."

There it was again, guilt. He didn't care for it at all. "That's because Daddy didn't work very much," Drew pointed out.

The words had no effect on Jeremy. "My daddy was fun," Jeremy said wistfully.

Fun. Drew doubted very much if he could be *fun*. But he had enlisted in this war for Jeremy and knew that he was going to have to score some direct hits. Otherwise he had no hope of gaining Jeremy's approval. Without that, the boy wouldn't come willingly with him to New York. And then he'd have an even worse war on his hands. With Anastasia.

Drew looked at the open, upturned face. "Just what was it that your dad did to be fun?"

Jeremy chewed quickly so he could answer without a mouthful of cereal getting in the way. "He played trains. Can you play trains?"

"I don't know," Drew answered honestly. "I never tried." He couldn't really remember playing when it came down to it. There was a vague recollection of a set of toy soldiers in gray and blue uniforms, but he couldn't actually remember ever playing with them. They had stood at attention, lined up on a shelf. He had no childhood to draw on.

Cereal forgotten, Jeremy was out of his seat and grabbing Drew by the hand. "I gotta set o' trains in the playroom. Daddy put 'em up." He was tugging Drew out of his chair urgently. "C'mon and see."

"What about your breakfast?" Drew pointed toward the bowl. He had absolutely no desire to "play trains." He had an office to set up.

"Breakfast first, young man," Irene said sternly.

For the life of him, Drew wasn't certain if she was just addressing Jeremy or if he was included in the reprimand. To further confound him, Irene placed a plate of bacon and eggs in front of him.

"I don't eat breakfast," Drew told Irene. "Just toast."

His statement fell on deaf, unsympathetic ears. Irene eyed the plate. "Shame to let it go to waste." She made absolutely no attempt to remove the dish.

"C'mon," Jeremy urged, wiggling back onto his seat. "Hurry up and eat so we can go and play."

"I can't go and play, Jeremy, I—"

Drew saw a look of disappointment paint the small features. Features that echoed Jonathan's. "All right," he sighed. "You show me the trains and we'll make them go around once, fair enough?"

Jeremy was wolfing down the rest of his breakfast. More milk joined the spots on the tablecloth as the spoon flew. "What's that mean?"

Drew searched for an explanation Jeremy would understand. He wasn't used to trying to simplify things. "That means we compromise."

"Huh?" The dark eyes stared at him blankly.

Drew heard Irene chuckle in the background. She was obviously going to let him work this out on his own. What the hell was a synonym for compromise? "I do something that you want and then you let me do something that I have to do."

"Oh." Jeremy's face lit up as he understood. "Sure. Fair enough," he sang out. He grinned at Drew as he repeated the new phrase.

Drew had a sneaking suspicion that there was a lot more of Anastasia in the little boy than first met the eye. Oh, well, he supposed he could spare half an hour. He ate his breakfast quickly and estimated that he could get to the office at around nine if traffic was light.

Chapter Five

The best laid estimates of mice and men often went awry, Drew decided sometime later. He was down on his hands and knees, attempting to successfully mount a derailed steam engine back on the track. He discovered that it was a lot more difficult than it looked. It took Drew three attempts before all eight stationary and two front mobile wheels made proper contact with the tracks.

The layout in the room was surprisingly elaborate. Jonathan had obviously been a railroad enthusiast. All those years they had spent growing up, and he had never known, Drew thought. The entire floor of the recreation room was covered with tracks, trestles and two complete villages with various people and animals populating the imaginary world. Jeremy had happily told Drew as much history about the growth of the two villages as he could remember while they ran the engines on alternating tracks.

Drew sat back on his heels, unconsciously tugging at the engineer's cap Jeremy had insisted he wear. That this had all been lovingly arranged by his brother left Drew totally in awe.

What else didn't I know about you, Jonathan?

"Can we run it yet?" Jeremy asked. He was wearing a smaller version of Drew's cap and lay sprawled on his stomach on the floor. He tapped the toes of his new sneakers impatiently against the indoor-outdoor carpeting.

Drew nodded, hoping that the engine would work this time. It had made the most feeble attempt at traversing the tracks the other two times. During both tries, the train had moved about three lengths of track forward, falling over at the first curve it encountered.

"One last time around and then I have to leave, or I won't be able to make lunch," he warned Jeremy.

As it was, Drew didn't think he really had a prayer of making it to the restaurant. Setting up his office was going to take the better part of a day. Which was just as well. He hadn't had a hamburger in years and hated anything that came under the heading of "fast food."

Jeremy solemnly took in the information. His hand hovered over the transformer. There were passengers waiting in the little station for the green and black engine to arrive. "Ready?"

Drew gave the signal. "Turn it on." He felt a certain surge of accomplishment when the train sped smoothly by him, even though he knew it was absolutely absurd to feel that way about a toy train. Still, he watched as it traveled by a tiny herd of black and white cattle on its way into the first village.

"You did it!" Jeremy cheered.

Drew was totally absorbed in the train's progress. So absorbed, he didn't hear the door behind him opening. He heard her laughter before he managed to turn around. Anastasia. She *would* catch him like this, he thought in embarrassed disgust. Her laugh was low and throaty, and made him think of a dark, smoky room where people drank whiskey and exchanged secret stories that no one bothered to remember.

He quickly got to his feet to face her. She had an amused expression and was staring at his head. He realized that she was looking at the hat Jeremy had given him. Belatedly, Drew snatched it off, crumpling it self-consciously. The indignant look he gave her had absolutely no effect.

"I guess you're surprised," he muttered.

He looked so adorably silly. And it touched her heart to find him this way because of Jeremy. She wished now she hadn't laughed so that she could have observed them a little longer. *Yes, Virginia, the man is human after all.* "Speechless."

Drew thrust the hat to Jeremy. "I sincerely doubt that." The woman probably even talked in her sleep. The sudden urge to find out utterly mystified him.

Daisy took the hat from Jeremy and turned it around in her hand, as if to study it. "It makes a very interesting statement." She raised her eyes to Drew. "Complements your suit."

Jeremy had no idea what they were talking about. But he knew that Daisy's appearance meant that she was going to keep her promise. Since his parents had gone away, he was nervous about other people disappearing out of his life. No one was more important to him than Daisy. He tugged on her hand until she bent down. When she did, he pressed petal-soft lips to her cheek.

"Hi, Aunt Daisy."

She gave him a proper kiss back and then pulled the brim of his hat down over his eyes.

"Hi, yourself." She rose so that she could face Drew. "So, what have you two men been up to?" She still couldn't believe that she had actually caught Drew playing with the trains. Jonathan had sometimes holed up here for hours, drifting off into another, simpler world with his son. But Drew wasn't Jonathan. Yet.

Drew saw the laughter lingering in her eyes. They crinkled slightly on the sides and seemed to glow, lighting up her face. It was an enticing picture. That still didn't mean he appreciated being the source of her amusement.

"We were playing trains, Aunt Daisy." Jeremy tucked his hand into hers easily, trustingly. She closed her fingers over his, thinking how warm it felt, having a child look to her for security. "Uncle Drew plays trains pretty good. I teached him how."

"Taught, baby, you taught him," she corrected affectionately. Daisy took Jeremy's hat off his head and tousled his hair. "We'd better get going."

The boy cocked his head quizzically, glancing at the clock on the wall. It was big, with a white face and black numbers, resembling the clocks found in old railroad stations. Jeremy was just learning to tell time and once in a while, the numbers became jumbled. "Is it 'leban-thirty already?"

"No. It's ten-thirty." She pointed out the numbers. "See?" The small face turned toward hers, waiting for an explanation. "I thought we'd go out a little sooner. I've got to deliver some shrubs early this afternoon. Is that okay by you, Tiger?" She began to walk toward the doorway.

Jeremy loved being consulted and nodded vigorously as he followed. "Sure. He's coming, too," Jeremy added as an afterthought.

She turned from the door. "Who?" Daisy looked at Drew. Jeremy had to be talking about one of his friends. He couldn't possibly mean Drew. The man was dressed for a power meeting, not lunch at Hamburger Delight surrounded by screaming children.

Sometimes he wondered how grown-ups kept track of anything at all. "Uncle Drew," Jeremy told her patiently. Who else would he be talking about?

Time to make an exit. "Well I—" Drew saw the way Daisy lifted a brow knowingly as she looked at him. Her laughter might be enticing, but her smug look had him wanting to strangle her again.

Think you know all the answers, don't you? Something perverse had Drew taking up the challenge. "Yes, Jeremy invited me along."

"He has to go to an office," Jeremy told Daisy quickly, holding her hand as they went down the stairs. He looked over his shoulder at Drew. "What's an office? Is it like Aunt Daisy's flower shop?"

Drew could just envision her shop. Chaos in a rectangular box with bills haphazardly scattered throughout. "Hardly."

"No, sweetie," Daisy said cheerfully as she opened the front door. She let Jeremy go out first. "Nothing living thrives there, I'm sure."

Definitely strangle, Drew thought. First chance he got. They didn't prosecute justifiable homicide and anyone who knew her knew it was justifiable.

Lost in thought, Drew was unprepared for the frontal attack.

"But you'll go to the office later, right?" It was a hopeful question, voiced by a boy who didn't appear as if he was going to graciously accept no for an answer. Jeremy took Drew's hand in his, linking small fingers through long, artistic ones. He smiled brightly up at Drew. "'Cause Aunt Daisy's here now."

Drew looked at Daisy over Jeremy's head. "Your timing is off." *As always.*

"On the contrary." She turned and walked toward her truck. "I think my timing is marvelous. You can follow us in your car if you like."

He was struck speechless as he examined the large, brightly painted truck. It was a flatbed with large lavender flowers painted on a field of white. Across the side was the logo. She belonged behind the wheel of a cabriolet convertible coupe or something equally as diminutive. Not a large truck used to haul who-knew-what. "You're going to drive this?"

"Sure, why not?" Next, he was going to criticize the clothes she wore. The man was a chauvinist. She dug deep for patience. "What's wrong with it? It's the company truck." She attempted to maintain a cheerful attitude, but he was making it difficult.

Drew circled the vehicle slowly and stopped at the rear. There were shrubs in it. Large ones secured with a chain to prevent them from falling over. "What are you carrying around with you?"

"*Ligustrum* for the Samuelsons," she said matter-of-factly, joining him at the rear of the truck. "I was planning to go to lunch with Jeremy, then swing by the Samuelson's house and plant their shrubs." She took Jeremy's face in her hand and gave it just the slightest affectionate squeeze. Jeremy pretended to make a face and she made a sillier one in return. "You can help me water them when I'm done."

"When *you're* done?" Drew looked at her. She made it sound as if she was actually doing the job herself. "Don't you have any help?"

She didn't care for his condescending manner. Did he think he could just walk in and take over her life as well as Jeremy's?

"Yes, I have help. I have lots of help. Normally. But Pablo's sick, Simon strained his back and can't do heavy labor for a while, and Eric has admirably gone back to college full time." She walked to the front of the truck and boosted Jeremy inside the cab, then secured the seat belt. "Unfortunately, that leaves me in a bind."

He didn't see a problem. "Why don't you hire someone else?"

Daisy got into the truck and closed the door. She leaned her elbow out of the open window. "I'm trying. But in the meantime—" she nodded toward the shrubs "—work has to get done."

Every time he gave her the benefit of the doubt, his original assessment returned. Crazy, completely, irresponsibly crazy. "You can't possibly lift those things."

Her annoyance gave way to amusement again. He did look cute when he got so worked up. "Why can't I possibly?" she asked, echoing his words.

She had to ask? "You're too...too..." He waved his hands in frustration. Didn't she realize she could get hurt? "Too damn stubborn is what you are."

Daisy nodded solemnly. "Maybe that's how I got them on the truck in the first place. By being too damn stubborn." She grinned at him, conveniently omitting the fact that she had had help.

He should just let her go and do the work. What did it matter to him if she hurt her back or wound up in the hospital? It would get her out of the way that much sooner and he could go home with Jeremy. No, not his concern, no, sir.

"Where is this place?" His tone was gruff.

"Three miles from Hamburger Delight. West." For good measure, she pointed, curious to see what Drew would say next.

He turned the situation over in his mind. The woman needed a keeper. How could she possibly believe she was equipped to take care of a four-year-old when she couldn't even take care of herself?

"All right, I'll help you." He bit the words off as if he had just agreed to a death sentence.

Daisy sat back in her seat, studying him. *Why* was he offering to help? "You'll get your suit all dirty."

She was mocking him, he thought. "Let me worry about my suit."

"Fine." Daisy raised her hands, palms up, in surrender. Far be it from her to turn down free help. She hadn't looked forward to doing the job and she had absolutely no problem about needing to do things on her own. Help was fine. Terrific. Even better if it came from him. If nothing else, it meant that there was a little bit of Jonathan lurking somewhere within that single-breasted suit.

She indicated his car. "Now, if you'll just follow me." She turned on her engine and watched Drew walk toward his car and get in. He looked as if he was muttering to himself. She couldn't keep the smile from her lips and didn't bother to try as she fastened her seat belt.

Jeremy leaned over as far as he could, held back by the massive seat belt that restrained him in two places. "How come you're grinning?"

"I think that Uncle Drew might just be a nicer man under all that gruff talk than he wants everyone to believe." And nice men, she thought, could ultimately be gotten to see things her way. Especially when it came to the care of a sensitive child who was attached to her.

Jeremy tried to puzzle that out for a moment and failed. "Why doesn't he want us to know he's nice?" It made no sense to him.

Daisy looked in her passenger mirror, making sure not to lose Drew. "I don't think he knows it himself."

Carrying a tray overflowing with French fries, hamburgers, sodas and one token black coffee for Drew, Daisy made her way into the outdoor portion of the restaurant. Drew followed silently while Jeremy had already blazed a trail for them. She found an empty table in the shape of a flattened mushroom and sat down on the closest toadstool. Drew looked uncertain whether or not to sit down at all.

"It doesn't bite," she assured him with a grin.

He scowled and then sat, careful to avoid a small, damp lime-green spot that had once been part of a Popsicle.

An enclosed pen with multicolored balls and a curved, royal blue slide leading into it provided the main source of entertainment for anyone under four feet tall. Squeals came from beneath the balls, belonging to children who had dive-bombed into the pen ahead of Jeremy.

Jeremy took one bite of his hamburger, then went barreling into the center of the pen.

There was no back to the toadstool and it was uncomfortably small. Drew realized that there was no right way to sit on a toadstool. He watched as Jeremy went clambering up the ladder on the other side of the slide. He was right about wanting to take Jeremy with him. The boy had no discipline.

"You should make him sit down and eat. It's better for digestion."

She shrugged, watching Jeremy enjoy himself. She was relieved that he wasn't sitting around, moping, although she knew it had to come someday. It was like waiting for the other shoe to drop.

"He's having fun. His digestion's taking care of itself." She pulled a French fry out of the paper container and ate it.

"It's a bad example."

She chewed slowly, her eyes on Drew's face. "Having fun?"

Why did she always insist on twisting things? "You know what I mean."

"Yes, I do." Her eyes held his as she wondered what was behind them. She was relieved that her initial wish was true. Deep down, so far down he probably wasn't aware of it, Drew really wasn't as cold, as strict as he liked to portray. Now it wasn't just a matter of keeping Jeremy safe with her. It was also turning into a matter of trying to pull this self-contained man out of the prison he had voluntarily walked into years ago. "Do you know what I mean?"

"Never."

She sighed and ate two fries before continuing. "Right now, Jeremy needs fun. He needs fun and love a lot more than he needs proper table manners." She watched Jeremy jump into the pen, balls flying everywhere, then scramble out for another turn. "We'll work that part out later."

Drew looked at the amount of fat and cholesterol represented by the items on the tray and frowned. "Along with nutrition?"

His attitude tickled her. This was a man who needed fun in his life as much as Jeremy did. He desperately needed to loosen up. "You don't like French fries and hamburgers?"

How could she be so blissfully uninformed? Everyone knew what junk food was. Poison in an appealing wrapper. "Do you have any idea what they're doing to your body right now?"

Because it irritated him, she bit into another fry. "Making it happy?" she guessed.

He tried not to watch the slow, sensuous movement of her mouth. She was doing this on purpose. "You're incorrigible, you know that?"

She sighed, dragging her hand through her hair. "If I didn't, you'd keep reminding me." She looked at the paper coffee cup. He had left it untouched. Probably needs a French name attached to the coffee bean before he'd deign to sip it. "You obviously hate the food and you look like you're ready to be shot out of a cannon at any minute. What are you doing here, anyway?''

"Jeremy asked me to come."

She sighed, stretching out her long legs before her, the heels of her worn boots resting on the black, scarred asphalt. For a short woman, she seemed to be all leg, he observed.

Daisy told herself to keep a rein on her temper. The man was trying. Pathetically, but he was trying. And you didn't encourage a flower to grow by hitting it. "I supposed that means you're not all bad."

"Thank you."

She sat up again, as if some mysterious force had suddenly energized her. "But with some effort, I'm sure you'll get there." Maybe it was time for a serious talk, without the boxing gloves on. This seemed like an innocuous enough place to do it, surrounded with children and their mothers. "Why do you want to take Jeremy away, Drew? You can see he's happy here."

She really didn't understand, did she? All she seemed to think of was playing and having fun. Those traits didn't go very far in the real world, not if you intended to make something of yourself. He ducked as a bright red ball went sailing overhead. Damn, this place was hazardous. "I want to see him reach his full potential. Happiness alone isn't everything."

"It is if you don't have it." She thought of how frightened she had felt those first few nights at Uncle Warren's house. And then at the boarding school when even Warren had shipped them away. "It plugs up an awful lot of holes."

She looked as if she were speaking from experience. He felt a vague curiosity as to what had caused that faraway look in her eyes, but he dismissed it. The less he knew about her, the simpler things remained. Jonathan had told him more than he wanted to know as it was. "The holes get larger if you don't have the proper education to face the world.''

"I don't see a conflict here." She broke off a piece of a French fry and tossed it to a scavenging starling that had wandered into the play area. "You can have happiness and get an education." The small bird struggled with the piece as he tried to fly and eat at the same time.

The sound of her delighted laughter curled through Drew's system like sweet potent wine. If he didn't know any better, he would say it had a drugging effect on him.

Two more birds hovered hesitantly a few feet away and she broke the remainder of the fry in two and tossed it to them.

She seemed to be more interested in throwing her food away than in eating it. "What are you doing?"

It was an odd question. "I'm feeding a bird." She stopped and realized why he might have asked. "Didn't you ever feed pigeons as a kid in New York?"

"No."

She wasn't surprised, just saddened. He had probably never done a single carefree thing in his life. She suddenly felt sorry for him, even though he was still the man who wanted to take Jeremy out of her life and turn him into a robot.

"Ducks?" she pressed. "Birds? Stray cat?" Had he even had a pet? "Anything?"

There was pity in her eyes and he couldn't for the life of him understand why. Why should she feel sorry for him because he never threw food at an animal? "You make it sound like a crime that I didn't."

"No, just a shame."

"Why?" It made no sense to him but he wanted to understand. Why, he didn't know and didn't try to explore. Knowing would make him as flaky as she was. "Because I didn't clog a bird's arteries?"

She stopped feeding the starlings and looked at him, a French fry dangling from her fingertips. "Are you always such a wet blanket, or do I get special treatment?" She turned all the way around on the toadstool to face him. "You can't possibly be as single-mindedly bleak and morose as you paint yourself out to be. This has to be an act, right?"

He wasn't going to get into an argument with her in a public place. Drew tried to turn away from her but found that when he turned sideways, he was in the way. A legion of small children kept running into him on their way to the pen's slide. He shifted around.

"You're babbling again."

He didn't fool her. "I think I'm coming damn near close to the truth and you don't like it. Emotions frighten you, don't they?" His expression darkened and she knew she was right. The man couldn't show any emotion except anger. She supposed it was a start.

He was about to tell her that it was none of her business, then stopped as Jeremy came running over for another bite of his hamburger. The boy barely broke stride as he turned to hurry back to the slide.

"Careful, Jeremy," Drew called after him. "You're going to throw up."

"No, he won't."

How did he know she was going to say that?

"Jeremy never throws up. He has a cast-iron stomach." She started to throw another piece to the one lone bird that remained, then decided not to.

"Even iron cracks."

She looked at him. Was he talking about himself, or her? "I'm counting on it. Here—" she held up the French fry in front of his mouth "—have one."

He lifted a brow. "Run out of birds to feed?"

She shook her head, her eyes on his. He did have beautiful eyes. Soulful eyes. Was there a soul behind them? "Found something that needs charity more."

Drew grabbed her hand in his to move it away. For some reason, he didn't. He left his fingers laced lightly around the small wrist. Her pulse was scrambling against his thumb. He watched the smile spread on her lips as she slowly fed him the slender strip of potato.

"Good?"

He wasn't even aware of chewing. All he was aware of was her, the light fragrance that wafted to him, the sensuous smile on her full lips. He was eating a French fry, for God's sake. Why did it feel like an erotic experience?

"Greasy," he murmured.

"There's something to be said for that, too." The words were hardly a whisper as his lips grazed the tips of her fingers, finishing the tiny bit of food.

She had felt something, Daisy thought. Something strange and powerful and just the slightest bit dangerous. It intrigued her.

The tingling sensation on her fingertips wouldn't go away.

A shout jarred their attention away from one another and toward Jeremy. The boy was standing on top of the last rung on the slide, waving to them.

"Watch me!" he crowed importantly just before he did a half gainer into the center of the balls two feet below. A barrage of balls went flying in all directions again as other children squealed with delight or indignation at being displaced.

"Jeremy, careful!" Daisy called out, half rising. "You don't want to squash anyone."

The warning brought only giggles from Jeremy and the children around him.

She had no idea how to go about disciplining a child. "That's it, make it sound like fun."

Her pulses still humming, Daisy sat a little straighter, a little more removed from Drew. "It *is* fun. Your trouble, Mr. Addison, is that you don't know the first thing about having fun."

"My trouble," Drew corrected her, "is sitting right next to me." He had never meant anything so wholeheartedly in his life.

Jeremy was exhausted, but they still had to drag him away from the play area.

"Are you really going to go through with this?" Drew nodded at the shrubs in back of her truck.

"This isn't a challenge, Drew." She bent inside the cab to secure Jeremy's seat belt. "This is my work. I'm sure you understand what work is."

"I understand." He closed the door on Jeremy, then walked around the front of the truck. "I just never expected to hear the word coming from you."

"Don't start," she warned.

Too late for that, he thought as he got into his own car. Something *had* started and for the life of him, he didn't know what to do about it, other than ignore it and hope it would go away.

Drew had no idea why he bothered to follow her. Anastasia was a damn stubborn woman who deserved to reap the consequences of her actions. But she was dragging his nephew around, so that meant that he had to keep an eye on them both.

The Samuelsons lived in a ranch-style house that was sprawled out on a third of an acre and looked far too large for them to be living in alone. They were an elderly, retired couple. They had the look of people who had weathered a good many storms in their lifetime and had been together forever.

They were both out front when Daisy pulled up in her truck. It looked as if they had been waiting for her. Mrs. Samuelson hurried to the rear of the truck before Daisy had even parked.

"Oh, these will look so lovely out front, my dear." Daisy joined her with Jeremy following in her wake. All signs of exhaustion had vanished in the short trip. "Are you sure you can handle this?" Mrs. Samuelson looked at her dubiously. Though they were the same height, the older woman was a great deal more sturdy-looking. "Maybe Mr. Samuelson could—"

The last thing in the world Daisy wanted was to have the older man sweating and possibly working himself up to a heart attack. She was more than capable of planting the shrubs by herself. She had done it before.

"I'm fine, really. You two just go inside and I'll call you when I'm finished." She looked at the bags of manure and leaf mold leaning against the inside of the flatbed. "It's going to take me a while."

Drew pulled the car up behind her, parking by the curb. When he got out, he was greeted with a broad smile and a warm handshake. Mrs. Samuelson had his hand in both of hers.

"You must be Daisy's husband," Mrs. Samuelson said warmly.

"God forbid," Drew and Daisy said at the same time.

Mrs. Samuelson looked completely confused.

"This is my brother-in-law, Drew Addison." Daisy hooked her arm through the woman's and gently led her toward her front door.

"You'll call if you need anything?" Mrs. Samuelson asked. "Water, iced tea, lunch?"

"I promise." Daisy turned around to catch the amused look on Drew's face.

"You're not half bad when you smile, you know?" she observed, passing him.

He had no response for that. He watched the way Jeremy shadowed her every move. At the very least, the boy would be in her way and he could get hurt. "Why don't I take Jeremy home?" Drew suggested.

"I don't wanna go home." Jeremy stuck his hands in his back pockets the way Daisy did as she surveyed the front yard. "Aunt Daisy needs help."

Truer words were never spoken. "I fully agree."

Daisy looked over her shoulder and quirked her lips into a fraction of a smile before bracing herself to tug the first bag of dirt from the truck.

Stupid, that's what she was. She didn't have the brains that God gave a gnat. Drew elbowed her out of the way. "I'll do it."

She looked at him. She was wearing jeans and a pink pullover while he was attired to address the chairman of the board. "You'll get your suit all dirty," she reminded him.

"I'll send you the cleaning bill."

Maybe there was hope for him yet. "Fair enough."

"Hey, I know 'bout that. Uncle Drew teached—taught—me," Jeremy said eagerly.

Daisy smiled at Drew before climbing onto the truck. "See, happy kids absorb things more quickly."

As he slid the second bag from the flatbed, Drew refrained from answering. Daisy worked the first container to the edge of the truck.

"I've got it." Drew yanked the container down, setting it on the driveway. He climbed on the back of the truck and pulled over the other two containers, then placed them next to the first one. Sweat was beginning to trickle down his back by the time he finished.

He frowned, taking off his jacket. He should have done that in the first place. "And now you're going to dig?"

She rolled up her sleeves and hid a smile as she saw Jeremy do the same. "Unless you know a better way to get them into the ground."

"Yeah, hired help." Drew let out along breath. "How many shovels did you bring?"

"One." She took it off the truck and turned to look at him, a lopsided grin on her face. "I'm not a two-fisted digger."

He attempted to take the shovel from her by placing his hand over hers on the handle. "We'll take turns."

She surrendered the shovel, wondering how long it would be before Drew gave up. Men who sat behind a desk for a living didn't tend to have much stamina as a rule. "Far be it from me to argue."

"Ha!" He stripped off his shirt, tossing it on top of the jacket.

Daisy's breath backed up in her lungs as she saw the ridge of muscles she had only glimpsed briefly the other night. His was not a body that came from a sedentary life-style. It was, in a word, gorgeous. She knew Margaret would be drooling right about now.

"Health club?" she guessed.

He dragged the first container over toward the front yard. Jeremy was holding on to the other side of the deep green plastic and running to try to keep up. "What?"

"The muscles." She tapped one finger at his biceps. "Work out at the health club?"

"No, I had them flown in."

She took the shovel from him and poked a hole in the center of the first bag of manure, preparing it. She poked a little harder than she might have. "Look, no one's asking you to do this."

He took the shovel from her. "Shut up before I find another use for this thing."

She stood back, her arms folded before her. "Are you always this testy, doing good deeds? There—" she pointed "—start there."

He broke ground. "I don't know. I'm not in the habit of doing good deeds."

And why he was doing one now was totally beyond him.

Chapter Six

Daisy watched Drew as he dug, wrestling with the almost impenetrable ground. His muscles rippled from the effort. Sweat glistened on his body and ran down his back in twisting, winding rivulets, creating an ache in Daisy that completely surprised her. This was Drew she was reacting to. For a moment, the realization took Daisy's breath away.

Except for the trousers, which were quickly losing their crease and gaining stains created by dirt and sweat in their stead, no one seeing him now would have ever taken Drew to be a high-powered executive. He looked like a laborer, one who could have easily caused, she thought, more than one female's heart to arrest. Fortunately hers was working just fine. Perhaps beating a little faster than normal, but it was almost eighty-five degrees and she *was* working. At least it was an excuse.

Daisy tried very hard not to stare as she dragged the five bags of leaf mold and manure into the yard. It wasn't easy. Whatever else he was, Drew was magnificent.

Drew felt his arms aching. He had met with annoying resistance each time he tried to push the shovel into the ground. The earth in Bel Air had a lot in common with Anastasia, he thought.

The shovel resounded with a tinny clunk as it hit something even harder than the earth. Drew bent to take out what looked to be a rusted length of pipe in the hole he was digging. He tossed it to the side.

Wiping his forehead with the back of his hand, he glared at Daisy. "What do you people have out here for soil, rock?"

Daisy dropped the last bag next to the others, then came up behind Drew and peered into the hole. It wasn't deep enough yet. "Close. It's clay that oozes and sucks your shoes right off if you try to walk on it when it's wet. It turns into cement when it's dry."

Difficult, he thought. Definitely like her. He shook his head in disbelief as he crossed his arms over the shovel and took a breather.

"It's surprising that anything grows here at all." He had begun to regret volunteering for this the moment he had taken the shovel from Daisy. Nothing was happening to make him change his mind.

"That's why I brought all these soil additives." She knew he wasn't going to be happy with what she was about to tell him. "It has to be deeper than that." She pointed to the hole. "Close to four feet."

Drew had never planted anything before but his own two feet on the ground. He had no idea if she was being unreasonable, but it would have been like her. He glanced at the shrub closest to him. While he had been battling the soil, she had worked the shrub free of its container and had methodically untangled some of the roots. "You're going to bury the whole thing?"

She smiled patiently and it annoyed the hell out of him. "The roots have to spread out if the shrub is going to grow. They need good soil. Actually, this soil is exceedingly nutritious, but it tends to be too hard for the roots on first contact." She indicated the mixture of leaf mold and manure she had been preparing. "We mix about twenty-five percent of that to the existing soil to help the roots along."

She took a step toward him. "You're obviously tired." Daisy reached for the shovel. "I can—"

Drew pulled the shovel toward him. "I'll do it." It sounded faintly like a growl. Digging these holes had turned into a matter of pride.

Daisy raised her hands. "Fine with me."

Shifting to stretch his back, he allowed himself an additional moment and then began to dig again. He could feel muscles straining from his forearms up to his neck and down his back. He was a good foot taller than she and probably had seventy-five pounds on her. The idea of her digging in this soil was ludicrous.

"How could you possibly think that you could dig in this soil?" he demanded. The woman was an airhead.

Daisy started mixing the second batch for the next bush. "I'm a lot stronger than I look."

He almost snorted, his eyes skimming her body. "Yeah. I hear barbed wire usually is."

She didn't bristle at the comment. "I did a lot of weight training when I was preparing for the Olympics. The three thousand meter run," she added. "I never really stopped."

Drew left the shovel where it was, stuck upright in the dirt, and turned around to stare at her. "You were in the Olympics?"

"No."

Just as he thought. She was spinning stories. He wondered how many she had told Jeremy and hoped that the boy didn't take after her.

"I did make the try-outs, though," she said matter-of-factly, sprinkling the dark soil into the powder-light brown leaf mold she had brought with her. She was aware that Drew had stopped digging and was staring at her. "A broken ankle kept me out of the actual competition." She sighed. It would have been nice, being able to compete, and possibly winning. "By the time I had healed enough to practice for the next games, I lost interest."

"I see." The woman should be a fiction writer, not a landscape consultant. She certainly had one hell of an imagination.

Daisy rose, dusting off her hands on her jeans. "What I didn't lose interest in was the weight training part of it. It only make good sense, keeping your body in shape. Don't you agree?"

"Yeah, sure."

He glanced in her direction again as she bent over to open the third sack of leaf mold and felt something twist sharply in his stomach. At least she hadn't exaggerated that part of her story. She had managed to keep in phenomenal shape—for a chronic pain in the neck.

It was hot and almost eerily quiet. Jeremy was inside the house, watching television with Mrs. Samuelson and scarfing down her homemade cookies. Because he could use the diversion, Drew decided to see how far Daisy would go with her fabrication. "So, how does an Olympic hopeful wind up planting shrubs?"

"I decided that I didn't want to be a lawyer." She worked out the proper ratio again, then sifted the mixture with her hands. The bright red garden gloves she wore clashed with her pink shirt. "I went into it with great dreams, but it turned out to be too cold for me, too bogged down in nasty technicalities that don't have anything to do with justice. I didn't like being concerned with the strict letter of the law and not the people whose lives it affected.''

She shrugged, dismissing a whole way of life as if it were nothing more than an unappealing meal. ''I tried a few other things, but this was what I liked best.'' She cocked her head as she looked at the shrubs. She could visualize them in a year's time, flowering, bright and green. It gave her a good feeling. ''Planting things, making them grow. There's something very simple and beautiful about that. Besides, I like nurturing things.''

''Whoa.'' Drew held up a hand to stop her before she went meandering down another twisting verbal road. He pinned her with a look meant to make her confess that she was lying. She looked at him innocently. ''A lawyer?'' Right, and he was a basketball player for the New York Knicks. Jonathan had never mentioned that she was a lawyer. Drew assumed the information would have been passed on if it were true. Wouldn't it? ''You passed the bar exam?'' He waited for her to say no.

''Yes.'' She looked at him as if she had done nothing more outrageous than state the ingredients of an angel food cake.

She was one cool customer. He could almost admire, in an odd sort of way, the way she let things roll off her tongue, if it wasn't for Jeremy. His nephew had been handed over to be raised by a pathological liar. What the hell had Jonathan been thinking of, agreeing to let her have custody?

''You passed the bar exam,'' he repeated. ''While you were single-handedly saving the rain forest and simultaneously performing open-heart surgery?''

Rather than look indignant or offended, she simply smiled. It was a Mona Lisa kind of smile that drove him crazy. ''You don't believe me.''

He laughed as he turned his attention back to the hole in the ground. Shovel met dirt with an accompanying grunt. "That's putting it mildly." He thought he saw her shrug carelessly out of the corner of his eye.

An olympic hopeful/lawyer who spent her time feeding birds at Hamburger Delight and planting shrubs for elderly people. Who was she kidding? He threw the dirt over his shoulder and pushed the shovel in again. Did she actually expect him to believe her? She might be crazy, but he wasn't.

He looked at the shovel in his hands. He was digging and she wasn't. Maybe something had to be reevaluated here. Later, when he had time.

Three hours had never moved so slowly or with such agony. But at last, at the end of that time, all three shrubs stood neatly lined up behind one another, evergreen sentries between the two adjacent gardens.

Drew thought they looked a lot smaller in the ground than they had in the containers. He stood for a moment, just looking at them. Not out of a sense of pride or accomplishment but because he needed a breather. He was beginning to have grave doubts that he could make it to his car unassisted. And he wasn't about to have Anastasia help him. Death before dishonor.

But he had done it. He hadn't let her dig so much as a single shovelful of dirt. Why, he didn't know. Maybe he had had something to prove—to her, to himself.

Or maybe she was contagious and he was going crazy. He was too tired to think about it.

Moving very carefully, Drew bent over and picked up his shirt and jacket from the grass where he had thrown them. He debated putting them on and decided against it. He couldn't bear the thought of anything against his hot, wet skin right now. Instead he slung both over his shoulder and turned to look at his car. It was parked behind her truck, a good fifteen feet away.

One foot in front of the other, Andrew. You can do it.

Daisy was busy loading the empty containers and bags onto the back of the truck. Drew passed her slowly as he walked to his car. She felt awful for him, but he had insisted on doing it himself.

She tossed the shovel on last, then wiped off her hands. "Are you going to the house?"

He nodded, dropping the jacket into the car. He needed a shower, he thought. Badly. "To change."

The way he said it, he made it sound as if he had plans. "And then what?" She shoved her hands into her back pockets as she leaned against the hood of his car.

"I still have an office to set up," he said doggedly. An office that he would have been getting well under way if it hadn't been for obstacles she kept providing.

Daisy looked at her wristwatch. "But it's after two-thirty." He couldn't get much done now, especially not in his condition. "Why don't you just call it a day and go soak in a hot tub?"

God, it did sound tempting. He could almost feel the water surrounding his aching body. Drew tried to make it a point to work out on a regular basis no matter where he happened to be in the world. But the workouts were nothing compared to the three hours' worth of digging he had just put in. He must have lost five pounds of water alone, despite the five glasses of lemonade Mrs. Samuelson had brought out for him.

But he couldn't give in. He was already behind, he reminded himself. "Later," he told Daisy as he dropped into the driver's seat. It took effort to pull his feet into the car. "After I get back." It hurt just to tilt back his head as he looked up at Daisy. "You?"

Why couldn't he just admit that he was exhausted and stop trying to be the man of steel? She shrugged in answer to his question. "I still have palm trees to pick out at the nursery."

He slumped back in his seat. "Don't tell me, you're planning to plant those, too?"

Well, she'd have to do those by herself. He was through being a good scout. He had no idea what possessed him to do it in the first place, except that she had looked so damn frail. Now she looked damn rested, while he probably looked as if he had spent the day in a coal mine.

"Relax." She laid a comforting hand on his shoulder. Her fingers were slippery from the perspiration she found there. Rather than wipe her hand, she slowly rubbed her thumb over her fingers. Drew had no idea why he found that extremely sensual. But he did.

"The wholesale nursery I do business with will take care of getting them into the ground. They had a full crew available. I just want to pick out the best specimens."

Like you, she couldn't help thinking. Even perspired and grumpy-looking, she had to admit that she had never seen a man with a build as good as his. At least not up close. Yes, Margaret would definitely be drooling right about now if she were here. If she were inclined to drool, which she wasn't, Daisy would have done so herself.

Daisy glanced over her shoulder and saw Jeremy running toward her. "Jeremy's going to help me pick them out." She stretched her hand out toward the boy. He moved into the pocket it created, like a small kitten seeking its mother's warmth. "Aren't you, Jeremy?"

After spending the better part of the past three hours inside the house with Mrs. Samuelson, watching cartoons and eating cookies, Jeremy was well rested and raring to go. "You bet."

Drew looked toward the Samuelson's house, unable at the moment to will his body into action. Just a few seconds more, he promised himself, then he'd turn on the ignition. He realized that Daisy was looking at him. There was just the slightest touch of sympathy in her eyes. The last thing he wanted was for her to ask him if there was anything wrong.

He sought to divert her attention away from him. "Why do they need such a big house? There's just the two of them, isn't there?"

Daisy curled her arm around Jeremy's small shoulders. "She likes to have room for the all grandchildren when they come to visit." It sounded like a greeting card type of life. One she had never had. Still, she was optimistic. "I hope I wind up like that someday. In a nice, comfortable marriage, looking forward to having my grandchildren come over to spend the weekend."

She sounded wistful, he thought. "First you have to get someone daring enough to marry you." He had almost said "foolhardy" instead.

Drew positioned himself carefully and pressed down on the gas as he turned on the ignition. Every bone in his body told him that he was going to regret this afternoon long before nightfall.

The man was a born romantic. "What a lovely thing to say." She straightened away from the car as it rumbled to life. She had no doubt if she remained, he'd probably use it as an excuse to run her over. Still, she owed him one. "What time do you think you'll be home?"

"Later."

The word hung in the air as he pulled away from the curb and drove down the street.

He was heading in the wrong direction, she thought, wondering how long it would take him to find out. She was grateful that she wouldn't be there when he discovered his mistake.

She gave Jeremy a squeeze. "There goes a very stubborn man, Jeremy. Come on." She turned toward the house. "Let's go tell Mrs. Samuelson we're finished."

He thought of the cookies. And the way Mrs. Samuelson had laughed over the cartoons. Not like a grown-up at all. "Can we come back and visit her sometime, Aunt Daisy? She's nice."

"Count on it." Daisy was rewarded with a very broad grin.

Daisy had just begun to lose the battle with her drooping eyelids. The book she was reading was slipping from her grasp when she heard the front door being opened and then closed.

Drew was home.

The thought telegraphed itself through her body, waking her up. She glanced at the digital clock on her nightstand. Eleven o'clock. He was a stubborn man all right. She shook her head and rose from her bed, the hem of her light blue nightgown floating down around her legs. She slipped her arms into the matching robe and tied the single ribbon at her breast. She had almost given up on him.

The stairs were a challenge.

They spread before him like a towering Mount Everest, daring him to climb and conquer. Swallowing an oath that encompassed both his fatigue and Daisy's existence on earth, Drew gripped the banister with sore, aching fingers and slowly made his way up. He was dragging himself up more than walking. It felt as if he had been shot through with lead and it was only a matter of time, perhaps minutes, before he would turn completely immobile.

Immobile but not numb. True to his prediction, every single bone in his body was aching wretchedly. There were blisters on his hands. One had broken open on the way home as he had gripped the steering wheel. It made holding on to the banister almost impossible. But if he didn't hold on, Drew wouldn't make it up to his room at all.

He briefly flirted with the idea of simply collapsing on the sofa and spending the night there. He was exhausted enough to do it. Except for the fact that Anastasia would find him there in the morning and probably gloat or cluck sympathetically, which was probably even more irritating. He wasn't about to give her the opportunity.

Five minutes later Drew stood on the landing and let out a sigh of relief. He had successfully negotiated the stairs, despite the fact that there seemed to be twice as many steps now as there had been when he had left this morning.

He looked down the hall toward his door. Just a few more feet and he'd be in his room. Mecca. Once inside, he planned to do nothing more strenuous than fall face down on the bed. He knew he hadn't the will or the strength to even undress. He was going to have to call his valet in New York and have the man express mail more suits and shirts out to him. Tomorrow.

Tomorrow was much too far away for him to even contemplate.

Miraculously reaching his door, he placed his hand on the doorknob, turned it and all but fell into the room.

He blinked. The lights were on. Had he forgotten to turn them off this morning? He would have scratched his head if the effort required to do so hadn't been too much for him. He looked toward the bed. There was a covered silver tray on it. Was he in the right room?

Right room or not, he was going to bed. Sitting on his bed, he stared at the tray. Whatever was under the lid, he hadn't the strength to eat it. He was about to push it aside when the fragrance drifted his way. He knew immediately that Anastasia was in the room.

She stood in the doorway, framed by the light from the hall. She looked a little like a wood nymph, come to plague him. Or were those banshees?

He looked about two yards past exhausted, she thought, feeling sorry for him. "You weren't kidding about later," she said as she walked in.

He was beginning to recognize that tone. "I'm tired, Anastasia. Could I have a reprieve tonight?"

She sat on the bed, keeping the tray between them. "From what?"

He was tired, but he wasn't dead. He couldn't help noticing that the robe was just the slightest bit opaque. All he saw was the nightgown beneath, but it was enough to stir an imagination he thought had gone to sleep. "You. I'm not up to sparring with you."

Daisy smiled and held up her hands. "No sparring. No gloves." She turned her hands front to back for his benefit. "See?"

He looked at her suspiciously. Was she about to offer some compromise in hopes that he was too tired to think? "Then what are you doing here?"

The man had a lot to learn about trust. "Returning a kindness for a kindness." She lifted the silver lid to expose a platter of food she had prepared herself. "Cold fried chicken." She thought of his lecture at Hamburger Delight. "Or don't you eat that, either?"

He loved fried chicken, but not at this moment. All he wanted to do was sink into a pillow and ignore the thousand pulsating points on his body. "I'm too tired to eat. All I want to do is go to sleep. Preferably not sitting up." It was a blatant hint.

She looked at the platter regretfully before replacing the lid. "You have to eat to keep your strength up."

Yes, against you. He tried not to watch the way the material moved against her breasts as she shifted. It was like trying to pull himself out of quicksand. The more he tried, the worse it became.

"I don't think I can chew. Everything hurts but my teeth." Right now he couldn't have tasted anything even if he wasn't exhausted. There were other appetites suddenly waking up.

Oh, my God, not with her.

"I'm prepared for that, too."

He hadn't the slightest idea what she was talking about. With effort, he rose from the bed. "Aren't Boy Scouts the ones who are supposed to be prepared?"

Daisy loosened his tie and then slipped it from his collar. "So are Girl Scouts."

The words, he was trying to keep his mind on the words, he told himself. "You were a Girl Scout?"

"Senior Girl Scout." She rose and removed his jacket, one sleeve at a time. He could only stand there and let her. Sudden movements were not advisable for him at the moment. For a number of reasons.

"Of course. I forgot. You went through vocations like some people go through tissues. Just how many vocations have you had?"

Placing his jacket neatly on a chair, Daisy removed the tray from his bed. "Three—no, four." She shrugged as she placed the tray on the bureau. "Enough to know I had found the right one when I came to it."

He couldn't turn his head, he couldn't move. Any movement would start up the pain again. "Isn't that just a tad unstable?"

"What, looking for happiness? I don't think so."

She was standing in front of him. As she considered his question, she undid the top button on his shirt. "Happiness again," he muttered. Damn, his throat was going dry. "Is that all you can think about?"

She eased the second button free. "What else is there?"

Drew opened his mouth, but couldn't think of a single answer for her. His brain had completely overloaded and was in the process of shutting down. The only thing he could focus on was her fingers as they slowly glided down his chest. He felt his skin heating. "What are you doing?"

"Can't you tell?"

He could tell. He could tell all right, and it wasn't going to work. She wasn't going to seduce him into relinquishing his claim to Jeremy. Even if she had the softest body, the firmest breasts he had ever seen. Not even if his hands ached now for a new reason.

"Anastasia, it isn't going to work."

"No," she agreed readily, "not if you keep your clothes on." She began to tug his shirt out of the waistband of his trousers.

He caught her hand. "I have no intentions of taking off my clothes. Any more of my clothes," he corrected.

"Suit yourself," she said, "but liniment is more effective if you don't apply it through material."

What was she talking about? "Liniment?" He blinked, trying to clear his head. She was muddling everything inside it. "What liniment?"

"This liniment." She held up the small bottle she had had tucked in the pocket of her robe. "It's what the coach used when our muscles were too sore."

"Coach," he echoed. "That would be the Olympic coach, right?" She never gave up, did she? But he was too tired to argue over this.

"Yes." She grinned, knowing exactly what had crossed his mind. She finished pulling his shirt free and pushed it off his shoulders. She saw something flame in his eyes then disappear just as quickly. She shut away her own tingle of excitement. It wasn't her intention to entice either one of them. "Sit."

"I'm not a dog." Drew's protest was not as forceful as he'd meant it to be. Surrendering, he sat.

Daisy climbed on the bed and positioned herself behind him on her knees. He was aware of every movement, every breath. His fatigue, his pain, faded behind a haze. He was aware of only her.

Daisy cupped her hand and poured liniment into it, then quickly rubbed it into his skin as she began to knead his tense muscles.

"Oh, God." He didn't know if he groaned the words or if they just echoed in his mind. He wasn't sure of very much anymore.

He wasn't relaxing, but that, she figured, took time. He had knots in his shoulders the size of hand balls.

"Good?" She grinned to herself when he didn't answer. Stoic to the end. *But you'll come around eventually.* "It's all right, you can admit it. I'll still respect you in the morning."

He leaned back slightly, into her hands, into her touch. He didn't know if he was responding to her massage or to her, or a combination of both, but it felt like heaven. He was on his way to becoming human again.

He turned and his bare arm brushed against her thigh. Sparks tap danced all through him. Maybe too human. Survival instincts erupted. "Do you ever shut up?"

She wondered if she was crazy, feeling sorry for him. "It's been known to happen." She squeezed his shoulder just a little too hard and enjoyed watching him wince. Served him right. "Are you asking me to stop talking?"

He knew that would bring on another debate. "My aspirations aren't quite that high at the moment." This was beginning to feel too good. Alarms went off all through him. "You don't have to do that." He moved his shoulders against her hand.

"Yes, I do." God, he was tense. "Unlike you, the milk of human kindness has not curdled in my veins." She leaned over him and he could smell her. Almost taste her, damn her. "I do appreciate what you did today, for whatever reason it was that you did it."

He wanted to keep it as simple as possible. For both of them. "You didn't look as if you could handle digging all those holes, that's all."

She poured more liniment and enjoyed watching him shiver involuntarily as she applied it to his back. "Since when are you concerned about me?"

"I wasn't concerned. I was just—" She was doing it again, making him trip over his own tongue. She had an uncanny knack for that. "Crazy, all right? I don't know what came over me."

Annoyed, he turned around so suddenly that she lost her balance and tumbled forward. Without thinking, Drew caught her in his arms.

Startled, she stared at Drew. "Well, this is an interesting position." She kept her voice deliberately flippant to hide the fact that her heart was suddenly threatening to leap out of her chest. "What do we do about it?"

He felt the muscles in his stomach contract into a tight fist. "I could just drop you on the floor."

She shook her head slowly, her eyes never leaving his. "Too violent. You're not given to violence."

He thought about his earlier urge to strangle her. It was still a viable choice for what she was doing to him. "I don't know about that."

Daisy raised herself up ever so slightly so that her mouth was just inches away from his. "I do," she whispered.

Her breath was sweet, tempting, and any resistance he might have had, had long since evaporated in the strong California sun. Without realizing what he was doing, or perhaps not wanting to realize what he was doing, Drew cupped the back of her head, threading his fingers through her hair.

He brought her lips to his.

He shouldn't be doing this when he was tired. He shouldn't ever do it, he emphasized, but definitely not when he was so exhausted, when his guard was nonexistent. It felt as if everything within him was completely, instantly undone. Something overwhelming was happening and he had no control over it, no control over his own reaction. It was as if his body had been invaded by an alien force.

The kiss deepened. He wasn't even certain if he was responsible for that or if she was. He did know that his arms tightened around her as he drew her body even closer to him.

Inexplicably, suddenly, he was transported into another world, a world of flashing lights and heat and sounds that buzzed in his ears. A world filled with needs, incredible, insatiable needs.

He wanted to make love with her.

His body hadn't an ounce of strength in it. There was no one single place where he didn't ache. And yet all he wanted to do was take her to bed with him and try to explore what it was that she was doing to him. He didn't even like her, for God's sake. Why would he want to make love with her?

He knew why, damn it.

Her head was spinning. She had wondered, in between the bickering, what it would be like to kiss him. Pleasant, interesting, arousing. Perhaps even boring. All these words had presented themselves to her.

Now she knew there was no word for it. What was happening right at this moment defied description. All she knew was that she wanted more. Much more. But not now. Not until she was prepared to handle it.

Heart pounding, she braced her hands against his chest and pushed until there was a wedge between them. She drew air into her lungs, trying to find her voice. And then she heard the noise.

Her mouth curved. "Should I take that as a compliment?"

Dazed, he looked at her. "What?"

"Your pants." She pointed toward his pocket. "They're ringing."

Chapter Seven

"Oh." Drew fought through the haze that had encapsulated his brain. He felt the phone vibrate ever so slightly against his thigh as it rang again. "That's my private line to New York."

At that moment they both stood up. Drew fumbled for the phone and took it out of his pocket. It looked like a small, elaborate calculator, Daisy thought.

She looked at the folded black object in Drew's hand. Daisy knew without being told that the incoming call wasn't personal. Nothing about this man was personal. "It's almost three in the morning in New York. Who would be calling you from there, the night watchman?"

"I've got someone patching me through on a three-way conference call to Japan. Tokyo, actually." He had forgotten that, Drew realized. It wasn't like him to forget. He was not forgiving of mistakes, especially his own. He had to get a better grip on things. This woman had him sliding in directions he had no desire to go in.

"Tokyo. Of course." She took a step away from him, testing the strength in her legs. They still worked. Sort of. She suppressed a sigh of relief. Saved by the bell. At least for now.

He just held the phone in his hand without lifting the cover, thinking of what he had nearly done. He must have been crazy, really crazy, to lose control that way.

"Better answer it before they decide to trade with someone else," Daisy advised. She glanced at the tray on the bureau as she began to retreat. "I'll leave this here in case you get a second wind." She ran the tip of her finger over her lip and remembered.... "Or a third one."

Drew extended the antenna and opened the phone before he was tempted to drag her back and do something he knew was utterly stupid, utterly out of character and utterly risky to his very way of life. He watched her as she left the room and wished that his pulse would stop jumping around so erratically. He looked away, but the sway of her hips beneath the light material was irrevocably burned into his mind.

"Hello?" he mumbled into the receiver.

Daisy eased the door closed and then leaned against it for a moment until she was sure she had regained full control over her knees. Right now, they felt as if they were going to buckle.

Who would have thought?

Who would have *ever* thought that the Iceman could kiss like that? Kiss her until her blood was boiling, her body was turning to fluid, and her head was spinning dizzily like some child's toy? Not in a million years would she have foreseen that happening. Daisy liked surprises, but this was an exception.

Or at least the verdict was still out on her ultimate reaction to the fact that the touch of Drew's mouth made her forget her name, her rank and her serial number, and had her wanting to throw all caution to the wind.

Well, this was probably as composed as she supposed she'd be for the rest of the night, Daisy thought. She straightened, moving away from the door, and slowly went to her room. She couldn't help wondering if this was what Alyce had felt the first time she had kissed Jonathan. If so, the Addison men were lethal.

Life returned to as normal a routine as was possible, given the circumstances. Jeremy returned to his pre-school the following Monday. Daisy moved her belongings from her apartment into the house and went to Showers of Flowers...and Things. And Drew went into hiding.

At least, that was the way Daisy saw it. Drew came down to breakfast every morning punctually at seven. He would consume two cups of black coffee and, occasionally, a piece of toast. When he spoke, it was to Jeremy or to Irene. Daisy noted that he avoided speaking to her as if she were the personification of the Black Plague. For the time being, she played along, wondering how long it would go on. Drew would leave for work long before they were finished eating.

And then they wouldn't see him again until the following morning, at which point the ritual was repeated. It went on like this for four days. When it looked as though the routine would continue indefinitely, Daisy made up her mind to wait up for Drew and beard the lion in his den. Or, more precisely, at the front door.

The man obviously had to be told what he was doing wrong since he was apparently too blind to see it for himself.

She had spent the better part of the morning working on the nursery's monthly inventory and the afternoon helping

Simon plant the Applegate's azaleas. When Daisy arrived home, it was to spend the evening playing with a very active Jeremy. There had been a party at the pre-school and Jeremy was wired on chocolate cake and red fruit punch. It had taken her awhile to get him into bed. By nine she was ready for bed herself. But she was absolutely determined to talk to Drew when he got home.

If he got home, she amended, staring at the grandfather clock that stood majestically guarding the foyer. It faced the front door. Daisy had dragged over a chair so that she was catty-corner to it. She wanted to be the first thing Drew saw when he came in. If she fell asleep, she knew the noise he'd make as he opened the door would wake her.

Ten-twenty-one.

What the hell did a man do "at the office" until ten-twenty-one at night? she wondered irritably. Maybe they'd have this talk early tomorrow morning. She debated calling it a night when she heard a car in the driveway. Speak of the devil.

It hadn't been one of his easiest days, but it had certainly been one of the better ones, Drew thought as he pulled up in the driveway. He had gotten inside information that there was a takeover being planned for one of his subsidiary companies. Normally he would have flown to the site, but there hadn't been enough time. The miracle of telecommunications had enabled him to stop the takeover before it had actually had a chance to gain any momentum and roll right over him.

Yes, he thought, getting out and slamming the car door, a very good day. He was tired, bone-tired, and looked forward to going to bed and sleeping the sleep of the victorious.

And then he saw her and triumph did an immediate about-face.

Ever since what he had mentally termed as "the unfortunate incident" in his room, Drew had been purposely avoiding Daisy. Work had been a handy excuse to hide behind. He hadn't liked his reaction to her, nor had he cared for the weakness that flowed over him when he had kissed her. Like a flash flood that had come from nowhere. And had nowhere to go.

She had something on her mind, he thought as he closed the door behind him, still facing her. "Loaded for bear," he believed the expression was. Was he the bear?

"Staking out new territory?" Drew gestured to the foyer, keeping his voice mild as he began to walk toward the stairs.

She was on her feet instantly, just as he knew she would be, following him up the stairs. He decided he was cursed, or doomed, or whatever word it was that meant he was destined to make one hell of a mistake. And probably very soon.

He kept walking. She was wearing that perfume again, the one that swept through his senses and scrambled his thinking processes. He wondered if he could buy the company and have the perfume banned from the market.

Daisy tried to stay calm, although waiting had made her agitated. "You've been working awfully late this week."

He responded without turning around. His room was within reach now. Maybe he could just shut the door on her, once inside.

"I work awfully late every week." She was making noises like a neglected wife and all he had done was kiss her once. There was a reason, he mused, why he had never bothered getting married. To avoid scenes such as this one.

He opened his door, but she had anticipated him. She was in the doorway before he could shut it. "So this is normal for you?" she asked.

He didn't care for her tone. "Yes."

All right, he thought, he was stretching it just a little. He did work long hours and felt exhilarated by it. But this time he was working longer hours to get the job done *and* to avoid her.

Drew would rather have had his tongue cut out than to tell her that she had him on the run. Why, of all the women who were available in the world, did he have to be attracted to a sharp-tongued, overly perky flake who had the annoying ability of turning his words inside out while simultaneously doing a number on his male hormones? What was worse, he had a feeling that she could very capably crack the very foundations of his nice, safe world—a world where the only risks he was asked to make involved business transactions. Emotions never came into play.

Lately, around her, nothing else *but* emotions seemed to be stirring. There was no justice in the world.

She leaned against the doorjamb, as leery of entering the room as he was of having her there. She crossed her arms in front of her, trying to look nonchalant. "So far, you're not making a very good case for yourself."

He turned and looked at her. Now what? "What do you mean, case?"

He was too busy to even remember why he was supposedly here, she thought. Typical. "You're never home. What kind of a life is that supposed to be for Jeremy?"

"A comfortable one." What did she want from him? "Look, real fathers go to work all the time." Unlike the Bohemian she had probably had as a father. Drew could envision her being raised by two misplaced hippies living in the last of the communes. That seemed to fit with the aura she gave off. Sitting cross-legged on the floor, weaving blankets, making pottery and doing nothing. That might suit her, but that wasn't him.

"Yes, they go to work, but they don't live there." How could this be the same man who had kissed her so passionately only a few days ago? Had he used up his entire supply of feelings in that one instance? For Jeremy's sake, she refused to believe that. "The important things are at home." She looked at him pointedly. "Or should be."

The woman didn't have a logical bone in her body. But then, he already knew that. It was why he was attracted to this life-threatening mass of contradictions and pulsating emotion that he didn't understand. "There are things that I have to take care of."

She blew out a breath, stifling an urge to beat on his hard head. "I appreciate that. But do you have to run the whole damn company?"

She didn't have the vaguest idea of what it took to run something like Addison Corporation. "What would you know about it?"

When he said something like that, she had no idea why she had reacted to him the way she had the other night. "I know that people in authority hire other people they trust and delegate responsibilities. They don't try to do it all themselves."

Oh, no, she didn't. She didn't use one set of rules and give him another. "Like plant shrubs?"

She knew he'd bring that up. "That was a temporary situation." She crossed to him and stood on her toes to face him. "I'm talking about a way of life."

The company *was* his life. Or had been. "The company is important."

"Of course it is." She threw up her hands. "But it's a thing, an entity." Didn't he understand anything? Was that man who had played trains with Jeremy in that ridiculous hat someone she had just dreamed up? No, it had happened. There *had* to be something inside of him she could work with, draw on. "We're talking about a small boy who won't always *be* a small boy and who needs memories built up now."

Drew sighed wearily. She could probably talk all night if he let her. "Where is this leading?"

There was nothing in his eyes, no spark of understanding. "Nowhere," she answered quietly, "if you're not listening."

This was what she wanted, wasn't it? Jeremy all to herself, by default. But if Drew didn't understand this, he wouldn't understand why she would fight his attempt to get custody of Jeremy and they'd be right back where they had started from. Square one. She was trying desperately to turn him into someone who would understand why Jeremy had to stay with her. She couldn't do that if Drew was in hiding.

Her eyes were like flames when she was angry, he thought. Damn it, he was getting distracted again. He had to exercise more control over himself. This shouldn't be happening, not if he didn't want it to. And he didn't.

"All right," he relented, "I'm listening."

Yes, but are you hearing? "Spend some time with Jeremy."

What was she talking about? "I see him every morning at breakfast."

Dead from the neck up. "You see the newspaper every morning," she fairly shouted then remembered that Jeremy was only two doors down the hall. She lowered her voice. "You don't have a relationship with that, either."

He should have known better than to try to conduct a rational, logical conversation with her. "You're babbling again."

The hours of waiting, of anticipating this conversation, took their toll. She simply reacted and took a swing at him, landing a punch on his arm. It didn't do any good. It didn't alleviate the frustration. It just hurt her knuckles. "I am making sense, you idiot. Can't you understand anything that's not printed on a spreadsheet or a legal document?"

He rubbed his arm, surprised. The blow had stung. "I can't understand you," he admitted freely. And he doubted he ever would.

She shut her eyes for a moment, gathering strength. The man had a head like a rock. And she suddenly despaired that his heart wasn't far behind. "I'm not asking you to understand me. I don't matter. Jeremy does. You came barging in here, demanding him." She grew angrier at the very thought of his actions and the possible motives behind them. "He's not an acquisition, a takeover to crow about." Inadvertently, she had struck very close to home. "He's a little boy who needs a hell of a lot more attention than you've been giving him."

Because he knew he had been absent more than he normally would have, Drew conceded the point to her. "What do you want me to do?"

Finally. Exhausted from the effort, she sat on the edge of the bed. "Take him to the park."

"Park?" he echoed.

He looked so bewildered, she had to smile. "You know, the place where they have slides, green stuff, swings. Anything sound familiar here?"

Drew had never gone to a park as a child. He hadn't the vaguest idea why that would be a pleasant experience for anyone. "And exactly what am I supposed to do with him at the park?"

Was he serious? Maybe he *did* work all the time. Maybe he had been born working. "Anything he wants you to. That's the idea of taking him."

Maybe she had a point at that. He loosened his tie and undid his collar button. "I'll see."

He wasn't going to get out of it that easily. "Tomorrow."

If she wasn't the pushiest woman on the face of the earth, he'd hate to meet the woman who held the title. "I'm going to work tomorrow."

Why didn't that surprise her? "It's Saturday," she pointed out.

"So?" He began to take his jacket off and then thought better of it. Though they were arguing, on another plane, he was still reacting to her, reacting to the fact that she was sitting on the edge of his bed and he wanted her in it. With him.

She sighed. "You're absolutely hopeless." She gave up, angry with herself for having cared, angry with him for existing in her life and Jeremy's. "Go ahead. Go!" She waved her hand at him, rising. "Go to your office, to your meetings and to your ringing pants' phone—"

"Cellular phone." His voice was so damn patient she could have screamed.

Her eyes grew dark as her voice lowered. She began to speak slowly, with emphasis. The change, so unusual for her, made him pay attention. "But just remember this conversation when you try to get custody of Jeremy."

He was an insensitive brute and would always stay that way. He couldn't be made to change, or see reason. She would see him in court, she thought, and that would be that. Daisy turned on her heel and began to stalk out the door.

"What if it rains?"

She was an idiot for giving him another chance. Hands at her sides, she turned around.

"This is California. Haven't you heard the song? It never rains here. Except for the rainy season," she added, her lips quirking into a small smile. "And if it does, you'll play trains with him again, or see a movie, or watch cartoons—"

"Cartoons?" he asked incredulously, disdain dripping from his voice.

"Drawings that move," she felt bound to explain. "You must have heard of them." She couldn't help the grin that rose to her lips as she imagined him watching with Jeremy. That was something she might even videotape and save for posterity. "There're a lot of them on Saturday morning. You have your choice."

He picked the lesser of the evils, or so he hoped. "I'll go to the park."

Daisy nodded. "Smart move."

Not by along shot. "No, a smart move would have been if I had sent my lawyers out here instead of me." A lot smarter, he thought, feeling an ache forming just by being here, alone with her.

She smiled sweetly. "I would have carved them into little pieces and sent them back in a box. Figuratively speaking, of course."

"Of course." It sounded silly, but somehow, he could see her doing just that. "So why am I so lucky?"

She patted his face the way a mother did with a slightly slow child. "You're family."

No, I'm a hell of a lot more than that. And less than that. "Are you going to come along?"

The question surprised her. She wasn't certain which way he would have preferred it. "Do you want me to?"

No, I don't want you anywhere close by. He thought of being alone with Jeremy and how awkward that made him feel. Perhaps inadequate might have been a better word, but he didn't want to think about that now. "Yes."

The smile she gave him before she left the room haunted his dreams that night. "Then I'll come."

Margaret ran the nursery on Saturdays. Daisy wasn't thinking about work when she picked up the phone as it rang on their way out the door.

Margaret didn't bother saying hello. "You know that palm tree order for the mall?"

Daisy had an uneasy feeling in her stomach at Margaret's wording. "Yes?"

"Well, that's just it. They only got one. The order was for eight. They've got to get them put into the ground before the men can start on the brickwork. I can't reach anyone at the Keeline Nursery and the customer is screaming for blood. Or at least more palm trees. He keeps saying things about deadlines and forfeiting fees."

"I've got Steve's private number at his house." She noticed that Drew was listening and frowning ever so slightly. "I'll call him and get back to you."

"Steve?" Drew asked as she hung up. It was absurd to think she hadn't had a life before he appeared, yet the fact that she did irked him in a way he found troublesome. What was coming over him? He didn't care if she did cartwheels naked in the snow, so why did it matter if she had a man's private number?

"The owner of the wholesale nursery." She pulled her personal phonebook out of her purse and started thumbing through the pages. "We've got a little problem with an order."

Shoe on the other foot. "Surely that's not going to make you miss our outing to the park?" The sarcasm was three inches thick.

He was enjoying this, she thought. "No, I just need about a half an hour to unscramble this. You two go on ahead." She saw the dubious look enter Drew's eyes. Unless she missed her guess, he didn't want to go. "You can't miss it. It's just three blocks away." She pointed vaguely in the right direction. Drew didn't move. "A simple little playground," she persisted, "with sand and swings. I'll be there as soon as I can."

"We can wait." He leaned against the counter as she thumbed through her telephone book. Jeremy was restlessly moving from side to side.

"You might, but he can't." She ruffled Jeremy's hair. "Right, Jeremy?" She looked at Drew and wondered if he was afraid to be alone with Jeremy for some reason. Why else was he hesitating?

"But you'll come?" Jeremy looked uncertainly over his shoulder at Drew, then shifted his gaze anxiously to his aunt.

"Of course I'll come. I promise," she added when the anxious expression didn't leave Jeremy's face.

"You know," Drew drawled slowly, "work shouldn't just take over your life like that."

Rather than get annoyed, she laughed. Let him have his moment. It was harmless enough. "Shut up and go have fun, you two."

It took a little longer than she had hoped, necessitating a quick trip to Keeline itself. On the way back, she made a quick side trip on impulse. It was almost an hour later before she pulled up to the playground.

It was a mini-playland for children and had been one of the main reasons Alyce and Jonathan had decided to settle in this development as opposed to another. The play area was well equipped and well maintained. It had everything to fuel a child's imagination, from an elaborate swing set to a miniature old pirate ship for the children to explore.

It took her a few minutes to locate Drew and Jeremy. They were by the swings. Drew was absently pushing Jeremy with one hand. The momentum was dismally listless. In his other hand Drew held his cellular phone. The conversation he was engaged in held all of his attention.

Damn, wasn't he ever going to learn?

Daisy's good humor evaporated. She had to work at curbing her temper. She didn't want Jeremy to witness a testy confrontation. She managed to wait until Drew ended his conversation.

As Drew said goodbye, Daisy crossed to him. "Finished?"

She had startled him, appearing out of nowhere that way. "As a matter of fact, yes."

He stopped pushing Jeremy altogether as he retracted the antenna and flipped the phone closed. Just as Drew was about to put it in his pocket, Daisy snatched it out of his hand.

Now what had come over her? "Do you want to make a call?"

She shook her head as she dropped the offending object into her purse and then closed it.

"Just what do you think you're doing?"

"Freeing you," she said cheerfully. She nodded at Jeremy. "He needs your undivided attention, remember? Hi, Tiger." She kissed the top of the boy's head. "Are you having a good time?" One look at his solemn, bored face answered her question.

Now that she was here, Jeremy wriggled in his seat, holding on to the chains on either side of him. "Push me high, Aunt Daisy. Uncle Drew doesn't know how." The last statement was uttered with childish disgust.

It was difficult, but Daisy came to Drew's defense. "That's because he was only using one hand. He can do a lot better when he uses them both." She gestured Drew toward Jeremy. "All yours, Drew."

She stepped back, folding her arms. He had hoped that she'd take over instead of confiscating his telephone and utterly confounding him in the space of two minutes. He should have known better. He looked at her stance. Both feet were planted firmly on the ground and she looked as if she was monitoring him. "Are you going to rate me?"

"Just enjoying the view, Drew, just enjoying the view." She grinned to herself as he began to push Jeremy again. "By the way, next week's Halloween."

Why did he have this sinking feeling in his stomach that he wasn't going to like what was coming? "So?"

She shrugged. "So, I took the liberty of ordering your costume."

He stopped pushing. "My what?"

"Costume. The thing you put on your body when you go trick-or-treating. You're not pushing, Drew," she pointed out.

He didn't like having her watch his every move. He wasn't used to it. It had been a long time since he had felt himself accountable to anyone. "I'm also not going trick-or-treating."

"No, not technically," she agreed. "But I thought it would be fun to dress up when we took Jeremy around the neighborhood."

Jeremy twisted around in his swing and she could see by his broad grin that he approved of the idea. Alyce and Jonathan had dressed up and taken him last year. She felt this might help ease things a little for him.

But obviously not for Drew, she thought, seeing the disgruntled expression on his face. "You've got to be kidding."

She grinned. He wasn't getting out of this one. "Do I look like I'm kidding?"

Drew was beginning to believe there wasn't a reasonable bone in her body, but he was going to try to reason with her anyway. Something told him he would have gotten better results discussing philosophy with a shoe. "Halloween is . . . when?"

"October 31st. Same day it is every year."

He ignored the sarcasm. "It's a week night." And that should have been the end of it.

Daisy was unfazed. "I'll give you a note to take in to the office if you oversleep."

The woman did not live in the real world. "Why don't I just quit altogether?"

The sarcastic question appeared to go right over her head, as far as he could see. "That's entirely up to you, but it might not be such a bad idea to consider." She ignored the glare he gave her. "Jonathan used to only go in part-time."

Drew pushed a little too hard, but Jeremy only squealed with glee. "That's because I ran the business and besides, there was the money he inherited."

She looked at him innocently. "You didn't inherit any money?"

"Yes, but—" He gave up trying. "Never mind." He pushed silently for a few minutes, aware that she was still watching him. "You don't know my size," he pointed out triumphantly. And there was no way he was going in for a fitting.

She smiled, conjuring up a memory. "Oh, I had a pretty good idea."

She was referring to the night she had walked in on him, he could tell. Trust her to bring that up. Well, she could bring up anything she wanted. He wasn't going to put on a costume and he sure as hell wasn't about to go trick-or-treating. And that was the end of it.

Chapter Eight

The box was on his bed when he arrived home from the office. It was a large, retangular white box with bold red letters that read London's Better Costumes across the front. He eyed it for a moment, prepared to ignore it and Halloween altogether. But curiosity got the better of him and he finally opened the box. The situation was not unlike the one he found himself in with Anastasia, Drew thought. He was prepared to ignore her and somehow, he just couldn't.

But he was working on it.

An involuntary laugh exploded from him when he held the top half of the outfit up against himself. A long, green jersey. Fawn-colored leather trousers and a bow and arrows remained in the box. It took him a few minutes to figure out that it was a Robin Hood costume. She wanted him to be Robin Hood. She was out of her mind. Stark, raving, certifiably crazy. If Drew had had any lingering doubts before, they were certainly gone now.

"Like it?" Daisy had heard Drew come home and had purposely waited until he had gone up to his room. She had a feeling he wouldn't be able to resist looking into the box. Few people resisted innocent temptation. The next step was getting him into it. For that, she had enlisted Jeremy's aid, carefully coaching the boy in what to say.

Drew turned to tell her exactly what he thought of the costume and her in no uncertain terms and then stopped. She was wearing a floor-length forest green dress made of velvet. It was cinched at a waist so small that it begged for a man's hand to span it, to let his fingers dip down to the enticing swell of her hips. The color of the dress brought out her eyes so vividly Drew felt as if he were hypnotized. She had done something to her hair, too, something that made it look like a dark cloud storming around her shoulders. Her bare shoulders. They were a creamy white and tempted him to gently glide his fingers along them. He ached just to touch her.

He found his voice, but it wasn't as easy as it should have been. "Who are you supposed to be?"

The way he looked at her made her forget, for a brief second, that they were, at bottom, adversaries engaged in a mental war over the welfare of a child. The look in Drew's eyes made her feel warm, wanted.

She smiled at him. "Maid Marian, m'lord."

His eyes strayed to the bodice. It was cut deep and set off what he surmised was her best feature. Or one of them. He tried not to stare. "Maid Marian is going to catch a cold if she's not careful."

She had seen the appreciative look before he locked it away. *Gotcha.* "Robin wouldn't let that happen." She indicated the costume he was holding up against himself with her eyes.

"What?" He glanced down, forgetting for a moment that he was still holding the shirt in his hands. "Oh, no way. No damn way am I going to put this on." To emphasize the point, he tossed the costume onto the bed behind him. It landed on top of the bow.

Her grin grew mischievous. "Why not? It's the realistic model." She pointed to the pants. "A rugged, manly costume if ever there was one. I could have gotten you the one based on the Errol Flynn interpretation of Robin Hood." Her eyes were teasing. "I did have a yen to see you in tights, but I suppressed it."

"Thank you." He wanted to wipe the smirk off her face. He wanted to kiss it away until her lips were too numb to form a smile. Or to talk. It was something, he thought, to aspire to for the good of the world as well as for reasons of his own reawakening lust. He refused to view his reaction to her in any other terms. It was lust, pure and simple. Or maybe not so pure or so simple, but lust nonetheless.

He tried to keep his mind on the topic. "I am not about to make a fool of myself, parading around in any sort of ridiculous—"

He never got a chance to finish. Jeremy fairly bounded into the doorway, circumventing his aunt's wide skirt. It occurred to Drew, belatedly, that Daisy was bringing in reinforcements. Dressed in Lincoln green, with a hat held jauntily in place on his head by means of an elastic band beneath his chin, Jeremy looked like a miniature citizen of Sherwood Forest. He was holding tightly onto a large plastic staff that was as tall as he was.

"You have to come, Robin," Jeremy informed Drew. Authority rang in his voice that went far beyond his few years.

Commanding people around ran in the family, Daisy thought. She placed her hands on Jeremy's shoulders and ushered him farther into the room. She had rehearsed him well. "This is Little John, Robin," she explained to Drew.

"He can't go anywhere unless you lead. After all, you are the leader."

Like hell he was. Drew folded his arms across his chest and regarded this general in crushed-velvet skirts. "I'm surprised *you* didn't want to be Robin Hood."

She grinned, and it did something to him, damn it, no matter how hard he didn't want it to. "I thought about it." She spread out the skirt. "But we're a set and you would have looked silly in this dress."

And she didn't, he thought. Not silly at all. Too damn arousing is what she looked.

"Look, I—" It was a valiant try that never got off the ground, doomed before its birth.

"Please?" Jeremy looked up at him. "My daddy and mommy used to dress up a long time ago when they took me trick-or-treating."

"Last year," Daisy corrected him with a fond smile. This part he was adding on his own, and her heart ached for him. She didn't want him to forget his parents, ever, but she was afraid that their memory would make him too sad.

The accuracy of details wasn't important to Jeremy. He kept his gaze steadily on his uncle, hopeful. Waiting.

Those were Jonathan's eyes looking at him, Drew thought with a pang. He looked toward the bed at the costume he had thrown aside. The Jonathan he knew, the Jonathan he *thought* he knew, wouldn't have had the time to wear costumes and go trick-or-treating, or play with trains or eat French fries at Hamburger Delight. But the Jonathan Jeremy had known obviously had.

She saw Drew wavering. *Good.*

"At least try it on," Daisy urged as she moved to the bed. She picked up the heap from the box and brought it to him, her skirts rustling enticingly as she moved. "Who knows? You might get lucky. It might not fit." Although she knew for a fact that it would. She had called his valet in New York and had gotten Drew's exact measurements. Drew might think of her as being scatterbrained, she mused, but there was very little Daisy liked to leave to chance. Not when things mattered.

Drew took the clothes from her and saw Jeremy grin. "What's the point, then?"

"At least you will have tried." Turning, she ushered Jeremy out of the room. "Hurry up and change. Irene has dinner waiting for you. We've already eaten."

Drew remained where he was, staring in disbelief at the costume, at the leather britches that were hanging from his hands.

He wasn't moving. "Hurry," Daisy urged as she began closing the door. She peered in and pointed to the costume. "Or I'll come up and dress you myself."

He wouldn't put it past her, he thought. All right, he wasn't going to be completely unreasonable about this. He'd try on the costume. What were the odds that it would really fit him? And then he'd be off the hook.

It fit.

Drew scowled at the image in the mirror. It fit as if it had been tailored for him. He should have realized she would do something underhanded like this. Well, he wasn't going out and that was that.

He began to unlace the front of his shirt when there was a knock on his door.

He knew without asking that it was Daisy. "Go away." He doubted that she would, but he did his best to sound unfriendly.

"You decent?"

He yanked the lacings and found that he had somehow tangled them. "That never stopped you before."

Taking a chance, Daisy opened the door. "Is that an invitation?"

He looked up, frustrated by the lacings, frustrated by her. Most of all, frustrated by the hodgepodge his emotional network had become in such a short time.

"No, that was a curse, I just stifled it." He stopped fighting with the black ties when he saw the look on her face. "What are you grinning at?"

He looked like a sculpture, waiting for a pedestal. "You." She tilted her head, allowing herself a fuller survey. "I was right. You do look good in that." She felt her pulse quicken and decided to enjoy it rather than attempt to fight it or explain it away. It was much more pleasant that way.

For the first time in his adult life, he felt something akin to embarrassment poking holes in him. "I'm not wearing this."

She crossed to him, the bottom of her skirt whispering over the threshold. "Yes, you are." With practiced ease, she untangled the ties.

He wished she'd stop fiddling around his chest. He didn't want to feel her fingers on his bare skin like that. "I'm a full grown man. I know if I'm going to wear something or not. Look, I played it your way. I tried it on, saw how ridiculous I look, and now I'm taking it off."

He waved away her hands and saw that she had redone the slender leather ties.

She took a step back and her expression became serious. "Jeremy's waiting."

He wasn't going to be talked into this. It was a stupid idea and he wanted no part of it. "You take him."

Her eyes held his. "Yes," Daisy said quietly. "I will."

He knew what she meant.

He supposed there was no harm in indulging Jeremy a little, but he was going to feel like a first-class fool, walking around like this. With an annoyed huff, Drew gave in.

"Damn you, woman, do you always get your way?" He stalked out of the bedroom, wondering why he was *letting* her get her own way.

Her smile was broad, pleased and beguiling. Almost innocent, except that he knew better. "No, not always, but enough times to keep me trying for more." As he walked toward the stairs, Daisy—carrying Drew's bow—surprised him by linking her arm through his. "Your quiver of arrows is downstairs."

He lifted a brow before taking the first step down. "Don't tempt me to use them."

Her smile broadened. "I wouldn't dream of it."

The sound of her laughter was like a sexy, stirring melody against his ear. He liked hearing it. He just wished it wasn't at his expense. No, he amended. He wished she wasn't laughing at all. Because when she did, he forgot that he was angry, forgot that his ultimate goal was to show her how much better suited he was to raise Jeremy than she. He forgot everything except that she existed. And that he wanted her.

Irene looked up as they came down the stairs, her eyes growing huge.

"Not a word," Drew warned the woman as he descended. "Not a single word."

Jeremy was ready, eagerly shifting from foot to foot. He hadn't mastered waiting patiently very well. But he was four and allowed, Daisy thought. He looked so normal, so untouched by tragedy. With all her heart, she wished it was true.

Daisy glanced at Drew. "Can she at least smile?"

"No," Drew answered gruffly, yanking the bottom of the jersey down as far as it would go. "And neither can you. Let's get this over with."

"But dinner—" Daisy looked toward the kitchen. He was probably grumpier on an empty stomach and he was bad enough as it was. She didn't want him fine-tuned.

"I've already eaten at the office." He had stayed at the office a little longer in hopes that Daisy and Jeremy would leave without him. No such luck.

"Whatever you say," Daisy said sweetly.

Ha, that'll be the day, Drew thought.

"You'll have fun," Jeremy promised, eagerly linking his hand with Drew's.

He sincerely doubted that. He was going to feel like an idiot, but maybe it would be worth it, Drew thought, looking into the small face with its dancing dark eyes. Besides, he didn't know anyone here, except for Anastasia, and she didn't count.

Daisy moved to the hall table and picked up Drew's accessories. She curtsied deeply as she offered them to Drew. "Your weapon, m'lord."

There was a ready retort on his lips as Drew turned toward her. The retort evaporated, dried to dust. It matched the condition in his throat.

He looked down at her soft breasts, covered just enough with green velvet to stir his fantasies and make his blood run hot. To make him yearn the way he had never yearned before. Indulging physical urges was a matter that was very low on his list of priorities. While he wasn't exactly a monk, the term playboy could never have been applied to him and he was content that way. Relationships took too much time away from his work, too much effort. They involved risks he wasn't prepared to take. He didn't have patience for the niceties that were required, wasn't up to playing the social games that people were forced to play. He firmly believed that being in love tended to create havoc in a man's life. Though he had eventually grown to like his sister-in-law, Alyce had turned Jonathan's life upside down, thrown it off course. She had transformed Jonathan into someone Drew didn't know. That fact was becoming more obvious to him with each passing day.

And now this gypsy in green velvet and nerve-jangling décolleté was doing it to him. Messing with his mind until he couldn't hold on to a single thought and follow it to its conclusion. Until he couldn't make a stand and stay there if she wanted him to move. It had to stop.

He took the weapon from her, wrapping his fingers around the bow and quiver. "Thank you," he mumbled.

For self-preservation, he turned toward his nephew. In comparison, things were more simple if he thought only of Jeremy.

"Let's go, 'Little John.' We have some robbing of the rich to do." He ushered the boy out the front door a little quicker than he had intended. Jeremy giggled, fairly skipping out.

It was a warm evening for October, even by Southern California standards. The streets seemed to explode with ghosts and goblins, witches and warriors, and green turtles with nunchakus. There were creatures Drew didn't recognize, mingling with miniature rock stars and cartoon characters. Some of the trick-or-treaters were surprisingly tall. It wasn't a night just for children.

To Drew's surprise, he was not the only adult besides Daisy to be wearing a costume. There were a handful of other parents who were indulging in childhood fantasies for the space of an evening. Cowboys and space captains nodded at him as they passed on the street, herding costumed children in front of them.

Despite the company, Drew still felt incredibly stupid. He was doing this for Jeremy, he told himself. And to prove to this overly bubbly woman next to him that he was capable of going along with a child's request, although what that had to do with properly raising Jeremy was still beyond him.

He looked about as comfortable as a lambchop at a fox convention, she thought, watching Drew. Had he always been this way? What kind of a little boy was the father of the man who hung back on the street with her tonight?

She needed to know. For Jeremy's sake.

And for her own.

Jeremy came racing up to them, holding up his huge orange pumpkin with its newest bounty. He tripped on a raised crack in the sidewalk and would have fallen if Drew hadn't been quick enough to catch him.

Unfazed, Jeremy ran to the next house. Daisy trained her flashlight on the sidewalk just in front of the boy to illuminate his way. "You've never done this before, have you?" Daisy guessed.

She had an irritating habit of plucking topics out of the air. "What?"

"Gone trick-or-treating?"

"No." He didn't like the fact that she could read him so easily, not when he was having increasingly more difficulty accomplishing the same with her. She was a hell of a lot more complicated than he had first thought. "How could you tell?"

"It shows." She turned to him. The porch light from the house in front of them illuminated his eyes. Such sad eyes, she thought. "A lot of things show."

He didn't want her getting any closer than she was. On all counts. "Now Maid Marian claims to have x-ray vision, as well?"

He wasn't fooling her. In a way, she thought not for the first time, Drew was a lot like Jonathan had been at first. It's what gave her hope. "You keep backing away. Are you afraid of a relationship?"

He refused to look at her. The moonlight was highlighting her profile and made her look wanton and temptingly innocent at the same time. He didn't understand how that could be possible. Yet there she was, being both. She, and what she was doing to him, scared the hell out of him.

Drew stared at Jeremy instead. "I'm building one. With Jeremy, remember?"

The man required an awful lot of patience, she thought. "You know what I mean."

He watched ahead of where Jeremy was walking, making sure that the boy didn't trip again. Making sure he didn't trip up himself.

When Jeremy rang the bell, eerie laughter pierced the air. Jeremy jumped back, but then bravely held his ground. Drew didn't realize that the feeling he was experiencing was pride.

"Don't flatter me, Anastasia. I hardly *ever* know what you mean."

Then she'd explain it to him, though she knew she didn't have to. "Us," she said quietly. "You can't deny there's not something humming between us."

This time he did look at her, but he was careful to only look at her face. A lot of good that did him. The banshee had a face like an angel tonight.

"Nerves. Nerves are what's humming between us. You scare the hell out of me." He'd make her back away if she wasn't going to do it voluntarily. "I've never dealt with a female barracuda before."

The description hurt, but she refused to show him. "Is that how you see me?"

They were under a street lamp and he saw the flash of pain in her eyes. Guilt rose, sharp and bitter. "All right, maybe not a barracuda. Something a little more petite." He looked away. If he didn't look at her, he couldn't feel guilty. A least, it was a good working theory. "How tall is a shrew?"

"All right, you've made your point." There was a strange hollowness inside of her. But she'd get over it. She had gotten over a good many things before.

Daisy turned her face forward, grateful for the darkness. "But all I have is Jeremy's best interests at heart."

He might not see it, but he could hear the hurt. He told himself he didn't care. It was her own fault. But it didn't erase his guilt. "So do I."

She aimed the flashlight beam ahead of him as Jeremy and two clowns, one shorter than he, one taller, scampered up wooden railroad ties to the next door.

"I guess we still have two months left to hash out what those 'best interests' are supposed to be."

"Two months?" he echoed.

Why did he sound as if she had just said something strange? She was tempted to look at him, but didn't quite trust herself yet. "The bargain was for three months, remember? One month has already gone by, or haven't you noticed?"

He hadn't. It struck him as odd. He had expected to feel like a prisoner, marking time, yet the month had somehow escaped him, slipping away without his even realizing it.

The air was warm, the moon was shining, and he could only keep a tight rein on his thoughts for so long with her next to him, half wearing that dress. He wanted to go home. "Hasn't he had enough yet?" Drew asked gruffly.

The grinch was back. But at least he had been nice for a while. The lapses were going to have to be longer if she ever hoped to thaw Drew out and have him relinquish his claim for custody. "He'll tell us when he's had enough."

More of her unorthodox philosophy. It was comforting to find something to become annoyed about. Otherwise his thoughts left him wide open to things he had no intentions of succumbing to. "You're letting a four-year-old decide things for himself?"

No, he had never been a little boy, celebrating Halloween, sneaking foods he shouldn't have, enjoying stolen moments past appointed bedtimes. She hadn't been wrong in her estimation of him. But she had to change him if she had any hopes of keeping Jeremy from suffering a fate she'd had to deal with. She had to make Drew sensitive enough to understand that she was the only one who was able to meet Jeremy's emotional needs.

"It's Halloween," she said simply. "And he knows when he's tired."

Jeremy gleefully ran up to show them his pumpkin. It was almost filled to the brim. "Here, hold this." He thrust the staff at her. "I need both hands." In a flash, he was running off to the next house.

There was enough candy in that pumpkin to make any three children sick to their stomach. "You're not going to let him eat all that, are you?"

She wondered if he really thought she was so lax, or if he was just trying to bait her. "No, that I'll dole out to him."

Maybe there was hope for her yet. "At last, one sensible decision."

She curtsied and the light from the flashlight wavered on the cement before Jeremy. "Thank you, m'lord, that's very kind of you."

He took the flashlight from her and shone it on the path for Jeremy. "Why do I keep hearing a mocking tone in your voice?"

"Possibly because it's there," she answered with a smile. "Loosen up, Drew. You'll live longer." Still holding on to Jeremy's staff, she lifted her skirts and walked ahead of Drew. "Right now, it'll only seem longer."

They were out for a total of two hours. When Jeremy's pumpkin was filled, Drew thought that would be the end of the excursion. But Daisy merely took off Jeremy's cap, turned it upside down and transferred candy into it. That left Jeremy more room in his pumpkin.

Just as Drew was giving up hope of the night ever ending, Jeremy's energy suddenly petered out. They were more than a mile away from the house.

Daisy took the boy's hand into hers and led him away from the last house. No longer bouncing along, Jeremy's steps were small and shuffling. "I think Little John is tired," she told Drew.

Drew shifted Jeremy's hat to his other side. A candy bar fell. "Just like that?" He retrieved the candy bar from the sidewalk before she could tell him to. He was beginning to anticipate some of her moves and found a vague comfort in that. "He was fine five minutes ago."

Daisy looked down at Jeremy. His eyes were drooping. "Five minutes is a long time when you're four."

She sounded as if she was speaking from first-hand experience. But that was impossible. "You remember?" he asked sarcastically.

There was almost childlike wonder in her face. "Don't you?"

"No, none of it." His entire childhood was a blur, with only tiny fragments of memories scattered throughout his mind, surfacing when something accidentally triggered them. "And you don't, either." She couldn't convince him that she did. She was just making it up, the way she probably did a lot of other things.

"I have a photographic memory. I remember *everything,*" she said sweetly.

So did he, about her. And he didn't want to. But details seemed to haunt the recesses of his mind, ambushing his thoughts and diverting them at the oddest times. "Just my luck, you're a walking computer. But even computers have glitches."

"I don't." She knelt next to Jeremy and brushed his hair from his face. He looked completely exhausted. "Come here, Little John. I'll carry you back." She moved to pick him up when Drew placed his hand over hers. She looked up at him quizzically.

"You'll trip with that dress." He shoved the hatful of candy at her. "Here, take this. I'll take him."

She took the hat and inclined her head, as if submitting. "As you wish, m'lord."

"Yeah, right." Only when it went along with what she wanted.

Drew slung his bow over one shoulder, next to the quiver. With one swift movement, he swept the boy into his arms. Jeremy slipped his arms around Drew's neck and nestled against him.

Daisy felt something tug at her heart. "I wish I had a camera," she murmured.

Drew looked at her sharply. To blackmail him? The britches were beginning to itch. "Why?"

"Because you've got an expression on your face I'd like to capture on film. Then I could take out the photograph whenever I felt inclined to bash you over the head. It would make me pause." She smiled, then turned to lead the way back. "I think you're human, Drew Addison, no matter how hard you try not to be."

"I'm not trying not to be human," he insisted, talking to her back. Moonlight shimmered on it, making her skin silvery. "I'm being logical." Tucking the boy against him, he kept a protective arm around his shoulders and walked as quickly as he could.

It was getting chilly and she wished she had rented a cape with this costume. "Like I said, that's one of the reasons I didn't become a lawyer."

She was still sticking to that ridiculous story. "Because of the logic," he recalled.

"No, because the logic got in the way of mercy, in the way of people, of justice. In the way of all the important things. Logic is very low on my priority list."

He laughed shortly and Jeremy stirred against him. The boy had fallen asleep, Drew realized. "Why doesn't that surprise me?"

She merely shook her head. "Maybe it's because you're so astute. Let's go home, Robin, and put Little John to bed."

They walked quickly down a twisting sidewalk, pools of light from street lamps guiding their way. The populace on the streets had thinned down considerably. Only a few die-hard trick-or-treaters were still out. Here and there, dogs barked behind fences, guarding their families from the threat of fairy folk.

"So, this was it?" Drew asked, breaking the silence between them.

Lost in her own thoughts about Drew, his question left her completely disoriented. "What?"

"Halloween. This is it?"

What more did he want? It seemed full to her. "Yes, pretty much."

He had no idea what the attraction was. "They go from house to house, collect candy that'll rot their teeth and make them sick and then fall asleep before they eat any of it." It all sounded very illogical when he said it aloud. "I didn't miss much."

You missed childhood, Drew. "Oh, I wouldn't say that."

There was that tone again, as if she knew things he didn't. Though he knew the conviction had no foundation, he still couldn't help the fact that it annoyed him. "No, knowing you, you probably wouldn't."

She looked up at him just before she crossed the street to their block. "You don't know me at all, m'lord."

He felt something twist within him. This time he recognized it. It was that weakness again, that weakness he had felt kissing her, getting lost in her scent, her taste. He shut it away, grateful that his arms were filled with a sleeping boy. Otherwise he would have taken her into them. "I think it's best if we keep it that way."

She shrugged too nonchalantly to please him. "If you say so, m'lord."

He did. He just didn't know if he meant it.

Chapter Nine

Daisy had left the front porch ablaze with lights. They were there to guide the steps of small trick-or-treaters on the brick walk leading to the house. But the sidewalk was empty now. It looked like any other evening in Bel Air. The costumed children were in their homes, shifting through their loot and the magic was gone for another year.

Daisy hurried ahead of Drew and unlocked the door. She held it open for him as he walked through, carrying a fast asleep Little John.

Irene rose from the armchair where she had sat during respites between onslaughts of sugar-motivated children. On the coffee table in front of her was a large, clear bowl that had been filled to overflowing with miniature candy bars and lollipops. It was three-quarters empty now.

The housekeeper hurried over to the child she had taken care of since birth. "Is he all right?" Concerned, she placed a hand to Jeremy's forehead and sighed when she found it cool.

"He's fine," Drew assured her. He looked down at the boy's face. Asleep, Jeremy looked even younger than four years old. He was such a little guy, Drew thought, and this was way past his bedtime. "He's just put in ten miles on those snazzy new sneakers of his."

Out of the corner of his eye, Drew saw Daisy looking at him. She had an amused expression on her face. And then he realized why. Oh God, now he was exaggerating, just the way she always did. He was *talking* like her. Where was his own personality going? How did she keep infiltrating his soul this way when he kept shutting all the doors?

Daisy placed Jeremy's pumpkin and the excess candy he had gathered in his cap on the table next to the bowl. She had emptied eight bags of candy into that bowl. "Looks like you had a lot of trick-or-treaters."

"Not in the last half hour or so," Irene answered. "But before that, it was like a siege. I couldn't hand out candy fast enough."

Daisy looked at her watch. It was a few minutes past nine. "I think it's time to close up shop, Irene. Thanks for manning the door."

Irene nodded. "No problem." She eyed the remaining candy in the bowl. "Well, if there's no use for these almond coconut bars," she murmured, "I'll just take a couple or three." She slipped several miniature bars into her pocket. "Good night." Smiling, the older woman made her way to her bedroom.

"She's going to be up all night if she eats all of those," Drew observed. "Too much sugar."

Didn't the man *ever* loosen up? Daisy shut off the porch light and turned to him. "I suppose you don't eat candy, either."

He could smell another disagreement coming on. Better that, he thought, his vision skimming her low neckline again, than the other. "No."

He couldn't be for real. If it hadn't been for that moment of weakness last week, if he hadn't kissed her the way he had, she would have been completely willing to believe that he had been born sitting behind a desk, managing the corporation. As it was, the memory of that kiss was beginning to fade a little around the edges. She found herself yearning for a refresher course.

"I'd like to take you in for a blood test."

He looked at her, befuddled. "Why?"

"To see if you have any." She unwrapped one tiny bit of chocolate and popped it into her mouth, savoring it as it melted against her tongue. "*Everybody* likes candy of some sort or another."

Another broad, sweeping statement that wasn't true. He shrugged as he turned toward the stairs, shifting Jeremy into a more comfortable position in his arms. "I never got into the habit."

At times it was like trying to have a conversation with a robot. She only sighed and shook her head as she lifted her skirts and followed him up the stairs. What kind of a life did he lead? How could he even call it a life? It sounded so black and white, so devoid of textures, of excitement. She was beginning to amend her initial assessment. Compared with Drew, Jonathan had been wild and reckless when she had first met him.

Drew eased open Jeremy's door with his shoulder.

"I can take it from here." Daisy started to take the sleeping boy from Drew.

But he shook his head and continued holding Jeremy. "I've carried him this far, I might as well put him to bed, too."

The truth of the matter was, he wanted to put the boy to bed, wanted that tiny personal act to call his own. He had no idea why he suddenly needed these sorts of things, even as he fought against what he felt was a flaw in his personality. Maybe it was Jonathan's death, maybe it was the sudden brush with mortality that Jonathan's death represented. Drew didn't know, didn't want to analyze his reasons. He just knew he needed to do it.

She smiled. This was definitely a good sign. Maybe Iceman meltdown was in sight yet.

"Sure." She crossed the threshold and pushed aside the covers on the bunk bed, then moved out of the way as Drew gently laid the boy down. Daisy slowly removed Jeremy's sneakers.

When she began to cover Jeremy, Drew placed his hand over hers. "Aren't you going to finish undressing him?"

She shook her head. "I don't want to wake him. Besides, once upon a time, there were no such things as nightclothes." She tucked the blanket securely around the boy, then placed his arms on top of the covers. "People slept in their clothing."

Drew watched her turn on the night-light, then followed her out into the hall. "Going back to the dark ages?"

Daisy closed Jeremy's door. "Just giving you a piece of history." She looked at him, amusement lifting the corners of her mouth. "In case you wanted to stay in those leather pants and that jersey."

The costume. He had forgotten he was wearing it. Drew scowled as he looked down at his outfit. "You owe me for this."

She turned, her skirt whirling softly in the muted hall light, brushing seductively against Drew's legs. As she turned, he moved forward. His arm made contact with her breast. They both felt the jolt.

"What," she asked in a soft whisper, "is it I owe you, Drew?"

He had been fighting this feeling all evening. Fighting desire ever since he'd kissed her. And he knew that the battle was about to be lost. Royally. He didn't like losing, but in losing, would he win? Or would he only succeed in losing himself? He no longer had any answers, only questions. What would it be like to kiss her again, to hold her warm body next to his and make love with her all night? What would it be like to hear that smoky, silky voice cry out his name in ecstasy?

His eyes skimmed along the outline of her lips. "You've got a smart mouth, you know that?"

It curved as she tilted her head back. "So you keep telling me."

Unable to stop himself, Drew combed his hands through her hair. Silky black strands wound themselves around his fingers. He saw her eyes darken slightly as desire awoke. His own blood heated. "God only knows why I want to kiss it."

She could feel her pulse starting to throb. If he didn't kiss her soon, she was going to have to take matters into her own hands. "Maybe it's because you're a lot smarter than you let on."

Drew lowered his head, his throat hoarse. "This isn't smart." The words whispered against her lips. "It's stupid."

Daisy rose on her toes just enough to cut the distance between their lips to a fraction of an inch. "Whatever."

He didn't remember starting the kiss. He was just suddenly in it. Hopelessly, completely in it. Desire erupted within him instantly, throwing him off balance, leaving him confused, disoriented. A beggar in a land he neither knew nor understood. He had no frame of reference to draw on. He had never *wanted* a woman this way, with this intensity, never felt as if everything was melting around him. As if *he* was melting.

All from the heat of her mouth.

He had always done things slowly, methodically, with precision. He had always looked before he leaped. Not only looked, but surveyed and measured the terrain completely. All those hopelessly outmoded adages applied to the way he lived his life.

So what was this that was happening to him now? Why was he leaping along a tightrope without a net beneath him?

He wanted to absorb her, to have her wrap herself around him and never let go. He wanted morning to never come. And all he was doing was kissing her.

It wasn't all. It was everything. The beginning of everything. And the end.

Her blood sang as his kiss deepened, taking her to points uncharted. This was it. She knew it just the way she had known when she had settled on what she wanted to do with her life. No more meandering, no more sampling. No more wondering. This wasn't merely pleasant, or interesting, or diverting. This was everything. Pain, happiness, and complete and total enchantment.

This was it.

He was the one.

Startled, a bit frightened, Daisy pushed away, her eyes open wide as she looked at him. She was in love with him. Just like that. In love. The realization had her breath backing up in her lungs.

"What's the matter?" He had gotten carried away again, Drew thought. Thank God she had stopped it when she did. There was still time to retreat.

She kept her hands on his forearms. Her legs were the consistency of whipped cream and totally useless. "I don't think we should be doing this here," she murmured, trying to catch her breath. She didn't think she would, not ever again.

His breathing was ragged. He felt embarrassed by it and didn't reply. He just nodded, slowly filling his lungs. His head still spun a little, but he could navigate without humiliating himself. "I'll just go—"

She tightened her grip on his forearms. When Drew looked at her, confused, Daisy shook her head. "I didn't say I didn't think we should be doing this. I said we shouldn't be doing this *here*."

"Then—?" Was she saying what he thought she was saying? With Anastasia, he was never sure.

She wanted to laugh but didn't, knowing it would hurt his pride. He was so incredibly adorable when he was fumbling.

"Then," she said with a nod. There weren't any more words necessary. Her fingers linked with his, she turned toward her room.

He followed her, knowing he shouldn't. Knowing that what he should be doing was running like hell to his room and locking the door. Not to keep her out, but to keep himself in. He had a feeling that if they made love now, things would never be the same again. And he didn't want anything to change, not for him.

Yet he couldn't turn away, couldn't leave. He couldn't do anything at all but want her. It was like being addicted and not having the willpower to cut himself free.

Daisy pushed the door closed behind them. It clicked softly, but the sound echoed throughout the room and vibrated within their heads. Daisy looked at Drew, waiting. The next move was his.

He felt his throat growing dry again. "This is crazy, you know."

Her grin was warm, inviting and rimmed with mischief. Her eyes sparkled and teased. "Yeah."

It was crazy, but there was nothing else he could do. Drew gave in to the desire pumping through him, churning his adrenaline past endurable limits.

Needs ran headlong into needs as he crushed her body to his. He was acting so far against type that he had no idea who or what he was anymore. All he knew was that he was thirsty, so terribly thirsty and her lips held the sustenance he needed to survive.

Holding her to him, his mouth greedily drank in what she had to offer. His hands roamed her back, her shoulders, while his heart pounded and roared in his ears.

Still waters, she thought. It was true what they said about them, absolutely true. She never would have dreamed this need existed within him. Never would have dreamed that its twin beat in her own breast.

He needed to regain control over himself before he went too quickly, before he hurt her. Dragging air into his lungs again, Drew held her at arm's length. She was still encased in her costume, but now he viewed it as a barrier. A very cumbersome barrier.

He traced the outline of her décolleté with his fingers, watching her irises grow smoky and blur, feeling her breath as it stilled within her.

"How did people manage in the old days?"

This time she did laugh, but there was delight in it and he was unoffended. "They took things off, just the way they do now. Irene helped me with my zipper." She turned her back to him slowly. "Would you mind?"

Mind? There wasn't anything he wanted to do more. With hands that had grown suddenly clumsy, he unfastened the hook and eye above the zipper. He felt the slight tremor that went through her and it excited him. Slowly, he slid the zipper to its base, savoring the sight of her exposed back as it came into view. She had perfect skin. Skin that begged to be touched, to be worshipped.

He'd stopped. "Something wrong?" she whispered, feeling as if jelly had replaced her limbs.

"No, something right," Drew answered, his voice low. "Something very right."

Still behind her, he lowered his lips to her shoulder as he slipped his hands inside her bodice. His fingers cupped her breasts gently and he heard her moan his name as she leaned back against his chest.

Daisy's breathing grew short as she tried vainly to absorb all the sensations that were wickedly dancing through her.

Drew pressed his lips to the slope of her neck, moving with excruciatingly slow increments to her shoulders, her back. She began to shiver, needing the warmth of his embrace. Turning, she sought his mouth. As he kissed her over and over again, Drew slipped the long, trailing sleeves from her arms until the gown rested precariously about her waist.

She burned to feel him against her.

"It would help a lot if Robin took off his shirt," Daisy murmured against his mouth, tugging at the jersey in mounting frustration.

Completely steeped in her, in what was happening within him because of her, it took Drew a moment to hear her voice. "What?"

"Your shirt," she prompted, humor mixing with passion in her eyes. "Take off your shirt."

All he could do was look at her, at the way the light from the single lamp in her room bathed her skin. She was nude from the waist up and seductively uninhibited about it.

She was talking to him, wasn't she? He hadn't heard a word. "I—"

"Never mind."

Trying to curb her eagerness, hands shaking ever so lightly, Daisy unfastened the belt at his waist. Fingers flying, she undid the leather lacings at the front of his shirt, then pushed it up his chest and off his shoulders. Never once did her eyes leave his.

"Better?" she asked, fitting herself against him.

Drew's arms tightened around her, holding her closer. He could feel her breasts against his chest, feel the erotic sensation of her nipples as they hardened.

"Better." He smiled, brushing her hair from her face. Infinitely better. There were times, he had to admit, when she was actually right. So right.

Such as now.

He pushed the gown from her hips. It fell to the floor, gathering about her ankles like a dark green lake. All she had on was the smallest bit of nylon. Soft, dark green, opaque nylon.

She saw desire flame in his eyes as he looked down at her. "I wanted to match your shirt."

And then she grinned and he had a sudden urge to nibble on her lip and taste her smile. He began with her eyelids as they fluttered shut beneath his lips.

Her head fell back as everything sprang to life within her. "I've never made love with a man in leather britches before."

Drew moved back. His eyes held hers. "How many men have you made love with?" He had no idea he was going to ask the question until it was there, hanging in the air between them.

"Counting tonight?" Daisy asked in a breathless whisper.

"Yes." The word was stark, rigid. Yet he had to hear her answer.

"One." No one else mattered, not the way he did. She wove her fingers through his hair. "None before you." *And none after,* she added silently. *Not ever again.*

He didn't believe her. A woman like Anastasia, with her zest for life, with her way of breezing through everything, had to have had countless lovers, men who she brought down to their knees in mute supplication before allowing them to experience a moment in paradise. He hated everyone of the faceless legion.

And he didn't give a damn who she had loved before, so long as she loved him now.

"Make love with me, Anastasia." Drew breathed the words against her shoulder, letting them linger on her skin like a love song that enveloped her.

Her hands were already on his hips. They felt taut and firm beneath her palms and she felt a shiver of anticipation pass over her.

She nipped his lower lip, gliding the tip of her tongue over it. His groan aroused her even more. "I wasn't about to suggest another round of trick-or-treating." Her eyes laughed, but it was that warm, inviting laugh that beckoned to his soul.

And he was racing to meet her. Racing even though he knew it meant his doom.

He felt her hands glide over his hips, his thighs, warming a path down as she tugged the britches from him. His breathing became shallow, his desire demanding as he followed suit with the scrap of material she whimsically called underwear.

All the while, he was kissing her over and over again. Kissing her eyes, her throat, her lips, unable to sate himself. The hunger was ravaging him, raging within him, pushing him on to take more and more. And she gave it to him. Met him demand for demand. The bounty she offered without asking for anything in return was endless and it humbled him.

When he had made love to women before, he had never lost himself, never lost sight of who or what he was, where he was. The earth had never moved before. It moved now. But this was California. Earthquakes were common in California, weren't they? And she was responsible for every one of them.

Colors filled his head. Colors and sights and sounds without definition, beyond description. And they were all originating from her.

A frenzy overtook him that he had to fight back. He wanted to plunge himself into her, to claim her, to make her his. But he wanted to go slowly, to savor every moment as if it were his last. For perhaps it would be.

But when they tumbled onto the bed, too weak to stand, he had no resistance left. He had to take her now. As he tucked her beneath him, his body poised, his eyes on hers, he linked his fingers with hers one by one.

"You knew, didn't you?" he asked, anticipating the answer. She had known, somehow known from the start, that they would wind up this way, here in her room, on the brink of discovery. On the edge of disaster.

She smiled, her eyes caressing his face. She could see by his look that he could almost feel her touch. "Didn't you?"

Yes, damn it, he had known. Some faraway part of him had known. Known that she was his undoing, just as Alyce had been his brother's. Perhaps he had known even at the christening, when he had first met her.

But he didn't want to think where this was going, where it would ultimately lead. All he wanted to think of was this moment.

And to somehow make it last forever.

As Daisy moved to accept him, he knew he was undone. She wrapped her legs around his body, holding tight, and the journey began.

It wasn't peaceful, did nothing to soothe. That part of it was over. Instead, they rode, wild and sweating, destined for a land they had never been to before. And they rode together.

When they came, spent, near exhaustion, to the threshold, they cried out each other's name.

But only Daisy heard.

Drew raised his head from where he had it pillowed against her breasts. It seemed like an eternity later. Or perhaps a lifetime later. His lifetime.

Because he couldn't completely fathom the magnitude of what had happened, the entire experience was almost hazy for him.

"Was I too rough?" he asked, concerned. Her lips were blurred from the imprint of his and he was afraid there might even be bruises, ready to rise. He felt as if he had been possessed. There was no other term that could quite adequately cover what he had felt. She had been a madness that had filled his blood.

"No. It was wonderful," she assured him.

Even the words took effort to say as she breathed slowly, languidly. She saw the furrow on his brow and her heartbeat quickened. He was withdrawing. So soon?

No you don't, not yet.

Daisy propped herself up on her elbow. Her hair rained down on his shoulder, synthesizing his skin. Drew could only stare, wondering how it was possible to feel aroused again when he was half dead from exhaustion.

The smile began slowly, lifting the corners of her mouth then spreading to her eyes like the sunrise on a prairie. Maybe he was only a quarter dead, Drew amended.

"Want to do it again?"

He rubbed his hand along her hair. The spirit was willing, but the flesh was weak. "In about two days, maybe, if I recover."

Humor. Very good, she thought. She'd melt the Iceman yet.

Watching his eyes, she feathered her fingertips along the light sprinkling of hair on his chest. She saw something stir within the depths. "Maybe I can stretch this out for two days," she mused.

Then she lifted her hand and slowly traced the path her fingers had taken, this time using the tip of her tongue. She felt his stomach muscles quiver beneath her breast.

Dingdong, the Iceman's dead.

She was doing it to him. He had no idea how, or where the sudden surge of stamina was coming from, but she was doing it to him. Arousing him, making him want her again. Making him crazy.

And madness, he had to admit, had never looked so inviting.

Reaching for her, he cupped her face in his hands. Daisy looked up, a question in her eyes.

"Come here," he urged her. "I think I've just recovered."

She grinned and began to oblige, sliding the length of her body along his. She felt his response as his body grew harder, more aroused. Her grin widened.

"It's a miracle," she murmured just before she covered his mouth with hers.

Chapter Ten

When Daisy woke up the next morning, she was alone in her bed. The imprint of Drew's body was still there, but the sheet was cold. He had obviously left her side some time ago.

Sitting up, she ran her hand through her hair and let it fall in a tangled wave against her bare shoulders. Had he gone to his own room during the night for form's sake, concerned that Jeremy might see them together? It would have gone a long way in comforting her if she could have believed that to be true. But Daisy knew that was crediting Drew with being a little too aware of the way a child's mind worked. Drew had some distance to go before he reached that point in his emotional development.

But he was definitely improving, she mused as she stretched her body, remembering the way his hands had felt, gliding along her skin last night. The way he had felt, loving her. He had already come a long way from the stuffed shirt who had stood on her doorstep four weeks ago.

Well, she was going to get no answers lying here, she thought. She rose and threw on the first robe she pulled out of the closet. It was pale yellow and floor length, and it felt sleek against her bare skin, reminding her that she was nude. She wasn't used to sleeping that way. Thoughts of last night brought a sensual smile to her lips.

Knotting the sash, she noted the time. Just barely six o'clock. But she doubted very much if Drew was asleep. If she knew him, he'd be awake, holding what had taken place between them last night under a microscope, scrutinizing it from every possible angle. Taking the magic out.

She knocked softly on his door. There was no answer. She knocked harder. Still nothing. Perplexed, Daisy raised her hand to knock once more before trying the door when she heard him say, "Come in."

He sounded impatient, as if she was intruding on his space.

The man was a bear the morning after. Something else to work on. Well, she hadn't believed that he was going to make a total transformation just because they had made love last night. Even she was more realistic than that, Daisy thought as she opened the door.

There was a suitcase laying open on his bed. He was packing.

Daisy stared, the happy glow she had been savoring vanishing like a puddle of water in the hot noon sun. She forced a nonchalant smile to her lips as she walked into the room. "Going somewhere?"

He felt every muscle in his body become taut. He didn't want to face her, not yet. Pretending to be preoccupied, he took fresh socks from the drawer and placed them into his suitcase.

"Um, yes. New York." Drew shut the drawer, then opened another. "There's a board meeting I have to attend. I—"

He turned, angry at himself for fumbling, angry at her for making him fumble. It was the truth, damn it. There was an emergency situation and he had to go. Why did it sound like a lie when he told her? Trying to regain some order in his life, he had checked in with the New York contact this morning. There was a major crisis going on that left unchecked would have far-reaching repercussions and yet it sounded like a pitiful excuse he was making up just to avoid her. Why?

Because he was going for more than one reason and he knew it. He was leaving because it was necessary and because he needed space. He needed time to clear his head, to find that rational person he had always been. And he couldn't do it here, not with her so close by.

He saw she was still waiting for him to complete his sentence. "Look, I can't miss it."

He was being too defensive. "I'm not saying anything," she said rather coolly. *Coward.*

He haphazardly threw in a handful of underwear on top of the socks, not bothering to fold them. "No, but your eyes are."

"You're not intuitive enough to read eyes yet, Drew." Still maintaining the smile she didn't feel, Daisy began to roll his underwear into neat little tubes and replace them in the suitcase.

"Don't."

She raised her eyes to his innocently. "I've seen what you have under these, I can pack them for you. Besides, one of my friends is a flight attendant. She showed me how to pack more efficiently."

She took the shirt from his hand and rolled it, as well. "When did all this happen?" She placed the shirt next to the underwear. "This sudden need for a meeting, I mean. Did you get a call from your pants' phone?"

She didn't believe him, he thought. Well, why should she? It all sounded suspiciously convenient. Make love and run. "It came up this morning. I phoned." He pressed his lips together. "This morning," he repeated unnecessarily. Damn, what had she done to him? Why couldn't she have just left him alone? This was getting too tangled for him, too complicated. He could plow through a seventy-page legal document with ease, but emotions, especially *these* emotions, were something he was a novice at. And expert status was too far away to attempt.

Placing the last shirt into the suitcase, Daisy perched on the edge of the bed and folded her hands in her lap, resigned to the turn of events. "So, how long are you going to be gone?" *You say forever and I'll cut your heart out, here and now.*

He shrugged without looking at her. "A day, maybe two. Maybe longer. I'm not sure." He walked into the bathroom for his electric razor and a few other items.

She watched as he dropped them into the case. Again, he didn't bother to arrange them. He was definitely nervous, she thought. Or guilty. "Are board meetings always this uncertain?"

He didn't know how long this was going to take. That much was true. "The meeting's about a takeover. I thought I squelched it last week. Obviously not. This thing seems to have more heads than a Hydra."

Just like his feelings, he thought, looking at her. He no sooner shored up one front, getting things under control, than another one opened up. Even now, he was reacting to her. It was six in the morning. Why did she look so good? It didn't seem right.

"But you are coming back?" Daisy lifted a brow when he didn't reply immediately. "The bargain, remember? Jeremy," she prompted.

He remembered. He remembered very well. If he hadn't made the bargain, if there wasn't a child's future at stake, Drew knew he wouldn't be returning. To return to the scene of the "crime" and voluntarily continue in this unsettling situation without the motivation that Jeremy provided would be nothing short of insane. If there was anything Drew hated, it was not being in control, not knowing exactly what it was that he was doing. And with Anastasia, there was only the unknown, the uncertain.

"Sure I'll be back," he said, his voice harsh. "Why shouldn't I be?"

She got up from the bed and shrugged, the robe sliding down her shoulder. She adjusted it, aware that he was watching her every move. Did he expect her to pounce on him? "I don't know. Maybe because you've got this fugitive look on your face, a little like Richard Kimble, running from the police."

He was fiddling with the lock and made himself stop. "Who?"

She shook her head. Why had she expected him to know? "You probably don't watch old reruns on T.V."

He let the lid drop on his suitcase. "I don't watch television."

She hung her head in mock defeat. "Boy, I sure can pick 'em."

He didn't hear her. "What?"

"Nothing." He couldn't help the way he was, she thought. That part was up to her. The least she could do was set his mind at ease. At least for now.

She laid both hands on his shoulders and waited until he looked into her eyes. "Don't worry, Drew, I'm not asking you to make an honest woman out of me. That's something that's passé." A small smile creased her lips. "Unless you believe in love and romance and silly things like that."

She might not be asking him to marry her, but she was asking for something. Something he couldn't give. Commitment. "Um, Anastasia, what happened last night—"

"Was beautiful," she said quickly, "and I'm not going to let you spoil it by dissecting it, or looking for the logic in it—"

Logic? "There wasn't any." Making love with her had to be the most illogical thing he had ever done in his life. And the most exciting.

"Exactly." She dropped her hands from his shoulders. "And that's just the way I like it."

He didn't begin to understand her. Not on a conscious level at any rate. Unconsciously he could ascribe a dozen meanings to what she was saying, all of them confusing as hell. He dragged a hand through his hair. "God, you are the most frustrating woman—"

She turned from the doorway, looking over her shoulder. "Got you stirred up, don't I?" She smiled wickedly. He'd be back and that was all she needed to know right now. "It's a start."

She paused, wondering if it was necessary to remind him. She took a chance. "Don't forget to say goodbye to Jeremy."

Drew looked at his watch. It was too early. "He's sleeping."

It *was* necessary to remind him, she thought with an inward sigh. Just when she thought he was learning. "So, wake him up. He needs to hear goodbye followed by hello in his life."

The woman definitely needed to come with an instruction manual. "Can that be translated into something someone with a logical mind can follow?"

She crossed to him again. "You can't just slip out of his life conveniently for days at a time." *The way you seem to be able to do out of mine.* "He needs to know where you're going and that you'll be back. He's still on very shaky ground, emotionally."

Drew saw no evidence to substantiate what she was saying. Jeremy appeared to be as cheerful as any other four-year-old. She was creating problems where there weren't any. "He seems fine."

Daisy wasn't convinced of that. There was something in Jeremy's eyes, something that told her the worst was yet to come. He had accepted his parents' death too easily after the initial shock had faded. She wished with all her heart that Drew was right, but she had a feeling that she was.

"People are full of surprises when you lift the lid. Even little people." She touched Drew's arm, imploring. "Wake him up. Trust me on this."

Trust her.

How could he trust her? About this, perhaps, if he stretched it. But not about anything else. She was the one who brought total chaos into his orderly mind, into his orderly life. How could he trust someone like that about anything? The only thing he could trust her for was to do more of the same.

He snapped the locks on his suitcase closed one at a time. "All right. And when I get back, we'll talk." Gripping the handle, he began to walk out of his room.

"Or avoid each other," she murmured as she followed close behind him.

He heard and pretended not to. Because she was probably right. Drew didn't want to talk, didn't want to think, didn't want to feel until the serenity returned. Well, he amended, not serenity exactly, but a kind of peace. A lack of personal turbulence at the very least.

"By the way, why are you taking a suitcase?" she asked just before he went into Jeremy's room.

"Carrying clothes in my teeth is cumbersome."

He wasn't prepared for the pure delight that he heard in her laughter. For a moment he felt his tension abating, as if he wasn't really running for his life. As if all he was doing was simply going to a meeting in another city for a short while with every intention of returning. Willingly and eagerly.

"I meant, if you're going to New York, you have an apartment there. With clothes and a razor. Why was it necessary for you to pack anything at all?"

She was right. He didn't know why he had packed, except that perhaps it symbolized something to him. A neat, orderly withdrawal. "Maybe I just wanted something to hold on to."

"Fine." She took the suitcase from him and placed it on the floor. As he looked at her, almost spellbound, she placed his hands on her waist, rose on her toes and took his face in her hands. "Hold on to this until you get back."

And she kissed him, effectively disintegrating what was left of his functioning mind.

Drew sat in his penthouse apartment, looking down on the city. From the twenty-second floor, it didn't look dirty or cold, or disinterested. It looked like a city of shining lights and tall buildings that stretched to touch the sky. A twinkling jewel-studded necklace for him to appreciate. Alone.

He missed her.

Damn it, he missed her, missed the sound of her voice, the smell of her hair, the sight of her quirky smile. The taste of her mouth.

He'd been gone only four days and he felt as if it was an eternity. What was happening to him?

He had hoped by returning to New York that everything that had happened in California would become a blur, a memory that would slowly fade. That's the way he had always reacted to traveling before. All his trips to Japan, to London, to Paris seemed like trips that had happened to someone else after a few days back. Reality was here, at Addison Corporation. And on the twenty-second floor of the Templeton Building where he had lived for the last eight years.

Or at least it had been. A little more than a month ago.

The Hydra had been completely beheaded yesterday. The takeover was permanently terminated. He could have caught a plane for the west coast last night, but he didn't. He had purposely remained another day, trying to recapture the old feeling. The feeling of belonging. It eluded him like a whimsical butterfly fluttering through a field of wildflowers.

He banged a fist on the coffee table and his coffee cup shook dangerously. What had she done to him?

He had only been gone from the New York office a month, an insignificant month. In that time he had been in daily contact with the people he normally dealt with via telecommunication hook-ups and fax machines, as well as constant calls on his "pants' phone."

The term had him smiling despite himself. It was supposed to be as if he were still there, in New York. As if, by maintaining this sort of visual contact, he could fool himself into believing that he hadn't actually left at all.

But he had left. He hadn't been in New York. He'd been in a house in Bel Air, living with a woman who seemed bent on redecorating the interior of his soul. Escaping, it should have given him a sense of overwhelming relief to be here, safe and sane in his apartment.

It should have.

But it didn't.

He took a sip of his coffee and pushed it aside, dissatisfied. As dissatisfied as he was with being in New York. He felt as if he had left a piece of himself behind in Bel Air. Part of his sanity, no doubt. He rose and walked to the huge bay window. The city lay at his feet, a beguiling panorama. What more could he want?

He knew the answer but refused to admit it to himself.

He pressed his hand against the cool glass and looked out. Right now, what was she doing? What was Jeremy doing?

When he had reluctantly woken the boy up before he left, Drew had been surprised by a display of tears. Still sleepy, Jeremy had thrown his arms around Drew's neck and just held on, without saying anything at all, only crying. And then he had let go and quietly said goodbye. It had been almost spooky for Drew. Did four-year-olds act that adult?

Drew turned his back to the city and eyed the telephone on his clear coffee table.

No, he wasn't going to call. He was stronger than that.

He hadn't a clue how four-year-olds were supposed to behave, really. He hadn't a clue about anything anymore. Why else would he feel, absurdly so, that he didn't belong in the very place where he *did* belong? The restless feeling threw him off balance completely. It was like trying on a favorite pair of shoes that had worked their way to the back of the closet and discovering that after all this time, they pinched.

He was going crazy, he thought, and would probably reach that destination soon since he was flying back tomorrow morning.

Searching for a diversion, Drew looked around his apartment and tried to picture Jeremy amid the white austere furnishings, the pristine white rug. Maybe he'd redecorate. White wasn't practical around children. Drew had no doubts that when the three months ended, Anastasia would give him custody of Jeremy. After all, she had to have seen how the boy held on to him. The boy loved him. That had been her point, hadn't it, for this enforced living arrangement? To see how Jeremy reacted to him. Jeremy was going to be his, just the way he had wanted. Drew was confident that he had everything going for him. The family name, money and the boy's affection.

He trailed his fingers along the top of the sofa. The day after New Year's he'd be back here permanently with Jeremy.

Just the two of them.

Drew had no idea where this strange, dissatisfied feeling was coming from. He'd be getting exactly what he wanted. What was the problem?

With a sigh, he picked up the telephone receiver, suddenly wanting desperately to talk to "the problem." He didn't know why, he only knew he had to. It was as if he was half sleepwalking through his life.

The telephone rang four times before there was an answer. He stayed on, waiting it out. He had no choice in the matter. He was even willing to settle for listening to the voice on her answering machine. In a way, it would have been almost preferable. At least that way, she wouldn't know he had called.

The receiver on the other end lifted and a sleepy voice murmured "Hello?" breathlessly against his ear. He felt something twist inside. He was beginning to recognize it for what it was. Raw desire.

Drew wrapped his fingers around a pencil so tightly he almost snapped it in two.

"Hello?" This time Daisy's voice was clearer, more alert.

"Hello, Anastasia. It's Andrew. Um, Drew. I just wanted to tell you that I was flying out tomorrow." Too tense suddenly to sit, Drew perched on the back of the sofa.

"You're coming home?"

Home. She made it sound as if the house in Bel Air was his home as well as hers. This was home. Here. In New York, not California.

If that was true, why was he arguing with himself about it? God, when he had flown out to L.A., he had had all the answers. Now he had all the questions instead and none of the answers fit.

He didn't respond to her question directly. "I'm taking the eight o'clock flight."

"A.m.? P.m.? In or out?"

She sounded awake now and her questions chagrined him. They shouldn't have been necessary. It wasn't like him not to give details like that automatically.

"A.m. I'm leaving JFK at eight in the morning." The ticket his secretary had purchased for him was on the coffee table. He flipped it open for the fifth time since this morning, checking to see if it was still there. Staring at it, Drew told her which airline he was taking.

"Fine. Then I'll meet you at LAX at ten o'clock, my time."

"You don't have to do that." He hadn't called to ask her to meet him. Had he? He wasn't certain anymore, but he didn't want her thinking he was asking. She might construe that to mean he was eager to be with her. "I know my way around."

There was a pause at the other end of the line and he thought he had lost the connection. And then she spoke again. "That's okay. You don't have to worry, Drew. My hands'll be on the wheel at all times."

"I wasn't worried about that." That sounded incredibly stupid. "I mean—"

Damn, what did he mean? He'd spent four days thinking about nothing else but her since he had gotten on the plane. There was three thousand miles between them. Three thousand miles between what he wanted and what he knew was wrong for him. All wrong. They had nothing in common except for the love of one child. Why couldn't he just be logical about this? He'd always been so logical before.

Logic had absolutely nothing to do with this. "I've missed you, all right?" He fairly barked the admission into the receiver. "Satisfied?"

"Not if you're not."

"Now who's dissecting things?" He rose and began to pace about the apartment restlessly. The sound of her voice was making him want her again and making him feel trapped at the same time.

"Must be the company I've been keeping."

He heard the smile in her voice and could see it in his mind's eye. Spreading slowly, lifting the corners of her mouth. He felt himself getting aroused.

What the hell was he doing to himself?

"How's Jeremy?" It was a safe topic—Jeremy's welfare—one about which they were both in agreement, at least in theory.

"He's fine. He keeps asking me when you're coming home." It was a good sign, she thought, his asking about the boy. Now if Drew would only realized that they all belonged together as a unit, everything would work itself out well. But that, Daisy knew, was going to take some time. She only hoped that she'd have enough. New Year's Day was not that far away.

There were a hundred things Drew wanted to say to her, yet nothing would come. It was as if his brain had disengaged from his tongue. "So, I'll see you tomorrow, I guess. But don't bother picking me up at the airport. I'll grab a cab. I might want to stop at the office first."

"Tomorrow," she promised.

The last time he flew to California, only a month ago, anxiety and agitation had been his constant companions on the trip because of Jonathan's death. They were back at his side again, but for a whole different spectrum of reasons.

Drew stared out the window, watching the cloud formations in the distance without seeing them at all. He felt like a man who no longer knew his own mind. He couldn't wait to arrive in Los Angeles, yet he didn't want to go. It was a little like standing in line, waiting for a ride on a giant roller coaster. It was both exhilarating and frightening at the same time.

Just like Anastasia was. Just like his feelings for her were.

It was a smooth flight all the way, if he didn't count what was going on in his stomach. When Drew deplaned, he bypassed the groups of people clustered at the luggage carousel, grateful that he had brought along only one suitcase. He didn't need more things trying his patience. He was agitated enough as it was.

He had no idea why he was scanning the crowd, looking for her face. He had all but ordered her to stay home. There was no reason to expect her to be here.

And yet, he hoped.

Maybe he should have stayed away a little longer, he thought. He needed more time to get a better grip on himself. The takeover had been stopped once and for all, mainly due to his efforts. Why couldn't he be this efficient with his private life?

As he walked toward the doors that led outside the building and to the line of queued-up taxicabs, he felt his left arm being taken while someone was simultaneously tugging on his right.

"Hi, stranger." The sultry voice washed over him, awakening every nerve in his body.

He could only stare at her, and grin like an idiot, he thought helplessly. "You came."

She brushed a kiss all too quickly against his cheek. "Did you ever have any doubts?"

Any answer he might have given was interrupted by the bouncing child on his right. "Uncle Drew, Uncle Drew," Jeremy yelled excitedly, still tugging.

Without thinking, only reacting, Drew scooped the boy up into his arms and hugged him.

Well, well, well, Daisy thought, *more progress.* At least he was coming right along on one level.

Uninhibited, Jeremy planted a wet kiss on Drew's cheek. It landed somewhere just beneath his eye. The boy threaded both hands around his uncle's neck and grinned broadly, relieved. Aunt Daisy had said he was coming back, but Jeremy hadn't been altogether certain until this moment. "What d'you bring me?"

Uh-oh. "Me." Drew had a sinking feeling that it wasn't quite what Jeremy was hoping to hear. At least, not exclusively.

"Oh." Jeremy's smile faded a little around the edges, giving way to a touch of disappointment.

"Was I supposed to bring you something else?" Drew stalled, his mind racing around. Was there anything in his suitcase he could pass off as a gift? He should have thought of that, he realized, when he was leaving New York. But he had never had a small boy waiting for him before.

"Hey, look, Tiger." Daisy nudged Jeremy's arm to get his attention. "Look what Uncle Drew has in his pocket."

As Drew looked down at the pocket in question along with Jeremy, Daisy pulled her hand up with a flourish, holding a wrapped package aloft. Though the package was small, its dimensions wouldn't have allowed it to comfortably fit into Drew's pocket.

Jeremy seemed blissfully unaware of that fact as he eagerly grabbed for the gift. Securing it, he planted another kiss on Drew's cheek. One that made Drew feel warm and guilty at the same time.

Drew set the boy down and looked at Daisy. He hadn't seen her carrying anything except for her small purse. "One of your many careers involve being a magician?"

"Pickpocket," she corrected. Her eyes were dancing and he had absolutely no idea if she was putting him on or not. After living with her for a month, he wouldn't put anything past her.

"You think of everything." He nodded toward the package.

"Not everything, but I'm working on it." And then her smile softened and he felt the sinewy strands of desire twist a little tighter in his belly. Daisy's lips brushed against his as she murmured, "Welcome home."

It wasn't his home, not really. But he no longer knew where he belonged. Except, perhaps, within the warmth of her kiss.

Jeremy was busy sending bits of wrapping paper flying as he unwrapped his gift, the latest action figure from a popular Saturday morning television program. That gave him a second, Drew thought.

Placing his suitcase on the ground next to him, Drew used both hands to secure Daisy in place. And then he kissed her the way he had been dreaming about kissing her since he had gotten on the plane to New York.

Time stopped. The world stopped. They were no longer in a crowded airport with people milling all around them and a little boy at their feet. They were at the beginning of the path that they had forged for themselves with the fires of passion.

Daisy looked a little stunned and very, very pleased when their lips parted. She touched his face in awe. "You really did miss me."

He held her for a moment longer, enjoying the way his fingers comfortably fit around her waist. "Yes, damn it, I really did."

"I've never been cursed at quite that way before," she told him, amusement highlighting her features. "I think I kind of like it."

She looked down at Jeremy. Typically the boy was making his figure do some tricks of derring-do he had recently seen on television. Beckoning, she took his hand in hers.

"Let's get out of everyone's way, Jeremy. It's time to go home." Ushering Jeremy toward the door, she linked her other arm through Drew's.

Drew knew he shouldn't let that sound as good as it did to him. His future lay in a totally different direction than hers did.

But at least, he thought as they walked to the parking lot, they had the present.

Chapter Eleven

At first glance, it seemed as if every parking space in the immediate area was taken, but Daisy had managed to find a spot not too far from the loading and unloading zone in front of Drew's terminal. As they walked through the electronic doors, Drew felt as if the actual land was greeting him. The air was warm, the sky sunny. A picture-perfect day. Five hours away, in New York, he had left behind a gray, overcast sky and temperatures in the thirties. An altogether nasty day. Somehow, it almost seemed like an omen.

Except that he didn't believe in omens.

He had to set the tone without further delay. He'd already lost precious ground by letting her know how much he had missed her. There was no point in perpetuating something that he knew had no future.

"I am going to have to stop at the office," Drew reminded Daisy as they reached her car.

She unlocked the passenger side and then walked around the hood to her side. "I never doubted it for a moment." Drew thought he detected a tinge of teasing sarcasm, or was that just his imagination? "We just wanted to see you before you went into hibernation again, didn't we, Jeremy?"

Jeremy was already in the backseat, orienting his new action figure to a world he had conjured up in his mind. He stopped and looked at his aunt quizzically as she got into the driver's seat. "What's hi-ber-na-tion mean?" He said the word very carefully, as if he was aware of forming each syllable.

Daisy strapped in, glancing at Drew out of the corner of her eye. "It's what bears do in the wintertime. Put your seat belt on, honey."

"It is on. You don't have to 'mind me. I'm not a baby." Jeremy cocked his head as he turned toward Drew. "And Uncle Drew's not a bear." Drew smiled at Jeremy for coming to his defense and Jeremy sat up straighter, proud of the recognition.

Daisy saw Jeremy's expression in her rearview mirror. A little male bonding going on here, she thought with a smile. "No," Daisy started the car, "not anymore."

Drew raised an amused brow. Daisy ignored him, concentrating instead on getting them out of the parking lot.

Several miles later, with the airport far behind them, they came to a stop at a red light. Major construction was all around them. A new community of one- and two-bedroom patio homes was going up, resting on the site of what had once been rows of decaying storefronts. On the corner was just the beginnings of a mini-mall to accommodate future residents' immediate needs.

Daisy scanned the area, then smiled to herself. Corner of Berekely and Yale. This was the place. The man at the Indigo company had been so pleased with her efficiency, not to mention her price, that he had recommended Showers of Flowers . . . to the man in charge of building this mini-mall.

"Look, Jeremy, there're your palm trees. They're going to be planting them in the ground by the end of the week." She pointed them out.

Jeremy scrambled forward, straining against his seat belt tether for a better view, his hands on the back of Drew's headrest. "Hey, yeah."

Four palms trees stood lined up in an uneven row near the curb. They were still in boxes, their long green fonds swaying in the breeze, combing the air like massive green spiders trying to climb up on smooth glass and succeeding only in sliding back down.

"I picked out those two," Jeremy told Drew proudly. "The ones over there." He jabbed a finger confidently toward the two palm trees on the far side.

There was no way Jeremy could possibly tell the trees apart, Drew thought. He was about to point this out when he saw the warning look on Daisy's face. The observation went unspoken.

"He did a good job, too, didn't he, Uncle Drew?" she prompted as the light began to change to green. She looked at Drew expectantly before stepping on the gas.

Drew half turned in his seat. "Couldn't have picked out better ones myself," he told Jeremy.

Jeremy puffed up his chest even further and then broke into pleased giggles.

Traffic was moderately light, despite the hour and the fact that half the area appeared to be under construction these days. Down with the old, up with the new. It seemed to Daisy as if large sections of Southern California were bent on getting a face-lift.

The construction had threaded its way haphazardly into the area where Jonathan had set up the Addison Corporation's annex branch office. Directly across the street, where

once had stood a seventy-year-old, eight-story office building huddling over a dilapidated stationery store and a candy
store that had long since been boarded up, a new fifteen-
story building was being constructed. It was just in the beginning stages, with silvery steel girders glistening in the sun
like a giant erector set creation in progress.

Daisy pulled the car up to the green section of the curb.
Drew unbuckled his seat belt and opened the passenger
door. "Don't forget where you live," she said as she
watched him get out.

He closed the door shut. "Don't worry, I won't." That
was just the problem. He knew where he lived. He knew, if
he was being honest with himself, where he belonged. And
it wasn't here.

"See you at seven," he told Jeremy.

"Make it five," Daisy advised amiably. Her voice hung
in the air as she pulled away from the curb.

He made it at five.

He hadn't really meant to, it just worked out that way.
Traveling in the air for five hours had made him extraordi-
narily tired.

Or at least that was what he told himself as he got out of
the cab in front of the house. It had nothing whatsoever to
do with the fact that he wanted to see her, nothing to do with
the fact that the importance of work somehow had waned
in comparison to the way he had felt when Jeremy had
thrown his arms around him.

Or when he had kissed Anastasia.

He was just tired, that was all. A man had a right to be
tired and come home, didn't he?

It was funny that he had never had these internal argu-
ments with himself before he had set foot on California soil
for more than a day at a time. Now it seemed to occur on a
regular basis.

He was about to insert his key in the lock when the door opened.

"Right on time." She'd hoped that he wouldn't revert back to his old behavior of staying late at the office, but she hadn't been certain. Seeing him here heartened her immensely.

For a moment Drew could do nothing but just look at her. Instead of her usual jeans and pullover, she was wearing a soft, feminine peach dress, with a flared skirt that showed off her legs to a fault. It made him think of peach sherbet. It was a silly thought, likening a dress to food. But it did remind him of that. He also remembered that he had a particular fondness for peach sherbet and the way it tasted as it melted on his tongue.

"What were you doing, watching for me?" He turned to look at her as she closed the door. The skirt swirled, brushing against her thighs, making him want to do the same.

"No," she answered solemnly, making him feel like an idiot for assuming that she had been. Of course she had better things to occupy herself with than standing at a window, waiting for him to come home.

And then her eyes gave her away. "Jeremy was." Even as she said it, Jeremy was emerging from his post in the living room, joining them. "Make a good scout, too, don't you, Jeremy?"

He lifted his head high as he fairly strutted before his uncle. "The best."

Drew dropped his briefcase by the hall table, where it would undoubtedly remain, he thought, for the rest of the evening. He had no desire to crowd his head with dry details. Not tonight.

"That's right." He placed a hand on the boy's shoulder. "Always be the best."

Jeremy raised his brows and looked to Daisy for confirmation. Daisy winked at him, brushing his bottom and scooting him along to the dining room. "Trying is what counts. Always try your best."

Trying without succeeding had never been enough for Drew. Success was all that counted. The world was filled with runners-up whom no one remembered. "Why does there always seem to be a difference of opinion between us?" Drew wanted to know.

"Because you choose to be stubborn." The statement was said matter-of-factly, with more than a trace of fondness. Daisy linked both her arms through his as she led Drew to the dining room. "But that's okay. You're allowed."

He shook his head as he sat down at the head of the table. He felt like a salmon trying to swim upstream during a monsoon. It wasn't easy, no matter how intent his goal.

"Welcome home, Mr. Drew," Irene said as she set a roast leg of lamb in front of him.

Drew looked to Daisy, but she merely lifted her shoulders innocently. "How did you know?" Roast leg of lamb was his favorite meal.

She spread her linen napkin carefully on her lap, wondering if he would be pleased or annoyed that she had set foot into his private world. "Orlando told me."

"You spoke to my valet?" Why hadn't the man said anything to him when he was home?

"Yes. At the same time I asked for your measurements for the Robin Hood costume."

She was a lot more thorough than he had given her credit for. If she had been a rival competitor, he would have been very leery of her, Drew thought, grateful that she wasn't. He glanced at Jeremy.

Or was she?

Dinner reminded him once more of everything that had been missing from his life as a child. When he was a young boy at home, dinner had been a quiet affair. He couldn't remember ever volunteering a single sentence, or ever hearing Jonathan relate a story. He and his brother spoke only when spoken to. Even his parents hardly ever said a word. The silence at the table each evening had been deafening.

After his mother had divorced his father, there had been boarding school. Dinner there had been a painful experience because he was so introverted. Jonathan had been there to protect him, to act as his shield, but dinner had never been anything pleasant to look forward to. Living on his own, dinner meant the consumption of fuel to keep going, or something that was going on while he was wooing a rival or getting a client to see things his way.

Dinner had never been like this, full of noise and laughter. Boyish laughter. Jeremy talked almost nonstop, filling Drew in on four days' worth of activities, predominantly his, although a few children at his pre-school did appear in the telling from time to time. With a wealth of information coming his way, Drew found he had difficulty keeping track of everything. Especially since Jeremy had a habit of backtracking to throw in yet another detail he had forgotten to mention.

Drew's head was swimming by the time Irene cleared away the dishes.

"Did you follow all of that?" Drew lowered his voice as they walked into the family room. Jeremy had a new electronic game he wanted to show Drew.

She grinned. Dinner had been a pleasurable experience for her, as well. Drew was still a little stiff, but he wasn't the solemn, restrained man he had been. She was confident that things would work themselves out to her satisfaction by the time the end of their bargain arrived.

"Every last word."

She had to be kidding, Drew thought. But, then, with her rapid-fire mouth, maybe she wasn't.

"Hurry, Uncle Drew, I want you to see this," Jeremy urged eagerly.

She gestured Drew into the room ahead of her. "Your public awaits."

Drew knew better than to groan.

Jeremy finally wound down around eight o'clock. Once in bed, he had insisted that Drew read a story to him. It had taken ten minutes to choose the proper book.

"It's called being selective," Daisy said to Drew, noting his bemused expression.

"It's called stalling tactics," he returned in a whisper to match hers. "I used them all the time myself."

She gave him a knowing look as he sat beside Jeremy's bed. "Yes, I know."

Drew said nothing. Instead he began to read. It amazed him that the live wire who had been fairly bouncing all over the family room just a few minutes earlier, fell asleep by the time he reached page three.

"I guess I didn't put enough inflection into it," Drew murmured with a smile as he closed the book.

Daisy took it from him and replaced it on the shelf. "He just ran out of steam." She tucked the cover around the little boy, thinking how much she loved him, how effortlessly he helped to fill the ache she had in her heart because of her sister's death. "It does happen."

Drew walked out with her. "It doesn't happen to you, not so's I've noticed."

She closed the door and turned around. "What have you noticed?"

Everything. Your fragrance, your hair, the way your hips move when you walk, calling to me. "That you smell good." Drew watched the smile curve her lips. "That you've got a wicked mouth—"

She couldn't help the laugh that rose to her lips. "You mean that in the best possible way, of course."

He fit his hands around her waist. He couldn't help himself. He didn't even remember doing it. It was just something that happened automatically. "Of course."

She let out a sigh. It was so good to have him here. "My wicked mouth has missed you."

He skimmed his knuckles along her cheek. "No one to be sarcastic with?"

"I'm never sarcastic. I just react." She brushed a kiss against his lips, savoring the taste she found there. Yearning flooded through her. "Like now," she said softly, her body swaying into his.

He was tempted, so sorely tempted. But it wasn't fair. Not to him, not to her. To let this go on really wasn't right. "Maybe we shouldn't."

She saw the war that raged within his eyes. The war between needs and doubts. She knew which side she wanted to win. "For an intelligent man, you certainly have some dumb ideas."

No, he wasn't going to allow himself to get carried away. She had to hear him out. He anchored her in place with his hands. "Daisy, as much as I want you—"

She tilted her head. He was much too serious. She was always in trouble when he became serious. "Go on, this sounds promising," she teased, hoping to nudge him out of his mood.

She'd found the right word to use. "That's exactly it, I can't promise."

Her eyes held his. Didn't he know anything about her yet? "Have I asked you to? Have I asked you to promise me anything?"

No, she hadn't asked. But it wasn't fair to take from a woman this way and not give her something in return. And he couldn't, no matter how much he wanted to. He couldn't give her what she needed, what she deserved. It wasn't in him to give.

He took her hands in his, holding them still. If she touched him, if she placed her hands on his chest, he couldn't think straight. She had a way of destroying his thoughts, except those that centered on her.

"Don't you understand? I don't know how to be intimate with you. I can kiss you, touch you, make love with you. But I can't be intimate. It's all locked up inside."

What had happened to him to tie him in knots this way? Was it the way they had been raised? Of course it had, she thought. From what Jonathan had told Alyce, there been no warm, nurturing love for the two boys as they had been growing up. Not even the smallest drop.

She feathered her hand along his cheek and cupped it. "Then let me set it free," she whispered.

Something broke down within him. Resistance crumbled. Drew dragged her mouth to his, thrown off balance by how much he needed to feel her mouth against his, to hold her body against his own.

Her kiss was warm, giving, loving. There was no thought to herself, only of him. He wanted to drop to his knees and beg her to love him.

He wanted to take her here and now, without a thought to tomorrow. Now was all that mattered.

He did neither. He absorbed what she had to give and demanded more, his mouth plundering hers. His blood roared in his ears as he pressed her closer, ever closer to him. He kissed her as if his very life depended on it, for at this one moment in time, it did.

She never ceased to surprise him. Even thinking he knew what he was in for, he was woefully unprepared. Each time it was the same. Astounding. Each time, it was different. Stronger, better.

He had to catch his breath, or go completely under. With his heart racing, he leaned his forehead against hers. "You have a hell of a way of conducting an argument."

She felt herself glowing as anticipation licked at the edges of her nerves. "I never argue."

He laughed, enjoying the way the sensation rippled through him, like sunshine. "Ha!"

"I cajole." Straightening, she opened the first button on his shirt. "I coax." Another button came free. "I reason."

He covered her hands with his own, but didn't remove them. "You haven't even got a nodding acquaintance with reason."

"Sure I do." She smiled into his eyes. "You're the soul of reason. And I'm acquainted with your soul."

Still cupping her hand, he turned it over. "It's right there in the palm of your hand."

She knew better. And so did he. "No, it's not. You still have it safely tucked away. And I wouldn't reduce your soul to such paltry portions."

She undid the last button. Splaying her hand over his chest, she thrilled to the heartbeat she felt beneath her fingers. His heart was beating fast. For her. "Now, are you going to make love with me, or do I have to hit you over head and drag you to my room, caveman style?"

He wondered if she would. She was a free enough spirit to indulge that fantasy.

"No dragging necessary." Allowing himself one small, swift kiss, almost chaste by comparison to what had come before, Drew lifted Daisy into his arms and carried her to her room.

She closed her eyes, savoring the sensation of being swept away. Her dress softly floated onto the gray-blue cover on her bed as he set her down.

The pace was slow this time, slow and lyrical. They both knew what was there, waiting for them. They took their time, deriving pleasure from the journey. Drew undressed her a layer at a time, his fingers exploring secrets he had just begun to discover the first time. She felt so delicate, almost fluid beneath his touch, yet he knew she was strong in the most subtlest of ways. She was just possibly the strongest willed person he had ever known, this woman who sighed beneath the lightest caress.

A series of flirtatious tiny buttons hid her from him. There must have been at least twenty of them running down the front of her dress. "How long did it take you to get into this?" he marveled.

"Longer, I hope, than it'll take to get me out."

He watched her eyes, thrilling in the way they clouded and darkened as he made his way patiently down to her waist, undoing the tiny pearl buttons one by one. The material finally parted, a silken peach curtain hanging on either side. She wasn't wearing a bra or camisole underneath.

His breath caught in his throat as he pressed a kiss to her breasts, first one, then the other. He'd been right. Peach sherbet was still a favorite with him.

"You're a mystery," he murmured, peeling another layer of clothing away. "A beautiful, tantalizing mystery."

He was learning, she thought, pleased. "Haven't you heard?" She arched to his touch as he slipped the dress from her shoulders. "Women like to be mysterious."

Slowly, ever so slowly, he removed the dress from her hips, down the long length of her legs, until he finally tossed it aside. She lay before him dressed in nothing more than panties and a smile. "I haven't noticed anything. Nothing but the sound of your voice, ever since I arrived in L.A."

She laughed, a soft, sexy, throaty laugh that hit him like a velvet-gloved punch straight to his abdomen.

The panties vanished, as did the remainder of his own clothing, forgotten obstacles as soon as they fell to the floor.

Drew caressed, reveled, dreamed, all the while heating her body as quickly as he did his own.

The kisses were deep and they both sank into them, into the darkness that was there just before the light.

It felt, she thought, arching into each gentle, sweeping stroke, as if he were memorizing every movement, preserving it for some future day when they would no longer be able to be this way together. A day when there was a continent between them.

She couldn't think of that, couldn't believe that it would happen. He was here with her now, and that was all she needed, all she wanted.

No, it was a lie. She wanted more. She wanted that soul he had flippantly said she had in the palm of her hand. She wanted it to open to her, to have him share more than his body with her. She wanted him to trust her enough to share his innermost feelings.

She was losing all orientation. The last time, when the lovemaking between them had been frenzied, she had hung on for the ride, exhilarating in the pace. Now that tempo was more indolent, more soothing, she fell in love with him all over again. There was gentleness here in his touch, compassion, thoughtfulness, all the things she *knew* he didn't know he possessed. She longed to make him understand. There was power in his graciousness.

She longed to stay lost with him forever.

The exquisite agony of wanting the rush to come, even while wanting to prolong the journey to that rush was once more warring within her. Within them both.

The urgency to pleasure one another increased.

She felt everything.

She felt only him, every caress, every shift of his fingers, every layer of his kiss.

Intrigued, empowered, he traced each one of her pulse points, sampling, watching as they throbbed. When he pressed a kiss to the soft skin inside of her elbow, he heard her moan and felt her shift insistently beneath him.

It brought a smile to his face. "I don't think there's any place where I can touch you that you won't react."

She laced her fingers behind his neck. "There isn't." Humor touched her eyes, rimming the passion. "Am I a science experiment now?"

There was no way to pigeonhole her. He'd learned that. "No, but you really are something."

She laughed, pleased at the simple compliment. "Very eloquent."

He trailed his fingers along the soft skin around her belly, watching in fascination as it quivered. "You chase the words right out of my head, Anastasia. You chase everything out of my head. All there is, is you, in broad, vivid colors."

"Why does that make you sound so sad?"

"Because it makes me realize what I've missed all my life. The colors. They were here all the time and I never saw them."

She offered herself to him. "Then stop missing them."

She made it sound so easy, so uncomplicated. She had an uncanny knack for reducing things to the smallest denominator. But it wasn't that simple. Not for him.

I'd probably scare you to death if I told you I loved you, she thought, aching to utter the words on her lips. To taste them and see how they felt before she pressed her mouth to his.

But she would wait and give him more time to discover what she already knew to be true. That he loved her. He just didn't know how to break down the barriers to reach her. They were barriers of his own making and he would have to be the one to dismantle them.

It was like making love to the wind. He could feel her against every part of his body, feel her essence vibrating within him, infiltrating, filling him. Holding him prisoner in its grasp.

The slow, steady pace evaporated as needs rose to a dangerous boiling point. His kisses became greedy, his caresses more possessive and she was there for him at every turn, wanting to be every woman he had ever loved, ever wanted. Wanting to be all things to him so that he would never turn away from her.

For if he did, she knew she would be lost. As lost as he had been when he had first arrived at her doorstep.

When they joined their hands, their mouths, their bodies, it was as if by some unspoken mutual agreement. And then they were speeding ahead, eagerly rushing to familiar territory, to the place where only they could enter. And only together.

She could hardly keep up. Opening to receive him, she felt his thrust as he filled her. She wanted him closer, closer; he couldn't be close enough. She would never get enough of him. Quickly, the explosions came, seizing them both and propelling them upward as if they were merely leaves caught up in a devil wind that blew in from the desert.

And when it was over, they could only hold on to each other, clinging to the sensations until they faded into mists.

"You know," she said in slow, measured words because she couldn't manage anything more, "for a man suffering from jet lag, you had an incredible amount of energy."

He felt the words rippling against his chest, felt the comfort of her warmth as her head rested there. Her cheek was just over his heart. A tranquilizing echo was passing between them. He allowed himself a moment to sift her hair through his fingers, glorying in the way it felt.

"You bring some unknown force out of me," Drew murmured has he watched her hair rain from his hand. The light from the lamp shone in it, trapped there, making it shimmer as if it were alive.

Daisy raised her head, keeping her hand on his chest. She liked feeling the beat of his heart, liked pretending it was doing it just for her. "Is the force up to another appearance?"

He lifted a brow. After what they'd been through, she could ask? "Tonight?"

She traced swirls along his chest, wiggling closer. "Tonight."

He grinned and let a sigh escape. "If you say so, but this time, *you* do the work."

She slipped easily on top of him and he could feel his fatigue melting away as if it had never been.

"Gladly."

But he didn't let her make the first move. His pride wouldn't let him.

Chapter Twelve

It had been busy from the moment they had opened their doors. Everyone, it appeared, wanted to have their landscaping completed before the holidays arrived. It wasn't until five o'clock that the hectic activity slowed. By six, Daisy had thanked her last customer, walked with him to the door and then quickly flipped the Open sign to Closed on the window.

"Ah, peace, ain't it grand?" Margaret murmured with a contented sigh. "Coffee's on me."

She went into the back office to pour them each a mug, leaving Daisy to transcribe the pile of order forms on the table into her order book. Later she would input them all into the computer to retain them on permanent file. But she didn't have time to wrestle with the temperamental machine now. Drew was coming.

At least she hoped so.

"Here." Margaret passed a blue mug with the words Boss Lady inscribed in fire-engine red across it to Daisy. "Milk, no sugar, just like you like it."

Margaret eased herself into a chair where clients normally sat, poring through albums filled with photographs of gardens Showers of Flowers ... had landscaped.

Daisy smiled her thanks and continued making notes in the book. Margaret took a sip, let the coffee wind its way through her, then looked thoughtfully at her friend. It was apparent to Daisy that she had been dying to discuss Daisy's relationship with Drew all week, but the opportunity had never presented itself.

"So how is it going with you and the Prince of Wall Street? You've hardly mentioned him at all since he got back from his business trip." Margaret leaned forward over the circular black marble table and peered at Daisy's face. "Is that a glow I detect?"

Daisy went on writing. "Could be the new rosebushes we got in this morning for the Monroes," she answered casually. "I think I'm allergic to them."

Margaret placed a hand on Daisy's hand, forcing her to stop writing and look up. "Hey, this is me. Margaret. You've talked to me about every man you've gone out with in the last seven years. The doctor, the airline pilot, the dance instructor, the—" Margaret stopped ticking off the different men on her fingers as the reason for Daisy's reticence suddenly seemed clear. She narrowed her eyes. "This one serious?"

Daisy gave up transcribing figures. She laid her pen down and picked up the coffee Margaret had brought her. It felt good going down. Margaret was getting better. "Andrew Addison, the First, is *very* serious."

As a rule, Daisy was never evasive. Margaret frowned. "You know what I mean."

Daisy held the mug with both hands, wishing the warmth would reach her soul. "He's not."

"But you are?"

Daisy nodded. "Very." She looked at Margaret. All her feelings were there in her eyes. "Margaret, I think he's the one."

For a second, all Margaret could do was gape. Daisy had always been so carefree, so blasé about her relationships before. It was almost impossible to believe that Daisy had actually fallen in love with anyone. It was usually the other way around.

"You're kidding. That's terrific!" Margaret gave Daisy a fierce hug. "Wow, this is more startling than when you finally decided what you wanted to be when you grew up—last year." The humor slowly left her face to be replaced with wistfulness as Margaret released Daisy. Margaret, Daisy knew, had been infatuated, but never in love, not really. "Tell me, I'm curious. How do you know you love him?"

That ranked right up there along with wanting to know the secret of life, Daisy thought. She didn't want to dissect why she loved him, though there were a hundred tiny pieces that went into it. The way he was with Jeremy. The way he held her. "How does anyone know? It's just there, that's all."

It was apparent by her expression that this wasn't what Margaret was hoping to hear. "Sounds like you're describing laundry detergent." She finished her coffee and set the mug down.

"Maybe." Daisy laughed. "During the spin cycle." That was what it was like, emotions all jumbled up, tumbling madly in a circle.

It was all the hint that Margaret needed. "You've been to bed with him."

To bed. That sounded much too mundane to express what had happened between them. Since he had returned, they had made love almost every night. "I've been to paradise and back."

Margaret had slid to the edge of her seat, her coffee forgotten. "So when are you getting married?"

They had made love, but she was still no closer to peering into his soul, to making him really open up to her, than she had been at the start.

"Married?" The word was followed by a short laugh outlined in sadness. "I don't even know if we're going to come to an amicable solution at the end of all this." *But I'm hoping for it.* She looked at the calendar on her desk. The days were flying by too fast. "I've got until New Year's Day to make the man see that Jeremy is better off with me—and so is he."

Margaret gave her hand a squeeze. "My money's on you, kid." She reached for her purse.

"Thanks." Daisy flashed her a smile. With a sigh, she closed her order book. "I need more than money, I need a miracle."

Margaret was rooting through her handbag, looking for her lipstick. "With me, it's a miracle if I have any money."

Daisy was more than happy to move on to another subject. The dilemma of Drew was causing her too many sleepless hours as it was. "Is that a hint for a raise?"

Margaret paused, an intrigued expression on her face. "Would it do me any good to ask?"

They both knew Margaret was kidding. Daisy paid her a generous salary. It was a known fact of life that had Margaret been earning twice the amount, she still wouldn't be able to hold on to a dime. She was too easily tempted. Margaret lived to shop.

"Asking's the easy part, Margaret." Absently Daisy glanced toward the window that looked out on the rear of nursery. "It's the getting that's hard."

Margaret applied the splash of color to her lips quickly. "We've stopped talking about my raise, haven't we?"

"Yes."

The bell over the front door jingled softly and Margaret frowned. "Can't people read?" And then she smiled. "Uh-oh, speak of the devil—or whatever."

Drew walked into the store and strode over to the table. He looked, Margaret observed, none too happy about being there.

"Well," he said to Daisy, "I'm here."

In contrast to his dour expression, Daisy grinned, relieved. "Yes, you are. I'll just go get my purse." She rose, taking the order book with her to deposit in the back office. "Close up for me, will you, Margaret?"

Drew shoved his hands into his pants' pockets and continued to look uncomfortable and restless.

"Going dancing?" Margaret finally asked when he said nothing.

He had no idea why he had listened to Daisy's behest. He had work to do. They were closed tomorrow. The entire building was closed tomorrow because of the holiday. He should be at the office now, tying up a few of the loose ends. Addison Corporation experienced its busiest season between now and the New Year. He didn't have time for foolishness.

And yet, he was here.

"Going to the grocery store," he answered.

Margaret looked at him a little oddly. "Is that what people do on dates in New York?"

He scowled, annoyed with the whole thing. Anastasia kept making the most inane demands on him. But he'd be lying if he didn't admit that a part, a very small part, he told himself, liked these traces of domesticity.

"I'm not taking her on a date. For some reason she's insisting that we shop for the damn Thanksgiving turkey together." He stared off toward the back office and wondered what was taking Anastasia so long. "Says it might be too heavy for her to carry." He snorted at the feeble lie. "I've seen her tote those fifteen-gallon things around."

He was cute, Margaret thought, even when there was steam coming out of his ears. She bet Daisy had her hands filled with this one. But if she knew Daisy, and she did, Daisy was more than equal to the challenge. "Maybe she just likes the company."

Drew took a look at Margaret for the first time. She didn't talk like any employee he had working for him. There was too much warmth in her voice when she spoke of Daisy. "Are all her employees this outspoken?"

"All her *friends*," she corrected him, "care about Daisy. She's a good person." The phrase "and you be good to her" went unsaid, but was clearly implied. Margaret continued studying Drew as she elaborated. "We were all a little worried that she wasn't going to find her niche in life. What with the lawyer thing not suiting her and that fling she had as a flight attendant, not to mention—"

Drew sat down in the chair Daisy had vacated. "You mean it's true?"

"Which 'it' are you referring to?"

It didn't seem possible. Everyone he knew had had a goal in mind while attending school, and then had gone out and reached it. Or at least tried to.

"All those things she claimed she did." He was at a loss as how to word it. "She really did them?"

Margaret had to bite her lip not to laugh at the confusion on his face. If Daisy didn't know why she was in love with

Drew, Margaret could have easily made out a list for her. Starting with incredible eyes and fantastic lips. "Yes."

There had to be an explanation. "Oh, I suppose she told you she did all those things."

"Yes."

Ah-ha, Drew thought. And then Margaret continued and ruined it.

"But I was in college with her, at least one of the colleges she attended." She saw the skeptical look rise in Drew's eyes. "The one she graduated from. And I was there for the celebration when she passed her bar exam." A faraway smile creased her lips. She could go on and on, but didn't. He didn't look like the type of man you could do that with. She smiled knowingly. Daisy was unusual. "You didn't believe her, did you?"

"No," he said simply.

No, he hadn't. But Anastasia was obviously a lot more complex than she pretended to be if all this was true. Why did she seem so flighty? And being intelligent, knowing what life was like, how could she be so everlastingly cheerful?

Margaret pushed her chair way from the table. Reluctantly, she stood up, taking the empty coffee mugs with her. "Daisy graduated first in her class from U.C.L.A." There was a hint of vicarious pride in her voice. "She gave the valedictorian speech."

That he found impossible to believe. "The woman who just went to get her purse?"

"The very same. Daisy's always had so much going for her, she's never known which direction to take. I always thought she could be anything she wanted to be." She laughed fondly. "So did Daisy. That's why she dabbled so much, trying out things until she made up her mind." Her eyes narrowed. "Nothing wrong in that, is there?"

Was he mistaken, or had her voice taken on a judgmental tone? Was he on trial here for some reason? "Are you her press agent, too?"

"Like I said," Margaret answered amicably, "Daisy's friends care about her."

He leaned over the counter as Margaret began to walk into the back room. "I appreciate the information, but what does this have to do with me?"

Dense. Handsome, but dense. Daisy did have her work cut out for her. "That's for you to figure out."

Daisy passed Margaret as she walked into the display area. "Has Margaret been talking off your ear?"

He was relieved to escape Margaret's close scrutiny. "Yes, but the woman doesn't hold a candle to you." He took her arm. "Ready?"

"Absolutely." She looked over her shoulder. "See you Monday morning, Margaret. Happy Thanksgiving."

Margaret leaned out of the back office, taking one last long look. They did make a very nice couple, she decided. "Have a nice Thanksgiving! And don't do anything I wouldn't do," she called after them as the glass door swung closed behind them.

Daisy smiled as they walked to the car. "That leaves us a very broad spectrum to choose from."

Drew had parked his car at the curb in the twenty-minute parking zone. She got in on the passenger side and buckled up.

Drew took the wheel. "I still don't see why you just don't go shopping by yourself." Why did he have to come along and suffer through this?

By now, his tone didn't faze her. Patience was needed. It probably always would be to a degree, but she didn't mind that, either. "Well, for one thing, I don't have a car, remember? It's in the shop."

Margaret had swung by the house early this morning to pick her up. Jeremy hadn't gone to pre-school. He hadn't been feeling well and had remained home with the housekeeper.

"For another, I thought this might be a good experience for you." She studied his profile. His was a bit more chiseled than Jonathan's had been, a little harder around the edges, the jaw set a little firmer, a little more stubbornly. She had already accepted the fact that she was facing a tougher challenge than her sister had. "Ever been grocery shopping?"

There had always been someone else to take care of that for him. In New York, Orlando did all the necessary shopping. Drew couldn't remember ever being inside a supermarket. "No, and I really haven't missed it."

Daisy leaned back, a smile playing on her lips. This should be interesting. "Never know until you try."

They had been going up and down the crowded aisles now for twenty minutes, Drew thought, while Anastasia debated the merits of one mushroom over another in the vegetable section, and agonized over which brand of cranberry sauce to use. Finally she pointed him toward the center of the store. Parallel rows of large, open freezers stood side by side in the center aisle. Cold air hovered mistily over a colorful montage of ice cream containers, frozen vegetables and meal entrées.

"So..." Drew looked at Daisy. "This is the frozen section." He folded his arms across his chest and rocked back on his heels. "Quite an eye-opening experience."

She led him to the meat department. "Sarcasm belongs at the check-out stands, not in the aisles."

The cart was already filled with all the items they would need for tomorrow's meal, except for the main one. It had taken some effort, but she had cajoled him into pushing the cart. With Thanksgiving one day away, Daisy was pleased to find that there were still plenty of turkeys to choose from.

She gestured him toward the rectangular freezer. "And now, sir, since it seems fitting, I'll let you choose the turkey."

He lifted a brow, eyeing her. "Is that some kind of a crack?"

"Only if you have a guilty conscience," she said sweetly. "Otherwise, it just refers to your being the head of the family." Both brows went up. "Don't turn pale on me, it's just a term to fit the oldest member of the family and since you're older than I am, you get the title."

His mind was on things other than turkeys. "How old are you?" He suddenly realized that he didn't know. It had never occurred to him to ask.

She pretended to look surprised. "Ah, a personal question."

When would he ever learn? He shook his head. "Never mind."

No, he wasn't going to shut the door, not when she'd waited so long to have him open one. She liked the fact that he wanted to know things about her, however indirectly the question had come up.

"I don't mind telling you how old I am. I'm twenty-nine." There was a woman behind him who was obviously trying to choose a turkey and Daisy and Drew were in her way. Daisy moved aside. "And you're thirty-two, so that makes you older."

He hadn't told her anything about himself, not even that. Privacy was something he guarded zealously. The less she knew, the less, he figured, she could use against him. And in this particular case, he had enough going against him, including his own willpower. "How do you know how old I am? Orlando?"

"Orlando had nothing to do with it. Jonathan mentioned it in passing once. As a matter of fact, he mentioned a lot of things." She grinned. "I probably know a great deal more about you than you'd want me to."

That's what he was afraid of. "Such as?"

She thought for a moment. "Such as you were afraid of the dark." She saw that he didn't like being reminded. But after all, he'd only been a child at the time. It was forgivable for children to be afraid of the dark. "Kids used to make fun of you and you cried—"

"I never cried," he said indignantly.

"I'd be very unhappy if I believed that," she told him quietly. "Besides," she continued, "there's nothing wrong with crying. It just means you're human." She smiled. "And I know for a fact that you're very, very human."

He murmured something unintelligible under his breath in reply.

There were things that would melt in a short amount of time in the cart. She nodded toward the freezer, pointing out one bird. "How's this one?"

He looked closer. The turkey was marked at twenty pounds and three ounces. "Isn't it rather large? Who else is coming?"

"No one, this time." She looked at a few turkeys, but decided her first choice was best. "Thanksgiving is for families."

"What do you mean, this time?" Drew asked suspiciously.

Was she planning a "next" time with a horde of people joining them? He didn't know anyone here. Besides, there wasn't going to be a "next time." He had made up his mind about that long ago. It was sticking to the decision that was becoming increasingly difficult.

Why was everything like pulling teeth with him? She was determined to thaw him out completely if it killed her. "I thought for Christmas Eve we'd invite some of Alyce's and Jonathan's friends and let you meet them."

Another shopper nudged them aside as she reached in for a turkey. Daisy kept a proprietary hand on the one she had selected. The cold hurt her fingertips, but she kept them there until the woman had made her selection and left.

"Why?" He wanted to know.

"Because you're supposed to be friendly around Christmas. It's the law. Besides, I thought you might want to meet some of the people who thought your brother was a terrific person." She frowned. "God, Drew, someone should have given you an instruction manual the day you were born. This should be inherent."

"What they should have done was given me one on you," he shot back.

Her mood dissipated and she laughed. "Then all the mystery'd be gone."

"And the confusion," he pointed out.

Daisy shrugged and turned to take out the turkey she had chosen. He knew perfectly well that she was more than capable of doing it, yet he still felt as if he should be the one taking it out. It looked unwieldy.

"Here," he said, nudging her aside, "I'll do that. You'll strain yourself."

She raised her hands, palms up, an amused smile on her lips. "That's why I brought you along."

No, she had brought him along to make him even more crazy than she already had. He dropped the turkey into the cart, squashing the bread beneath it. "Let's pay for this and get out of here."

She tugged the loaf out and frowned at it. "You're the boss."

He gave her a dark look, knowing she was laughing at him. "I guess we'd better get another loaf of bread."

"Good idea."

Yes, she was definitely laughing at him. He couldn't help thinking that it should have gotten him more annoyed than it did.

When they arrived home half an hour later, Irene met them at the door to help with the bags. "Jeremy's cold's gotten worse." She retrieved one sack out of the truck. "I've put him to bed."

"Thank you, Irene." Daisy picked up two of the bags.

Daisy looked remarkably unconcerned by the news, Drew thought. He hefted three bags, including the one with the turkey, out of the trunk and followed her into the house. "Shouldn't we call a doctor or something?"

"Not unless his cold gets really bad." She placed her bags on the kitchen table. "There're some children's cold remedies on hand in the medicine cabinet and there's still some cough medicine and decongestant left from the last time the doctor prescribed them." Irene was unpacking the groceries and putting them away, something Daisy always hated doing. "Let's go see the little patient."

The door to Jeremy's room was open. He looked absolutely miserable when they walked in. "I'm sick, Aunt Daisy."

She sat down on the bed next to him and stroked his hair. "Yes, I know, sweetheart."

"Does that mean I can't have the turkey tomorrow?"

"No, that means Uncle Drew'll carry you downstairs *to* the turkey. But think on the bright side. Maybe you'll be better by tomorrow."

He would have been disappointed, Drew thought, if she hadn't said that. It was nice to be able to predict some things about her, even small things.

Daisy kissed Jeremy's forehead. It was warm. "I'm afraid you've got a temperature, Jeremy."

Drew had always thought that was a ridiculous method to use. "Shouldn't you be using something more accurate than your lips?"

She turned to look at him. "I think they're pretty good at gauging things." Before Drew could say anything to dispute that, she looked at Jeremy. "It's my best tool, right, honey? Kisses away hurts, makes things better, takes temperatures."

Any second now, he was going to be nauseated. "Do you have time to bend steel with your bare hands during all this?" Drew asked.

She wasn't going to get drawn into an argument. He was still annoyed about being dragged to the supermarket. "If the occasion calls for it." She stood up. "Now, why don't you stay here with Jeremy while I see if I can find that medicine?"

"Will you play games with me?" Jeremy asked Drew hopefully.

It occurred to Daisy that Jeremy's voice sounded just a tad more pathetic. A born manipulator, she thought.

"Games?" she heard Drew echo uncomfortably as she left the room.

Daisy grinned to herself. Let him see that raising a child was no bed of roses, that it didn't go by the book, because what he was dealing with was a mass of exceptions with soft brown hair and big brown eyes. She'd be damned if he was going to send Jeremy to boarding school, and Drew couldn't raise Jeremy alone. He needed someone to help him. Preferably, someone who loved him.

When Drew came downstairs the next morning, he felt exhausted. It was his own fault, he thought. He had been the one to volunteer to stay up with Jeremy in case he needed something. The boy woke up every few hours, either completely stuffed up, unable to breathe, or coughing. Drew had swallowed his pride and woken Daisy up when he'd tried to put the vaporizer on and got nothing but sputtering hot water for his trouble. But the rest of the time he was determined to handle everything himself.

Consequently, it was eight in the morning, Jeremy was sleeping peacefully and Drew felt as if he had spent the night in a foxhole fending off enemy fire.

With a robe hanging open over his dark blue silk pajamas, Drew found his way into the kitchen. It wasn't easy when his eyes weren't focusing properly.

Daisy looked up from the turkey she was stuffing. She'd been up for more than two hours. There was a cherry pie baking in the oven to testify to that fact. Her heart softened as she watched Drew stumble in. "You look like hell."

Drew sank onto the closest stool at the breakfast counter. He propped his head up, afraid it would fall off if he didn't. "Last thing I need is a cheerful critic." He looked around halfheartedly. "Where's Irene?"

Satisfied that the turkey held all it should, she began to close up the bird. "I sent her home for Thanksgiving. She's staying at her sister's."

"Who's making dinner?"

She thought that fact was rather obvious. She gestured toward her handiwork. "I am."

"You cook?"

She looked at him incredulously before placing the turkey into the oven and setting the dials. "You have to ask?"

"Sorry, stupid question. I forgot I was talking to Superwoman."

He could be as sarcastic as he wanted to be. She was rather proud of her accomplishments, even if most of them had ultimately led her to a dead end. Knowledge was never wasted. "I spent six months at the Cordon Bleu." She had thought she wanted to be a chef at a fancy restaurant and eventually open up her own. But, as with other things, she had lost interest.

Drew's eyes were closing. "Naturally."

She began to clear off the counter, preparing for the next phase. "I got an A in everything, except for dessert."

Drew's eyes opened. Finally, something she didn't do well. "Everyone has to fail sometime."

She raised her eyes to his. "I got an A plus in that."

He blew out a breath, then got off the stool. "Why do I even bother?" he muttered. He crossed to the silent coffee-maker on the counter. It was empty. "How does this thing make coffee?"

She'd been so busy, she hadn't had time to set it. "Not at all if you don't put in the ingredients." Drying her hands, she left her work.

"Wise guy." He opened the cabinet overhead, not too sure what it was he was looking for, besides a can of coffee. Didn't these things take filters or something? "I need help here."

"Glad to hear you admit it." She turned him around and pushed him in the direction of the stool he had just vacated. "Sit down and I'll make the coffee." She took out the filters that were next to the can of coffee. "Jeremy still sleeping?"

She knew he was—she had looked in on the boy only fifteen minutes ago. Daisy had hated leaving Drew to take care of the boy on his own, but she felt that this was an excellent opportunity for him to see the worst side of parenting. She had stayed with Alyce and Jonathan so often, she felt like Jeremy's surrogate mother. But Drew had to be indoctrinated as to the difficulties involved with being a real parent. She wanted him to see what he was getting into. And that surviving it alone was even harder.

"Yes, which is more than I can say for me. God, I'm tired."

"Poor baby," she murmured. But she was grinning.

Within moments, the coffeemaker was making noises and dark liquid was trickling into the glass pot. "Want something to go with the coffee?"

"Yes." That had just slipped out. He hadn't even realized it was there, on his tongue, until he said it. He saw by the look on her face that she knew exactly what he was talking about. "Never mind, I probably don't have enough energy for that."

She slipped onto the stool next to him and smiled. He looked adorable with stubble on his face and dark smudges under his eyes. "You'd be surprised."

He didn't want to get himself started. It wasn't the lack of stamina. That would come. But he needed to exercise a little more self-control, starting now. They both knew this wasn't going to work out. "Don't you have to cook or something?"

She felt the hurt vibrating within her and told herself she was being too sensitive. But it still didn't go away.

"It was your idea." She got off the stool. The coffee was ready. She poured him a cup, then placed it on the counter in front of him.

He shrugged, trying to be nonchalant. "I've been known to have bad ideas occasionally."

She set her lips firmly. For the first time in weeks, she felt like hitting him. "I can think of one."

He knew what she was referring to, but he didn't want to talk about it. The time wasn't up yet. Later they would hash it out, but not now. Now all he wanted was a little peace and quiet.

She had resumed preparing dinner. He pointed to the bowl of potatoes she had peeled. They were bobbing in water. Why, he had no idea. "Need help with that?"

"That?" She looked at the bowl. "I'm going to make mashed potatoes later. Just what is it you would like to do?"

He shrugged. "Whatever you need me to do."

"Do you cook?"

He didn't answer her question. "I don't have a certificate from the Cordon Bleu, but any fool can mash potatoes."

She drained the potatoes and placed the bowl in front of him. The bottom made firm contact with the counter. "Fine, I guess that means you meet the job requirement. Here."

He stared at the potatoes for a moment. She hadn't given him a utensil. What was he supposed to use? "Um, Anastasia?"

She was busy washing lettuce. "Yes?"

"Do I just crush them?"

She laughed and the tension left her. With a twist of her wrist, she shut off the faucet. "Here, let me show you."

Chapter Thirteen

It seemed to Drew that the farther he attempted to retreat from Anastasia and his own confused, budding emotions, the farther she followed him into his world. There was no escaping her, or himself.

Thanksgiving turned out to be, as she had assured him, a family affair. And for perhaps the first time in his life, Drew felt as if he was part of a family. Until he had sat there, joining hands over the meal that included his contribution—incredibly liquidy mashed potatoes—saying grace, he had never felt as if he had really belonged to a unit. Up to that moment, Jonathan had been the only person he had ever felt close to. For the past ten years, the corporation had been his mother, father, wife, everything. If that seemed a little cold and bloodless at times, there were still deeply satisfying feelings to be garnered from watching the firm thrive and expand through his guidance at the helm.

Or at least there had been. Now he found himself not quite so content, not quite so satisfied. And it was all her fault.

He hit a key on his keyboard and the screen on his computer momentarily blinked, then jumped to a new spreadsheet. It would be over soon, he thought. There was a calendar on his desk, marking time. A little more than one more month and he would be back in New York with Jeremy. Permanently. And she would remain here. Drew couldn't ask her to give up her business. He knew what that meant. She belonged out here. And he belonged on the east coast, with Addison Corporation. He sighed, hitting another key. The future didn't look very good, at least for him.

He knew he had to accept that, accept the inevitable. He always had before. It was time to act like a responsible adult, not like some adolescent, cutting classes.

Yet the more he hid from her, the more he buried himself in paperwork, the more he wanted to be with her. The situation was driving him crazy. He couldn't wait until this madness was over.

He wondered if there was a way to make time stop.

Insane, he was going absolutely insane, he thought.

There was a knock on his door and he looked up, welcoming the diversion. Anything to stop thinking about Daisy…er, Anastasia. It seemed he was having a change of heart toward her. He straightened in his chair, turning it so that he could face the door. "Come in."

She did. Like the warm Santa Ana winds that blew in from the desert, she swept into his office, enveloping everything around her. She pushed the door closed behind her without bothering to look. "Hi."

He supposed that it had been just a matter of time before her invasion campaign brought her here. Still, he had to ask. "What are you doing here?"

Daisy came around his desk and stood next to him. She leaned a hip against the teakwood edge and her thigh brushed against his arm. The straight red skirt she was wearing was a good four inches above her knees, showing off legs that made his feel weak. She had topped off her outfit with a bulky black sweater that only hinted at what was beneath. But he knew. And desired.

"We are going Christmas shopping," she informed him blithely, as if they had spent the previous evening discussing the matter instead of her swooping out of the blue with this preposterous notion.

Drew sighed, pushed himself away from his desk and reached into his jacket breast pocket. Taking out his wallet, he flipped through until he came to a gleaming gold card. He removed it and held it up to her. "Here."

She looked at the plastic plate as if it was an eviction notice. With a shake of her head, Daisy pushed his hand away. "I don't want your charge card, Drew. I want you."

His brow furrowed. "Excuse me?"

"To go shopping with me," she clarified, knowing exactly what he was thinking. A look of mischievous pleasure filled her eyes. "Your other interpretation we can take up later."

Drew dealt with straight-talking people all day, or had, until he had come out to Los Angeles. But he certainly wasn't used to a woman being so direct about a matter he felt belonged behind closed doors. And with a tight rein around it, he reminded himself.

He tucked the card back into its slot and replaced his wallet. Every time he thought he knew her, he discovered something to blow apart his theory.

Daisy was determined to get him to go with her. She had left Margaret in charge of the shop and had reserved the rest of the day for shopping. "I have no idea how you shop in New York, but I require a personal appearance. Now let's go," she urged, straightening away from the desk. "The stores are jam-packed as it is."

He looked at his desk. Though orderly, it was piled high with work that needed to be taken care of. The computer was blinking, waiting for more input and there were reports that needed his signature. He couldn't possibly get away. "I'm too busy to go shopping."

She gave an encouraging tug on his arm. "That's the whole idea," she insisted. "Christmas shopping wouldn't be half as much fun if it wasn't hectic."

That made absolutely no sense. "Did anyone ever drop you on your head as a child?"

She laughed as she raised her chin. "No."

He placed a hand on top of hers to remove it from his arm, but the contact was pleasant and warmed him. He never seemed to be properly prepared for her. Drew left his hand where it was for a moment.

"They should have," he said. "Maybe it would have knocked some sense into it. But then, you probably would have thought happy thoughts and flown away."

Her eyes crinkled as she laughed again, delighted with the description and the fact that he had created it. "You're getting into the spirit of the season."

"I'm getting certifiably crazy is what I'm getting," he countered, but he was weakening. It should have surprised him, but it didn't.

"Whatever." Daisy tugged on his arm again, more insistently this time. "Now come on. You don't have any important meetings coming up today and nothing is due. This is the perfect day for you to take off and go shopping with me."

He stared at her. "How do you know that? How do you know I don't have anything due?" She'd said it with too much confidence for it to have been just a lucky guess on her part.

"I checked with your secretary." She winked and he felt himself responding. "I'm impulsive, but I'm not reckless."

"That is a matter of opinion."

He wondered what she would do if he dug in and absolutely refused to budge. But he was already leaning toward going with her. Why, he hadn't the slightest idea. He had always thought of the Christmas crowds as comprised of people who should have their heads examined for getting sucked into the retailers' paradise. On the other hand, as the president of a thriving corporation that supplied a good many things being purchased for the holidays, he had to condone it. It wasn't, however, a dilemma he normally found himself actively in the middle of.

He wasn't going to talk his way out of this. "You can leave the helm of your ship, Captain Kirk. The Klingons won't be attacking today. And don't tell me you don't know what I'm talking about," she warned quickly. "Leave me some illusions."

Drew had only a vague idea what she was referring to. Another television program he hadn't bothered watching. He liked the way she lifted her chin when she dug in. "If I refuse to go, you'll probably drag me."

Now he was getting the idea. She knew she'd wear him down. "By force, if necessary. Those are wheels on your chair, Drew. And I know how to use them."

He started to laugh. "How can I possibly be outnumbered by one woman?"

Daisy stopped tugging. Leaning over, she brushed a kiss on his lips. "Because that woman is me."

She had no idea, Drew thought as he rose to his feet, how true those words were. And how prophetic.

The mall seemed to be filled with Christmas decorations, wall to wall people and an incredible level of noise.

"How much longer?" Drew wanted to know.

He shifted packages and bags, searching for a comfortable position he knew in his heart didn't exist. They had already been to a bookstore and three separate sections in a department store. Shopping with her was like trying to mount a horse and getting only one foot in the stirrup before the horse began to gallop away. All he could do was run along beside her and try to keep up.

The next stop on her list was a confectionary store at the other end of the mall. She stepped up her pace, weaving in and out of tiny pockets of space in the crowd.

"Slacker." She laughed, tossing the word over her shoulder. "We've only been at this an hour. How do you do your shopping in New York?" She slowed down when she realized that he was falling behind. "Catalog or secretary?"

He didn't particularly care for the smug way she had hit the nail on the head. "The latter."

She waited until he had caught up before taking the escalator to the ground level of the mall. A long line of children and harried-looking parents curled around the base of the escalator, waiting to talk to the jovial Santa Claus seated in the center of the court.

"No grocery shopping, no Christmas shopping." She looked up at Drew and he could have sworn he saw just a flash of pity in her eyes. "What kind of a life did you lead, Drew?"

"A sane one." He got off behind her. Someone bumped into him, hitting his arm. He nearly dropped the packages he was carrying.

Daisy caught them before they had a chance to fall. They looked at one another, the packages braced between them. "That's your word for it. I call it dull." She straightened his packages, then turned to look around.

They were standing in front of a restaurant that served different kinds of crêpes. Despite the crowds in the mall, Daisy saw that there were still two tables left unoccupied within the restaurant when she looked through the opaque window. "I tell you what—if I feed you, will you stop being so cranky?"

Without waiting for an answer, she went into the restaurant.

"I am not cranky. " He tried his best not to hit anyone with his packages as they were led to a table by a young girl dressed in a French peasant costume. Drew was relieved to sink down into a chair. He deposited the packages next to his feet. "I just honestly don't see the reason for all the excitement."

They ordered and were quickly served. "You mean that, don't you? About not understanding the excitement. Besides Jonathan, didn't you ever have anyone to buy things for? Gifts that you *wanted* to buy yourself because you wanted to give someone a present?"

Taking a bite of the crêpe, he suddenly realized how hungry he was. "Jonathan and I didn't exchange gifts."

How sad, she thought. "Alyce and I did. We'd make little homemade things and hide them from each other. I still have the village she made for me one year." Her lips curved fondly as she remembered how excited she had been when she had unwrapped the gift. "She made it all out of shoe boxes. Alyce spent months collecting them, decorating them, adding in tiny details to the inside. It was the grandest present I ever got. I was nine."

He stopped eating and looked at her in disbelief. "And you kept it?"

"Of course I kept it. You don't throw away things that are made with love." He probably thought she was being foolish, but he would learn in time. Or at least she sincerely hoped so.

Daisy looked at the crowds of shoppers just beyond the restaurant window. "I guess that's why I like this so much."

he nodded in the general direction of the shoppers. "I
never got to do it as a child."

She turned and saw Drew looking at her as if he was see-
ng her for the first time. "You see, I do know what board-
ng school is all about, Drew. Alyce and I spent a couple of
Christmases there. Just us and the maintenance crew."
Separated from the memory by almost two decades, it still
hurt. "Our parents were too busy to come and get us, too
busy performing to spend Christmas with us. And Uncle
Warren always seemed to be somewhere else."

It astounded Drew how this charging dynamo had suddenly transformed into a small, hurting child right before his
eyes. "What did your parents do?" he asked gently.

"Avoided being parents, mostly." She picked at her food,
er appetite gone. "They were part of Tomorrow. The
Band," she added when he looked at her blankly. "They had
ne hit record in '74 or '75. They spent the rest of their lives
rying to get another one, I guess."

He didn't know what to say. He had never been good in
situations like this. "What was the song called?"

"Pretty Dreams." Her lips curved in an ironic smile.
Rather appropriate, don't you think?" She realized that
er voice had dropped to almost a whisper. She raised it,
rying to sound as if talking about this part of her life didn't
other her. "Anyway, having two daughters got in their way.
he other band members didn't have any kids, so Joe and
Annie left theirs with Uncle Warren."

She lowered her eyes to her plate. Funny how painful
things that she had accepted were when she verbalized them.
he felt the same emotions haunting her now as had plagued
er then.

"Except that Uncle Warren didn't know what to do with
two little girls any more than Joe and Annie did, so he
checked around and found a neat little boarding school in
oston. And we were shipped off like so much luggage for

the second time in as many months." She closed her eyes, reliving it. "God, that place looked so big when I first saw it." She opened them again when she felt his hand over hers. The lonely feeling within her evaporated and she smiled at him.

"How old were you?"

"Seven. Alyce was eight. She took charge," Daisy remembered. "She became my big, brave protector. I never knew how frightened she was until years later when we were talking about it."

Enough of this. Daisy forced herself to shake off the memory. "See, we've got more in common than you thought."

They did, except that inexplicably, she had turned out one way, and he another. She had become bright, sunny, extroverted, and he had withdrawn. The world hadn't offered love, so he had become self-sufficient and hadn't required any. He gravitated toward order and furthering a company. Things that didn't demand emotion from him, because he had none to give.

"That's what I don't understand. Having that in your background, having parents who were distant, why would this all appeal to you?" He gestured toward the shoppers outside the restaurant.

She really didn't see what his problem was with comprehending her reaction. It seemed self-explanatory to her.

"Because I didn't have it." He didn't see, she could tell. Daisy leaned forward across the small table for two, shutting out the restaurant, shutting out everything but Drew. "It's like spending years wanting ice cream and not having it. And then waking up one morning to be told that you are the owner of an ice-cream parlor." Her eyes almost glowed as she spoke. He could see it even in the dim atmosphere of the restaurant. "With five hundred flavors. You want to sample them all."

He had no desire to sample all of them. All he wanted was the taste of one particular flavor. If she were an ice cream, she'd probably be called peppermint candy, or perhaps, cinnamon spice. Something that left a tangy flavor that lingered on the tongue and on the mind.

He was beginning to understand, just a little. It frightened him in a way. It meant he was on her wavelength. "Is that why you went from job to job?"

She toyed with the coffee the waitress had brought, thinking. "Probably. I never analyzed it, but you could have something there. I didn't want to settle in a niche until I was certain that niche was for me."

She watched him over the rim of her cup as she drank. *And I didn't want to love a man until I knew he was the one I really wanted.*

Daisy set down her cup on the saucer. Turnabout was only fair. "What about you? I've told you my story. Now it's your turn to tell me yours."

He didn't like talking about himself. "I thought you knew my story."

"I do."

Over the years, Jonathan had told Alyce bits and pieces of his life and so Daisy had eventually heard about his younger brother. But that was second-hand. She wanted to hear it from Drew. How had he felt when he was growing up? What had he thought the first time he had walked into the boarding school?

"But I'd like to hear it from your lips." Her eyes skimmed over them and she sighed unconsciously. "Reinforcement I think you might call it."

"I thought you bored easily."

He was being evasive, she thought. "I don't get bored with certain things, things that I enjoy. I've seen *It's a Wonderful Life* at least twenty times."

He finished his coffee. The waitress drifted by and re
filled it. He nodded his thanks. "Is that a new movie?"

He was kidding, wasn't he? No, she decided, looking a
him, he wasn't. A smile bloomed on her face.

"Oh, have I got a treat for you." She laughed at the un
certain look on his face. He had the expression of the mar
who didn't know if he had picked the lady or the tiger
"Tonight, we're all going to watch a video. Thank you," she
said to the waitress as the woman filled her cup.

Wrapping her hands around the warm cup, she leaned
forward. It helped create an intimate atmosphere within the
eye of a hurricane. "Now come on, talk."

Maybe they had been better off shopping. At least tha
had left little opportunity for conversation. "You've cor
nered the market on that."

If he wanted to banter, he was out of luck. "You're no
getting out of this, Drew. Tell me about the boy you were."

He shrugged. "I don't remember." He saw her skeptica
look. She obviously didn't believe him. "Honestly, i
doesn't unfold for me the way it does for you. No sweepin
scenes, no years seen in wide-screen technicolor. Jus
snatches of memories I'd rather not rehash. I can't," h
added.

Don't shut me out again. Please. "Can't, or won't?"

She was juggling words again, but then, she was good a
that. "There's a difference?"

"There is," she answered quietly.

Even if he wanted to talk about it, he couldn't. He ha
locked everything away so well, he had lost the key. "Don'
you want to finish your shopping?"

All right, she'd let him retreat for now. But not forever
She finished the remainder of her coffee. "Okay, pay th
check with your gold card and we'll get back to it."

"I knew it. You just brought me along for my money," he teased, glad that the conversation had taken on a lighter one.

She didn't bother to deny it. "That, and I intend to have my way with you in the car on the way home."

That, he had to admit as he gathered the bags and packages she had purchased, sounded very promising.

That evening Daisy did as she promised. She rented *It's a Wonderful Life* and made him sit down and watch the movie with her. Jeremy was tucked in between them, his eyes wide, as the black and white movie flickered on the television monitor in the family room. Toward the end, despite his involvement, Jeremy's head began to droop.

Drew shifted the boy so that he would be more comfortable and saw the tear sliding down Daisy's cheek. "You're crying." Amazed, he took out his handkerchief and handed it to her.

She only nodded as she wiped away the tears. On the screen, people were pouring into George Bailey's house, offering their hard-earned money to help him in his time of need.

Drew could only stare at Daisy, mystified. "But you said you've already seen this movie."

She swallowed and nodded. The bell was ringing on the Christmas tree. Clarence had become an angel. "Yes."

Drew didn't understand. This, like everything else about the woman, made no sense. "How can you cry, then?"

She let out a huge, cleansing sigh as credits rolled up on the screen. Shutting off the VCR and the set, she turned to look at Drew.

"Don't you have a sentimental bone in your body?" She wiped away the last telltale trace of tears and handed the handkerchief back to him.

He pocketed it absently. "I have to admit, it was a touching movie, for what it was."

She wondered if she was hitting her head against a brick wall. "What it was, Drew, was a movie about feelings. It was about seeing the good in your life and being grateful for it." She was talking about him now, and not a fifty-year-old movie. Her tone grew urgent. "And realizing just how many people you touch in your life. How many you affect."

By his reckoning, he probably affected a great many people in the strictest sense of the word. "I make decisions every day that, in one way or another, have repercussions all over the world. That still doesn't make me want to cry."

She refused to give up on him. Somewhere in that health-club-earned chest beat a heart. And she was going to find it. "We'll work on it. Maybe after you've seen the movie a few more times, it'll sink in."

He wasn't about to sit through that again. At least, not tonight. "I think we lost someone." He nodded at Jeremy. The boy's body was curled up into his.

She brushed the hair away from Jeremy's face. "You want to do the honors and take him up to bed?"

She'd always hovered around him when he did it before. "Alone?"

He was teasing, she thought, pleased. Where there was a trace of humor, there was hope. She rose and took the tape out of the machine. "You're capable."

He moved Jeremy so that he could easily lift the boy into his arms. "I know I'm capable, but you always seem to want to supervise."

Daisy turned and looked at Drew with Jeremy. They made a nice picture together. "I think you're ready for your first solo flight."

It was silly to feel that her approval meant something. He was used to taking his own lead, making major decisions that affected thousands of employees. But there was a glow within him that he couldn't deny.

When Drew came downstairs several minutes later, he found Daisy in the dining room. The results of all their hours of shopping in the mall was spread all over the table, dripping from the chairs, onto the floor. Colored foil was flying every which way as she wrapped, oblivious to his return.

He leaned against the doorjamb for a moment, watching her and wondering if there was some way to harness all this energy. If there had been such a creature as Santa Claus, all his helpers should have looked like this, Drew decided, incredibly sexy and ethereal.

"Couldn't wait, could you?" he asked, amused.

She swung around, surprised, then threw a roll of foil, making it unfurl. A sheet of silver draped over the box on the table, catching the overhead light and winking it about the room like trapped stars.

Daisy looked at him accusingly. "You're not supposed to be down yet."

He straightened and crossed to the table. "I didn't know there was a prescribed length of time for putting a little boy to bed. What's this?" With the tip of his finger, he pretended to lift the edge of the foil. She slapped his hand away.

"That's your present." Daisy wedged herself between Drew and the table, blocking his access to the box. "You'll just have to wait until Christmas morning."

"Present?" He couldn't begin to describe it, but there was a strange feeling building inside of him. Almost a bittersweet sadness. It tugged at emotions he had no idea what to do with. "You bought me something?"

Why would that surprise him so much? she wondered. "Yes."

"When?"

He had been with her the whole time. She had shopped for Jeremy and gotten presents for Margaret and several other people whose names he didn't recall, though she had told him. There hadn't been anything in the purchases that remotely resembled something he might use. When had she had the opportunity to get him a gift?

Daisy grinned, well pleased with herself. "When I sent you off to the gift-wrapping department to get Margaret's present specially wrapped. Remember?"

He had thought it odd at the time, seeing as how she hadn't wanted any of the other gifts wrapped. But he had just chalked it off to Daisy being her usual confusing self.

The rectangular shape beneath the silver foil curtain intrigued him. "You actually bought something for me?"

Hadn't there ever been a Christmas for him filled with warmth and wonder? Not even once? "Hasn't anyone ever bought you anything?"

Embarrassed, he flushed. "Well, yes," he began to lie. "No—never mind."

She put down the scissors in her hand. He needed her. "I see I have my work cut out for me." She turned her body into his.

Without even thinking, Drew placed his hands on her waist. It was becoming a habit, he realized. "Daisy, don't get carried away." There was more he wanted to say, about the need to be careful, about being adult about the situation they found themselves in. About their being two very different people.

But he never managed to say any of that. The smile on her face was seeping into the corners of his soul, blotting words from his mind. "What?"

"You've never called me Daisy before." She laced her hands together behind his neck, fitting her body comfortably against his. "I think, Mr. Addison, that I am getting to you."

"Getting?" he murmured. Inclining his head, he nipped at her lower lip and heard her contented moan. Tomorrow would come soon enough, he thought. For now, he'd enjoy tonight. "I think we should be using the past tense in this case."

"Always so proper." She rose up on her toes, moving in closer still.

The rush was beginning, pulling him in. "No—" he lowered his mouth to hers, already losing himself in her "—not always."

It took Daisy a long time to get back to wrapping gifts.

Chapter Fourteen

It happened gradually, without his being consciously aware of it. He had taken to cutting back the time he spent in the office on Saturdays until it had dwindled down to a few hours at most. He was on his way out this morning to put in a couple of hours when he heard the commotion outside the house. It sounded as if there was a truck pulling up the driveway.

Daisy was at the front door, shouting a greeting to someone. Drew looked past her shoulder. There were two men seated in the cab of a truck and they appeared to be making a delivery. He thought he recognized them from her nursery. Looking closer, Drew could make out the contents on the back of the truck from where he stood. They were bringing a Christmas tree.

"It's a real tree." He'd been surprised that here it was, three days before Christmas and she still hadn't put up a tree. He had been waiting to see some artificial monstrosity take root in the living room. After all, this was California. It never occurred to him that she would use a real tree.

"Yes, I know." About to wave the men into the house, she stopped and looked at the frown on Drew's face. "You don't approve of real trees?"

He eyed the bound specimen as one of the men—Simon, he thought—climbed onto the truck. The tree looked to be about ten feet tall. "I don't approve of fires."

Daisy opened the unlatched double door, then worked the stops on the stationary door. Both doors would have to be opened to accommodate the tree and its base. "I'm not planning to set it on fire, I'm planning to decorate it."

Slowly, Drew had been changing his mind about her, finding Daisy to be more stable and conscientious than he had originally believed. Maybe he'd been too hasty. "That's irresponsible."

The second door stuck and she gave it a whack with the flat of her hand. It wiggled. "It would be more irresponsible not to decorate it."

"You know what I mean." He waved at the tree. "Why can't you be like everyone else in Southern California and have a pink tree or a silver tree?"

She swung the door back, allowing the men enough room to carry the tree in without having to maneuver it. Looking at Drew, she fisted one hand on her waist. "Because, in case you haven't noticed, I'm not like everyone else."

Drew sighed. Without realizing it, he tightened his hand around the handle of his briefcase. "I've noticed, I've noticed."

She caught her breath as Simon stumbled when he lowered the tree down to Pablo. Pablo, wider, squarer than his partner, managed to right the tree without damage. "And with everything else being so artificial these days, we need a real tree. Jeremy needs a real tree."

He understood that, but he understood what taking needless risks meant more. "Don't you ever read the newspapers?"

He wasn't going to let up, was he? she thought with an inner sigh. Well, he might as well work this out of his system. "Faithfully."

She was being obtuse on purpose. Doggedly, he pushed on. "About how many homes are burned to the ground by Christmas trees?"

She curbed the urge to help as Simon and Pablo struggled with the unwieldy evergreen up the walk. "I think all the trees responsible have now been brought to justice and locked up."

Why had he expected to talk her out of this? He hadn't one shred of evidence to prove to himself that she was a rational human being. "You're not taking me seriously."

She looked up into his face, smiling brightly before turning back to the men. "I'm doing my best not to, yes." She gestured Simon and Pablo through the door. "This way." Pivoting on the balls of her feet, she led them into the living room.

Drew followed, his trip to the office temporarily abandoned. "I can't believe you'd sacrifice something living for a few days' pleasure."

She looked at him as the two sinewy men righted the tree in the center of the room. That would have been his way, she thought, two and a half months ago. Now he was championing defenseless trees. *Yes, Virginia, there is a Santa Claus and Christmas Eve is full of magic.*

"I'm not. Thanks, guys, I really appreciate this." She slipped Simon an envelope she knew he would split with Pablo and saw them to the door.

"But—" Drew ran out of steam as he looked down at the base of the tree. Rather than being mounted in a stand, the

ree's base was surrounded by wood measuring approxi-
nately eighteen inches or so on all sides. "What's that?"

Daisy crossed to the tree again. "It's called a box." She
apped it with her toe. "The roots are in that. Once Christ-
nas is over, I'm going to plant it in the backyard near Jer-
my's tree house."

She placed a hand on Drew's shoulder, the contact con-
eying her feelings even more aptly than her words. "I al-
vays hated Hans Christian Anderson's 'Fir Tree.' Cutting
lown some beautiful, thriving thing just to string lights on
t for a little while seemed horribly thoughtless to me." She
an her fingers over the tips of the green branches. It had
ust as much right to live as anything else. "But I do love the
cent of real pine and Christmas trees. Don't worry about
ires, I'm taking all the proper precautions."

There was no arguing with her, but he had to have his say.
Ie had seen a tree burn once. It had gone up in flames in
econds. The sight had left a lasting impression. "You're not
mnipresent."

She winked, kissing his cheek. "No, but I'm working on
." She knew in his gruff, blustery way, he meant well. He
ust hadn't learned how to express himself properly. Lucky
or him she was learning how to read between the lines.

"Is it here? Is it here?" The excited cry pierced the air as
eremy ran down the stairs, holding on to the banister with
oth hands as he flew.

"It's here." Daisy laughed as she stepped out of Jere-
ıy's way. He came tearing into the room, then skidded to a
alt in front of the tree. His head fell back as he tried to take
in from close up. The tree looked to be a hundred feet tall.

"Wow. It's so big!" Eagerness spilled out from every
ore. "Can we decorate it? Can we, huh?"

Daisy tried to look solemn and failed. His excitement was
fectious. She was so relieved at the way he was handling
e holidays. She had been dreading that the first Christ-

mas without his parents would turn into a time of tears a\
sadness for the small boy. She could have saved herself a l\
of grief and worry. Youth had a resilience that she wishe\
she could share in. "I take it you mean now?"

Jeremy hopped from one foot to another. "Sure."

"Drew?" Daisy raised her eyes questioningly toward hi\

For a moment, he didn't know what she was asking hir\
For permission? That certainly wasn't like her. And then\
occurred to him. "You want me to help decorate it?"

She spread her hands wide. "It's the family tree. A\
you're family." She glanced at his briefcase. She was again\
his working on Saturdays. "You can send that thing \
ahead to the office. It'll get a head start for you."

He had wanted to go over the latest reliability report \
the satellite components his subsidiary company, G.\
Aerospace, was supplying to NASA. There was a proble\
according to the latest stats and he felt better being on t\
of everything.

Like her, a tiny voice whispered, coming out of nowher\
He banked away the thought. And the urge.

"Please, Uncle Drew, please?" Jeremy, his dark ey\
dancing, pulled on Drew's arm, trying to steer him aw\
from the front door and all the responsibilities he had \
ways placed first in his life.

Helpless, Drew looked toward Daisy for a way out of th\
He should have known better.

"I need someone tall for the lights. It's a large tree."

"If I wasn't here, you'd find a way." Drew was con\
dent of that. Nothing got in this woman's way. Jeremy w\
still looking up at him in supplication. With a sigh, Drew\
the briefcase drop from his hands. "All right, I guess I c\
stay and help for a little while."

He had changed, she thought with a smile. He was\
longer a man who could, in good conscience, send off a \

tle boy to boarding school. He wasn't locked up in his ivory tower on the fortieth floor any more, either.

"Come on," she told him, "you can help me fetch the decorations out of the rafters in the garage."

Jeremy kept a death grip on Drew's arm as they walked out. This was important, special, and he meant to have his Uncle Drew there.

Three hours later, Daisy leaned back and surveyed their handiwork. Jeremy was still tossing fistfuls of tinsel at the glittering tree, but for all intents and purposes, it was finished.

"I think it's the best tree ever." She looked at Jeremy. "What do you think?"

He pitched another fistful. Crinkled silver strands rained down. Most of them landed on the rug. He seemed blissfully unaware of that fact as he grabbed another handful. "It's gonna be," Jeremy answered with a secret smile.

Daisy cocked her head and studied the boy. "What are you up to?"

Dark eyes widened innocently as thin shoulders rose and fell elaborately. He couldn't tell. If you told, wishes didn't come true. His mother had taught him that. "Nothing."

Daisy laughed and gave him a little hug. More silver strands hit the rug. Irene was going to have a great time vacuuming the rug tomorrow. "That's the most potent 'nothing' I've ever heard."

Jeremy dusted his fingers off. His dark corduroy pants had tinsel attached everywhere. "It's a magic tree, right, Aunt Daisy?"

Her smile faded just a little as she wondered what he was thinking. "Yes," she said slowly, "it is if you want it to be."

"I do." Jeremy shut his eyes tight.

Having returned the ladder to its place in the garage, Drew entered the living room. He had to admit that it was the best-looking tree he had ever seen. And the first he had ever decorated. That went without saying. She knew, he thought. It was part of the reason she had used the boy to help convince him. He was secretly glad she had.

He wondered why it was so hard for him to open up and why he had to be all but dragged to do things that he ultimately found enjoyable. Old habits, he supposed, died hard.

He took a look at Jeremy. The boy's eyes were practically screwed shut. "What are you doing?"

Jeremy opened his eyes again. He had shut them so tightly, for a moment it was hard to focus in. "Wishing."

"For what?" Drew asked. Whatever it was, he was certain Daisy had covered it. She had brought more toys into the house in the past week than were normally found in the warehouse of a toy factory. There he went, he thought, appalled, exaggerating again. She *was* getting to him. In more ways than one.

Jeremy shook his head. "It won't come true if I tell." He smiled confidently. "But it'll be here Christmas morning."

Daisy ruffled his hair, hoping that he wouldn't be disappointed. It would have helped if he had confided to her what he wanted for Christmas. "Santa'll do his best," she promised.

"And God?" Jeremy asked, suddenly solemn as he looked at the manger scene he had set up beneath the tree with only a little help from his aunt. Shepherds and wise men were lined up, kneeling before the Christ Child. "This is about God, too, right, Aunt Daisy?"

Daisy gathered him to her. He *was* missing his parents, she thought. "And God, too."

He wiggled out of her grasp, a wide smile on his face. "Now we gotta set up the trains, Uncle Drew. Around the tree," he said when Drew looked at him blankly.

"I've never set up a track," Drew began, trying to ease his way out of this.

"That's okay." Jeremy took his hand in his own. "I'll show you."

Drew looked over his shoulder toward his briefcase. The fine Italian leather case was now buried beneath opened, gaping boxes that had contained the decorations. Oh, well, it would keep.

"Okay, but I'm going to need a lot of help," Drew told Jeremy.

"Not any more," Daisy murmured, taking his arm. He was coming along just fine.

Drew misunderstood. "You're helping?"

"I have been all along."

Drew wasn't certain if they were still in the same conversation as he allowed himself to be led away.

The house was filled to bursting. Drew looked around, fascinated. It looked as if Daisy had invited the whole town to her Christmas Eve party. She called it theirs, but it was clearly hers. Her party. He didn't know anyone here.

Which was why she kept insisting on introducing him to absolutely everyone. Every time he broke away from one group, there she was again, latching onto his arm and directing him toward someone else. The consummate party giver, he thought dryly.

He took temporary refuge by the punch bowl, needing to be alone for a minute. Names and faces swam through his mind. He knew Margaret, of course, and several faces looked familiar from the funeral. But the rest were all mingling together. He was never any good at parties when business wasn't the prime reason for gathering.

He sipped punch and wondered when he could be alone with Daisy.

As he scanned the room for her, he saw Jeremy sitting on the sofa near the tree. A sense of camaraderie filled him and, abandoning his glass of punch, Drew made his way

over to the boy. He dropped down next to him on the sofa
Dressed in his party clothes, Jeremy seemed very intent a
he stared at the lights on the tree. They were the old
fashioned kind that bubbled continuously, and apparently
had mesmerized Jeremy.

Drew looked at them. They did have a hypnotic effect. He
blinked and turned toward Jeremy. "Hi. What are you do
ing?"

Jeremy fidgeted a little. "Waiting."

He looked around. There were several other children close
to Jeremy's age, but he was apparently ignoring them at the
moment.

"Oh, for Santa Claus," Drew realized.

Jeremy started to say something, then closed his mouth
again and nodded. "Yeah, for Santa Claus." He regarded
his uncle for a moment, obviously puzzling over some
thing. Finally, he asked. "Do you believe, Uncle Drew?"

"In Santa Claus?" No, he had never believed. There had
been no one to perpetuate the myth for him or to make him
believe. Reality was something that had been fed to him very
early in life. There was no room for make-believe and wishe
coming true. It had been a very stark childhood, he thought
suddenly feeling deprived.

Jeremy wriggled and scratched. The wool slacks wer
itchy. "Yeah, do you believe in Santa Claus?"

No, Drew thought. Jeremy wasn't going to have the kin
of life he had had. "Sure, doesn't everyone?"

Jeremy looked heartened by his uncle's verification
"There's this girl at school, Shelly, and Shelly says it's jus
your mom and dad, not Santa."

Drew supposed that he could tell Jeremy the truth. H
had the right opening to work with. But he looked at th
small upturned face and decided that Jeremy would see hi
share of reality when he grew up. He had seen more than h
should already. Childhood should be the time for magic. H

smiled to himself, thinking that Daisy would approve of the thought.

"She's a very mean little girl," Drew answered. He was rewarded with a relieved smile. Drew tucked his arm around the small shoulders. "Santa's real." He leaned back, trying to put himself into Daisy's mind. What would she tell him? "He's a magic elf who's made up from all the goodness in your heart."

Jeremy frowned for a moment, thinking. "What if you've been bad?"

"Santa Claus always finds something to work with," Drew assured him. The answers were easy, he realized, if he just pretended to think like Daisy.

It was then that he saw her. Daisy was standing off to the side, listening to him. He saw a tear sliding down her cheek. He half rose in his seat. "What's wrong?"

She wiped it away with the heel of her hand. "This is better than Clarence becoming an angel."

Sometimes it was hard to keep up with her. "Who?" And then he remembered. "Oh, the movie." He shrugged, self-conscious at being caught acting sentimental. It wasn't something he saw himself doing well. He rose from the sofa. "I think I'll get some punch."

Margaret drifted over just as Drew left. "Hi, Jeremy, how are you doing?" She made herself comfortable beside the boy. "Excited about tomorrow morning?"

He liked Margaret, liked the way she smelled, all pretty, like flowers. He liked the funny way she talked sometimes. And she let him have doughnuts even when Aunt Daisy said he'd had too many. "You bet."

"Excuse me for a moment," Daisy said to Margaret. "Entertain her, Jeremy."

He wasn't getting away that easily, she thought, going after Drew. Daisy wove her way through the crowd, exchanging words in passing with several people. She noticed that a very vivacious-looking woman had cornered Drew. Daisy recognized her as the date of one of Jonathan's friends. From the look on her face, the woman had obviously decided that Drew was far more her type.

Wrong.

She had never been jealous before, never experienced even a twinge of the annoying emotion running through her. It was taking a healthy-size bite out of her now.

"Excuse me." Daisy elbowed the blonde aside, flashing the woman a smile as she took hold of Drew's arm. "I'm afraid I have to steal him away from you. His wife and twelve children are looking for him."

"When did I have time for twelve children?" he whispered, amused.

"What you should have had time for was learning about barracudas," she returned in the same tone of voice.

"That innocent-looking girl?" He knew he was baiting Daisy and he was enjoying himself immensely.

"Girl? She's older than I am." Or looked it, anyway, Daisy thought. "I have something to show you." Still holding his arm, she ushered him to a doorway.

"What is it you want to show me?" He looked around and saw nothing out of the ordinary. There were people in the dining room. People in the kitchen, from what he could glimpse. But nothing or no one unusual.

"That." Daisy pointed to the archway overhead. "Mistletoe, Drew."

He glanced up at the green sprig and then looked at her face. "You never struck me as an old-fashioned girl."

Easily, Drew cinched her waist with his hands. For a moment, it felt as if she was wearing nothing beneath her glistening silver wrap-around dress. His imagination began to take flight and he had to work at harnessing it.

She let her head drop back slightly as she laughed. "That's because I want to keep you guessing."

"You've succeeded admirably. Do I get to kiss you now?"

She had done this to him, he realized, taken away his dis-comfort. Relaxed him. Melted him. While he was the last word in competence as far as heading a huge corporation went, his interaction with people limited itself only to busi-ness. The man he had been three months ago would have never wanted to kiss a woman in the middle of a crowded room. Now he wanted nothing else.

"Try not kissing me and see what happens."

His hands slipped up her back. No, no bra, either. She was nude under that, wasn't she? His pulse quickened. "I'm not brave enough."

She raised her mouth to his. "Smart man."

Because they were in a crowded room, it was a fleeting kiss, barely hinting at the passion that existed beneath. But it was enough to make her yearn.

She opened her eyes again, pulling herself back from brink of desire. But even now, her pulse was unsteady. She left her arms wrapped around his neck. "I can get rid of all these people," she murmured.

"With a wave of your hand?" He looked around the im-mediate area. He hadn't minded this party nearly as much as he thought he would. It was almost pleasant. But being alone with her would have been infinitely better. "I don't doubt it. I don't doubt that anything is possible with you."

I hope so, oh, I hope so.

If he felt that way, then perhaps he would stay, she thought. The way Jonathan had before him. But Jonathan had had a brother who could take things over. Drew didn't. He had to run the company himself. Besides, it meant a great deal to him.

She'd give up her business, she decided, if he asked her to. It would be hard. She was happy doing what she was do-ing. Being a landscape consultant was her calling. But she knew at that instant that she would give up everything just to be with him and Jeremy. Nothing else really mattered.

But he had to ask. It wasn't something she could volunteer.

He saw the sudden shift in her eyes and wondered at it. Was it something he had said? "You look sad."

She shook her head, wishing her emotions didn't show so readily. "I'm just thinking."

"About what?"

She didn't want to tell him. What if he didn't feel the same way about her as she did about him? Yes, he had changed, changed a great deal, but what if that really just involved Jeremy and not her? What if she was just a pleasant interlude, a phase, a ship in the night? For the first time in long, long time, Daisy felt uncertain.

"Nothing." She linked her hand with his. "Come on, let's get you circulated."

He thought of the blood that had roared through his veins just at the merest touch of her body to his. He thought about the fact that he intended to find out if his impression that she wasn't wearing anything beneath her dress was accurate as soon as everyone left. "I think you've already accomplished that."

She could read his thoughts and she laughed. "I mean talking to people. You still haven't met Jonathan's poker buddies."

That took him by surprise. Jonathan had never liked card games. "Jonathan knew how to play poker?"

"No," she grinned, "but he played anyway. I think Jeremy could have beaten him. I know I did."

"Why doesn't that surprise me?"

"Maybe you're getting used to me."

"Never."

She wondered if he meant that the right way. She hoped so. Daisy ushered him in the direction of a group of m

ear the fireplace. Her lips still tingled, making her antici-
ate a night to remember.

"Well, that's all of it," Daisy muttered, placing the last
ift she had for Jeremy under the tree. She sat back on her
eels. It looked like a child's idea of paradise. The base of
he tree was draped in white cloth and an explosion of gifts
ittered the area all around the perimeter.

She looked at Drew, who had dragged in the sackful of
ifts from her hiding place in the garage. "You looked like
ou had a good time tonight."

"I did." The fact still astonished him. A room full of
trangers and yet he had enjoyed himself. Daisy made it
mpossible not to. He took her hand and helped her to her
eet. "Of course, it's nothing compared to the time I'm
bout to have."

She placed her hands on his forearms. She loved the way
is muscles felt beneath her fingers. "Oh? With anyone in
articular?"

"Someone very particular." He toyed with the bow at her
ip. "I've been wondering all night. What happens when I
ull this thing?"

A smile teased her lips. "Why don't we go up to my room
nd see?"

Impulsively, he kissed her, unable to resist. "That is the
est idea you've had in a long time."

"I'll see if I can come up with a few more tonight."

With his arm around her, Drew walked up the stairs with
aisy. There was another mistletoe at the head of the stairs.
rew took full advantage of it.

Her head was spinning as she pulled herself out of the
eep kiss. "Do that again and I don't think I'll make it to
y room."

He laughed and drew her closer, delighting in her, de-
ghting in the evening.

She stopped to peek into Jeremy's room before enterin
her own. The boy's even breathing was the only sound in th
room.

She thought again what an immense comfort it wa
hearing that sound. She turned to Drew. "Probabl
dreaming of all the presents he's going to get."

Drew's hand rested comfortably on the swell of her hip a
he peered in over Daisy's head. "I forgot to ask, did yo
leave any toys in the toy stores for other parents to buy?"

She closed the door softly. "You're exaggerating."

"I never exaggerate." He led her to her room, shutting th
door behind them. "You, however, have this distinct ten
dency to do that."

She leaned into him, her body tempting his, her war
breath tantalizing his skin. "Would it be an exaggeration t
say you've been driving me crazy all night?" she asked i
nocently.

He wrapped his arms around her. "I don't know, wou
it?"

"No." She shook her head slowly, her eyes on his fac
"An understatement. A vast understatement." She place
his hand over the bōw at her hip. "Want to unwrap one o
your presents early?"

"I've been counting on it all evening." He tugged on th
tie. As it came undone, the entire dress parted, seductive
hanging open from her shoulders. Just as he had surmise
she was completely nude beneath it.

Desire came, full blooded and demanding as he ran h
palms over her sleek body. "Isn't that a rather dangero
outfit to wear in public?"

She felt the glow beginning, growing as his hands strok
her body. "I had a sailor's knot on the tie earlier. I undid
while you were in the garage, getting Jeremy's presents."

"A sailor's knot," he echoed. "If you tell me that yo
were an admiral in the navy, I'll—"

She lifted her chin, her eyes teasing him. "You'll what?"

He laughed. "I'll probably believe you."

"You're coming along, Drew. You're definitely coming along."

He lifted a brow. "Not yet, but I plan to."

Drew tossed aside her dress and took her into his arms, fanning flames that had refused to be banked all evening.

New and different, but the same, that was the way he felt about the sensations that ripped through him each time they made love. He knew what to expect, yet there was always more, so much more. An entire treasure trove for him to get lost in. He had no doubts in his heart that it would always be that way.

Unless—

He stopped thinking. He refused to think about anything. All he wanted to do was feel the life-giving forces coursing through his blood the way they did each time he was with her.

He framed her face. "This is the best Christmas Eve I've ever had."

Daisy began to unhook his belt. "Oh, no, the best Christmas Eve you've ever had is yet to be."

And she was right.

Chapter Fifteen

Light was nudging its way past filmy white curtains in
Daisy's bedroom. Reluctantly she opened her eyes and the
blinked as she tried to make out the numbers on the cloc
next to her bed. It was a few minutes after six.

Christmas morning.

Why wasn't Jeremy knocking on her door, begging her
come down with him and see what Santa had brought? He'
been so anxious the night before. No, she thought, pensiv
would have been a better word. He had talked about wai
ing. Patient, she mused, like his father.

And his uncle.

Daisy smiled, remembering the way Jeremy had looke
last night in his jacket and matching slacks. Like a litt
man. Her little man. She looked at the wall that separate
her room from his. He was probably exhausted from sta
ing up so late at the party.

Daisy turned and propped herself up on her elbow. Drew was still asleep. It seemed to be a day for sleeping in, she mused, watching the way his chest rose and fell as he slept. He'd stopped slipping out of her bed before dawn a few days ago. She liked the feeling of waking up in the morning and finding him next to her.

But for how much longer?

It was exactly one week until the end of their bargain and he hadn't said a word about it, about the future. Not one word. Not a single hint of what was going to happen once the three months were up. She hadn't brought it up, either.

Maybe it was because neither of them wanted to hear the words, she thought, pressing her lips together. What if—?

No, today was Christmas. She wasn't going to spoil it by wondering and worrying over what was to be. It wouldn't help matters, anyway. She was content in the fact that he obviously loved Jeremy and understood his needs. He'd do what was best for the boy. They both would. If Drew had to return to the east coast because his career was there, so be it. She'd go, too. She knew she wouldn't be able to function very well here if her heart was three thousand miles away.

It would be nicer, she thought, if he'd ask her to go, but she'd made up her mind one way or another. Nothing in this world was going to separate her from Jeremy. Or from Drew.

Lightly, Daisy touched her lips to his, and Drew stirred. She did it again, with a little more feeling, and he opened his eyes, surprised. "Hey, sleepyhead. Wake up. It's Christmas morning."

He threaded his arm around her, holding Daisy against him. "So it is," he murmured, trying to clear the sleep from his brain. He shifted, stretching his body against hers. "Want to celebrate early?" He could hardly believe, even now, that the words were his own. He had seen her coming a mile away three months ago, a banshee bent on shaking up his very foundations. He'd been just as bent not to let her disturb one brick.

Now look at him. He'd plunged from his fortieth-floor office just as surely as Jonathan had. Without a net. And loved it.

She tugged teasingly on his lower lip with her teeth, then pulled away, laughing as he started to deepen the kiss.

"Later. First, we have a little boy to take care of." She slipped out of bed and picked up her robe. She saw desire flicker in Drew's eyes as he skimmed them over her nude body. Pushing her arms through the sleeves, she knotted the sash securely at her waist. "I think it's rather strange that he's still sleeping."

Drew glanced at the clock. "It's a good habit to get into at six in the morning."

"Christmas morning?"

Drew threw the covers off and planted his feet on the floor. "You're right, it is odd." He pulled his slacks on and followed her out into the hall. "I'm looking forward to seeing his expression when he unwraps that engine you bought him."

"*We* bought him" she corrected. "This isn't a competition."

Not any more. He'd won all the marbles. And she had gotten caught in her own trap. By trying to change Drew into the type of man who understood that Jeremy was a sensitive boy with needs, she had inadvertently fashioned someone she was now hopelessly in love with.

Drew took her hand. "Come on. I might get lucky and find some mistletoe along the way."

She kissed his mouth quickly. "You don't need mistletoe. Now let's wake him up before I get carried away."

"You?" Drew opened his eyes wide in wonder and surprise. "Never."

"Don't be wise," she murmured, opening Jeremy's door slowly. "Honey, are you asleep? It's Christmas. Santa's been here."

She stopped, her smile freezing. The covers on Jeremy's bed had been thrown back, as if a boy had recently risen in haste. His bed was empty.

A nervousness began to seep into her system. She wasn't completely sure why. Instinct. "Drew?"

He heard the slight note of anxiety in her voice and glossed over the situation for her benefit. "He probably didn't want to wake you and just snuck downstairs. Let's go."

He didn't need to urge her. There was something not right about this. She could sense it in her bones. Jeremy *always* wanted her to be part of things, especially since his parents had died. Daisy flew down the stairs, the hem of her robe trailing after her.

"Jeremy," she called out. "Jeremy, are you in the living room?"

He wasn't there. The gifts were exactly where she had placed them around the tree the night before, neatly wrapped and untouched. Panic began to build. Why wasn't he down here?

Though he knew it was useless, Drew circled the Christmas tree. The boy wasn't playing some sort of prank. He wasn't hiding behind the tree. Drew looked at Daisy. "Where is he?"

She shook her head, trying to think, squeezing back her tears as if they had depth and breadth. "I don't know. You check all the rooms upstairs. I'll look down here."

There was no reason why Jeremy should be hiding from them, she thought. Why wasn't he answering?

She went through the rooms quickly, calling. Irene's door opened before Daisy could knock.

"What's the matter?" the housekeeper asked, wrappin
her robe about her thin body.

"It's Jeremy. I can't find him."

Lines of concern popped out on the older woman's brov
"Shall I call the police?"

"No, no, not yet." Daisy dragged her hand through h
hair, trying desperately to think. Her thoughts were scatte
ing frantically in all directions, dandelion seeds in the bri
fall wind. Where would he go? And why? He'd never do
anything like this before. Why now? It didn't make sense
her.

With Irene on her heels, Daisy started to return to t
living room. As she hurried by the sliding-glass door in t
family room, she noticed that it was unlatched. She kne
she had checked it last night when the guests left. It w
locked then. Could Jeremy be in the yard at this hour?

"Wait here," she told Irene and then hurried out.

She looked around. The backyard was spacious with
miniature waterfall on one side and an elaborate swing s
near the house. The trees that bordered the fence on all thr
sides provided shade, but were too close to the fence f
Jeremy to play behind.

He was nowhere to be seen.

That left only one place to try. His tree house.

Holding her robe against her, she hurried barefoot ov
the wet grass. "Jeremy," she called up to the tree hous
"Are you up there? Jeremy, answer me. Please."

There was no reply, only a soft noise that sounded like
distant mockingbird. Or a muffled sob. Instinct had h
climbing up the wooden ties that Jonathan had nailed in
the tree.

She found Jeremy huddled in the corner, his hands co
ering his face. He was crying.

She knew it. She had known that something was wro
from the moment she woke up. Crouching, she half crawle

half shuffled on her knees into the tree house to reach him. "Oh, baby, what's the matter?"

He had wanted to be alone, to cry his heart out and empty out the pain. Now that she was here, Jeremy threw himself into his aunt's arms and sought out her warmth. "They didn't come."

Rocking him against her body, she stroked his hair. His wet face dampened the front of her robe. "Who, baby? Who didn't come?"

His cheeks shone with tears as he raised his head and looked at her. "Mommy and Daddy. They were supposed to come back. It's Christmas and they were supposed to come back to me."

She could feel her heart breaking. This was why he had taken his parents' death so well. He'd been waiting for Christmas, waiting for them to return, because Christmas was the time for miracles. How could she make him understand something that she didn't completely accept herself?

She felt tears gathering in her own eyes as she tried to answer him. "Oh, darling, they can't. They want to, but they can't."

He pushed himself away from her, angry, hurt, confused. "I thought if I wished real hard, they'd come back. You know, like a present for me. Christmas is magic. You said so. Uncle Drew told me so."

He looked as if he felt that everyone was lying to him, Daisy thought. It was a horrible thing for a four-year-old to believe. "Some things are beyond magic."

Jeremy hung his head. Two tears fell from his eyes onto her robe. "No, they don't want to come back. They don't love me."

She took hold of his arms and forced him to look at her. "They did love you. We all love you, sweetheart." Her voice was fierce, stern, as she tried to get through to him. She saw the hesitation, the desperate need to believe. To understand. "It has nothing to do with love. When people die, they can't come back, no matter how much they might want to." She gathered him to her and held on to him tightly. "You know that turnstile you got stuck in at the drugstore last month?"

Jeremy hiccuped, rubbing his fists against his eyes. He nodded. " 'Cause it only went one way."

"That's right." She kept her voice soft, soothing, hoping to calm him down. "That's kind of what life is like." She stroked his head. "It only goes one way. Forward. And your mommy and daddy have gone forward to the next level. Heaven. And someday, when you're a lot older, you'll join them."

Jeremy's small eyes searched her face. "And you and Uncle Drew? You'll come, too?"

Her heart ached at the compliment he had just given to her. To her and Drew. "And Uncle Drew and I will come too," Daisy assured him with a smile, blinking back her tears.

"Where are we going?"

When she turned around, Daisy saw Drew looking in trough the tree house window. She could see by the expression on his face that he had overheard everything. His tone had been inordinately gentle when he asked his question.

Jeremy wiped away the telltale tracks of his tears with his knuckles. "To heaven."

"Now?" Drew looked down at his robe. "I'm not dressed for it."

Jeremy sniffled and a half smile began to form on his lips.

"Besides," Drew continued, snaking inside the small quarters, "there are all these presents under the tree and I'm not sure about what kind of postage to put on them so we can mail them to heaven after you." He grinned at Daisy, knowing he was crowding her into a corner with his frame and enjoying the contact. "What do you say that we go and open them now instead of sitting in this tiny house?"

Jeremy let out a big sigh, then manfully nodded his head. He was his father's child. Even at four, he understood that there was no use in crying over what couldn't be. "Okay."

Daisy turned her head away from Jeremy, into Drew's shoulder. "Nicely done," she murmured under her breath.

"I was going to say the same to you. Never thought of life as being a turnstile before." He raised his voice as he looked at his nephew. "Why don't you go on first and I'll help your aunt down?"

Jeremy was already clambering out of the window as Drew turned toward Daisy. "Or were you a sherpa guide in the Himalayas, too?"

She gave him a shove with the flat of her hand. "Just go, wiseguy. I can climb down." She began to move past him toward the opening, but he placed a hand on her shoulder to stop her.

"In that case, let me go down first." He purposely raised and lowered his eyebrows as he looked at her robe. "I might like the view from the ground."

She laughed, her own tears drying. "Just take Jeremy into the house, all right?"

"Will do." He lowered himself out the window and climbed down agilely. Jeremy was waiting for him at the base of the tree. As Daisy watched, Drew took the boy's hand in his and led him into the house.

It was going to be all right, she thought. The other shoe had dropped and the worst was over. Jeremy would start to heal now.

When Daisy entered the living room a few minutes later, ripped wrapping paper had just begun to pile up on the floor beside Jeremy. The boy still looked somewhat subdued, but the magic of Christmas morning was slowly beginning to penetrate and dissolve the aura of sadness.

Daisy sat on the sofa where she could have a good view of Jeremy as he opened his gifts. She noted the loving expression on Drew's face as he observed Jeremy. The man was a far cry from the Iceman who had come in out of the rain three months ago. She had melted him just as she had set out to do. The rest was going to work itself out now. She just knew it. They would take joint custody of Jeremy and she would move to New York. It wasn't simple, but it would work.

Satisfied that Jeremy was all right, Drew leaned a hip against the arm of the sofa, next to Daisy. "Are you going to open your presents?"

She shrugged. "Not right now. I'd rather watch him." She saw the surprise and the joy as Jeremy unwrapped an airplane for the action figure "Drew" had brought him from New York. "Besides, I have a pretty good idea what everyone gave me. You drop enough hints, you're bound to get some of the things you mentioned."

"Oh?" His tone was so innocent sounding, it had Daisy looking in Drew's direction. He was rummaging through the gifts farthest from Jeremy. "What about this box?" Rising, he brought over a rectangular box wrapped in scampering Santa Clauses.

Daisy stared at it. She didn't remember that one. It looked like a shoe box. "Shoes? I didn't hint for shoes." She turned the box around slowly. "There's no card on it."

Drew was back on the arm of the sofa. Perched, as if he was too agitated suddenly to sit properly. "Why don't you open it? Maybe there's one inside."

Intrigued, suddenly inexplicably nervous, Daisy unwrapped the paper. It *was* a shoe box. A decorated shoe box. Windows were cut out on all sides and there were trees drawn on the back. A tiny sign on the front proclaimed Showers of Flowers . . . and Things.

Pressing her lips together to keep from crying, she raised her eyes to his.

Drew slid from the arm of the sofa down next to her on the cushion. "For your collection. I thought maybe your village might need a nursery." He felt a little foolish as he shrugged. "It seemed appropriate."

Tears rose again, this time from sheer joy. "It's beautiful. You did this for me?"

"Had to. Couldn't find anyone else to do it without making it seem as if I was crazy."

"You are," she laughed. "Wonderfully crazy."

She started to set the box down, to hug him, but as she slid it from her lap, she heard something move inside, sliding from one end to the other. It made a tiny thud against the box. Her brow furrowed as she took the lid off. Inside there was another small box, wrapped in the same sort of paper.

"Oh, yes." Drew cleared his throat, devastatingly anxious, "I thought—hoped, actually—that you might like that, too."

Jeremy was busy trying out the electronic drum set she had gotten him, but all Daisy heard was the buzzing in her ears as she tore off the paper from the small box.

Holding her breath, she opened it. Inside was a ring with a single, exquisite, square-cut emerald.

He had addressed huge auditoriums filled with employees and never experienced a single twinge of agitation. Nerves were slicing through him now like butterflies with razors for wings. "I thought that since you liked green so much, Maid Marian, you might want an emerald instead of a diamond for your engagement ring."

Her hand shook as she held the box. She couldn't even take the ring out. "Engagement?" Daisy repeated, her voice low.

He was floundering, he thought. "Engagement. You know, the thing that happens before you marry someone?"

Her mouth felt dry as her palms became damp. Was he serious? "Marry?"

"There seems to be an echo in here. If I say yes, will I hear the same word in return?"

She was going to start babbling any second now. Daisy lowered her eyes and stared at the box in her hand. "I don't know what to say."

She was going to say no, Drew thought, feeling his stomach muscles tighten. "That's a first." He licked his lips nervously. "Do you want to think it over?"

Daisy shook her head emphatically. "No."

The word cut through him like a carving knife. "No, huh?"

"I don't have to think about it." The words dripped from her mouth almost in slow motion as disbelief gripped her. He wanted her. He really, really wanted her. Forever. It *was* working out. They'd have each other and Jeremy, as well. *Oh, Alyce, Jonathan, I wish you were here to see this. You made all this happen.* "I've been thinking about it for a long time already."

He wasn't going to let her say no. He *couldn't* let her say no. She had to marry him. He couldn't go back to life the way it was before he had come out here. It would be too bleak, too empty, too meaningless for him now. Having felt the sun, he refused to reenter the cave and do without it forever more. She'd made him take risks, emotional risks he had never wanted to take. He wasn't about to go on free falling without her.

All the things he used to convince reluctant clients began to fill his head in jumbled order. He planned to keep talking until he wore her down.

He took her hands in his. "Before you say anything, let me have my say. This is a perfect way to solve our bargain. Jeremy needs both of us, not just one. I've already set wheels in motion to transfer the bulk of Addison Corporation's headquarters out here. That building that you saw going up across the street from the office?"

She remembered the one he was referring to. "Yes?"

"I bought it. It's going to be Addison Corporation's new home office. Now I need a home to go to. A real home, not a penthouse apartment where I just sleep. I want a real family to come home to, not just a valet." His eyes held hers as he searched for a sign that she understood what he was trying to tell her. That he needed her. That he couldn't live without her. "I need someone who knows how to make me laugh, not who knows my suit measurements."

Jeremy laughed as he pulled the string on a dinosaur doll and it gave him another flippant answer. Drew looked at the boy over his shoulder, then turned again to Daisy. "I want to adopt Jeremy. I *need* you and Jeremy. I've never been in love before, so it took me a long time to realize what was going on. But I love you, Daisy, and I'm not about to let you say no. Tell me the word I want to hear."

She didn't know whether to laugh or cry. A little of both was happening. "Idiot."

He raised a brow. The look on her face told him it was going to be all right. "That wasn't quite the word I was looking for."

She threw her arms around his neck. "What in heaven's name made you think I'd say no?"

"Because you never say what I think you'll say." Relieved, he felt his heart slide back into position out of his throat. "Then it's yes?"

"It's always been yes." She laughed. "Right from the first moment I heard your pants ringing for me."

Drew pulled her onto his lap, his mouth finding hers. And then they both heard bells ringing, accompanied by drumroll thanks to Jeremy's new electronic drum set.

* * * * *

Take 4 bestselling love stories FREE

Plus get a FREE surprise gift!

Special Limited-time Offer

Mail to Silhouette Reader Service™

3010 Walden Avenue
P.O. Box 1867
Buffalo, N.Y. 14269-1867

YES! Please send me 4 free Silhouette Special Edition® novels and my free surprise gift. Then send me 6 brand-new novels every month, which I will receive months before they appear in bookstores. Bill me at the low price of $2.71 each plus 25¢ delivery and applicable sales tax, if any.* That's the complete price and—compared to the cover prices of $3.50 each—quite a bargain! I understand that accepting the books and gift places me under no obligation ever to buy any books. I can always return a shipment and cancel at any time. Even if I never buy another book from Silhouette, the 4 free books and the surprise gift are mine to keep forever.

235 BPA AJH7

Name	(PLEASE PRINT)	
Address	Apt. No.	
City	State	Zip

This offer is limited to one order per household and not valid to present Silhouette Special Edition® subscribers. *Terms and prices are subject to change without notice. Sales tax applicable in N.Y.

USPED-93R   ©1990 Harlequin Enterprises Limited

MORGAN'S MERCENARIES

by Lindsay McKenna

Morgan Trayhern has returned and he's set up a company full of best pals in adventure. Three men who've been to hell and back are about to fight the toughest battle of all...love!

You loved Wolf Harding in HEART OF THE WOLF (SE #817) and Sean Killian in THE ROGUE (SE #824). Don't miss Jake Randolph in COMMANDO (SE #830), the final story in this exciting trilogy, available in August.

These are men you'll love and stories you'll treasure...only from Silhouette Special Edition!

Silhouette®

SPECIAL EDITION

WILD RIVER TRILOGY

by Laurie Paige

Come meet the wild McPherson men and see how these three sexy bachelors are tamed!

In HOME FOR A WILD HEART (SE #828) you got to know Kerrigan McPherson. Now meet the rest of the family:

A PLACE FOR EAGLES, September 1993—
Keegan McPherson gets the surprise of his life.

THE WAY OF A MAN, November 1993—
Paul McPherson finally meets his match.

Don't miss any of these exciting titles—only for our readers and only from Silhouette Special Edition!

Silhouette

From this
day
forward

Coming in August,
the first book in an exciting new trilogy from
Debbie Macomber
GROOM WANTED

To save the family business, Julia Conrad becomes a "green
card" bride to brilliant chemist Aleksandr Berinski. But what
more would it take to keep her prized employee—and new
husband—happy?

FROM THIS DAY FORWARD—Three couples marry first and
find love later in this heartwarming trilogy.

Look for
Bride Wanted (SE #836) in September
Marriage Wanted (SE #842) in October

Only from Silhouette Special Edition

If you enjoyed this book by

MARIE FERRARELLA,

don't miss these other titles by this popular author!

Silhouette Romance™

#08869	FATHER GOOSE	$2.69 ☐
#08920	BABIES ON HIS MIND	$2.69 ☐
#08932	THE RIGHT MAN	$2.69 ☐
#08947	IN HER OWN BACKYARD	$2.75 ☐

Silhouette Special Edition®

#09652	A GIRL'S BEST FRIEND	$2.95 ☐
#09675	BLESSING IN DISGUISE	$3.25 ☐
#09703	SOMEONE TO TALK TO	$3.29 ☐
#09767	WORLD'S GREATEST DAD	$3.39 ☐

Silhouette Intimate Moments®

#07496	HOLDING OUT FOR A HERO	$3.39 ☐
#07501	HEROES GREAT AND SMALL	$3.50 ☐

TOTAL AMOUNT	$	
POSTAGE & HANDLING	$	
($1.00 for one book, 50¢ for each additional)		
APPLICABLE TAXES*	$ _____	
TOTAL PAYABLE	$ _____	
(check or money order—please do not send cash)		

To order, complete this form and send it, along with a check or money order for the total above, payable to Silhouette Books, to: *In the U.S.:* 3010 Walden Avenue, P.O. Box 9077, Buffalo, NY 14269-9077; *In Canada:* P.O. Box 636, Fort Erie, Ontario, L2A 5X3.

Name: _____

Address: _____ City: _____

State/Prov.: _____ Zip/Postal Code: _____

*New York residents remit applicable sales taxes.
  Canadian residents remit applicable GST and provincial taxes.

MFBACK2

HE WA

"No one defies me or intentionally provokes me here, and certainly not a—"

"A woman? Is that what you were going to say?"

He grabbed her so quickly she didn't have time to react. He pulled her out of her saddle, halfway across his lap. His hard chest crushed her as his mouth found hers in a burning, searing kiss that sent currents of heat down her torso.

He had expected her to fight him. He had not expected to become caught up in this irresistible spiral of desire that threatened to devour him.

Books by Deborah Cox

Desert Dreams
From This Day Forward

Available from HarperPaperbacks

From This Day Forward

 DEBORAH COX

HarperPaperbacks
A Division of HarperCollinsPublishers

HarperPaperbacks   *A Division of* HarperCollins*Publishers*
10 East 53rd Street, New York, N.Y. 10022

Cover illustration by Jim Griffin

First printing: August 1995

Printed in the United States of America

HarperPaperbacks, HarperMonogram, and colophon are
trademarks of HarperCollins*Publishers*

❖ 10 9 8 7 6 5 4 3 2 1

For my critique partners—
Lorraine Carroll,
Sherrilyn Kenyon and Rickey Mallory.
Thanks for putting up with me!

And the measure of our torment is the measure of our youth.
God help us, for we knew the worst too young!

—Rudyard Kipling
"Gentlemen Rankers"

Prologue

New Orleans, Louisiana, March 1885

Dear Jason,
I am pleased to inform you I have located a
suitable candidate to fulfill the position of wife
and companion. Her name is Caroline Marshall.
I am well acquainted with the lady and can say
without hesitation that she meets the require-
ments you set forth in your letter. I am confident
you will find her pleasing to the eye and an intel-
ligent companion.

I am most gratified with your decision to
marry. I have sensed a growing loneliness in
your recent letters. Melanie and I believe that
you have made a splendid decision.

Therefore, the marriage by proxy has been
performed and preparations are underway for

*your bride's departure for Brazil. I will write
again when passage has been arranged.*

   I wish you both happiness and good fortune.
                                    Your cousin,
                                         Derek

"It's done." Caroline Marshall Sinclair placed the
quill in the inkstand and stared at the letter on the
desk before her. Quelling the doubt that rose in her
breast, she reread the missive. "Tell me I've done the
right thing."

Melanie Sinclair lifted the letter carefully, studying it for several seconds before replying. "It's amaz-
ing. I've seen Derek's handwriting hundreds of
times, but I could never have duplicated it so
closely."

"Well, I suppose if this doesn't work out I could
make my way as a forger."

Melanie laughed and returned the letter to the
desk. "I've never known you to be fainthearted,
Caroline. You were so sure this morning."

Sunlight from the open window glinted off the
ring on the third finger of Caroline's left hand,
reminding her of the vows she'd taken today, vows
that tied her forever to a stranger.

"Have you ever met Jason?" she asked, though
she knew the answer. She'd asked the question more
than once and had received a different reaction each
time. The words were always the same—*"No, but
Derek has told me so much about him, I feel as if I
know him."* The difference lay in the expressions,
the physical reaction which ranged from dreamy
contemplation to cautious optimism.

"No," Melanie replied, her mood reflective this

time. "All I know of him is what Derek has said over the years and what I've gleaned from—"

Surprised by the variation in Melanie's response, Caroline stopped studying her wedding band and glanced up at the other woman who stood gazing pensively out the window at the traffic on Tchoupitoulas Street. "What? Gleaned from what?"

"Oh," Melanie murmured as if she'd been called back from some faraway place. "Oh, the requests he's made over the years. Jason has very definite ideas about what he wants—the exact kind of books, the exact kind of furnishings, the exact kind of fixtures and glass and door facings for what must be a giant of a house."

A tremor of fear rippled through Caroline's body. Yes, Jason Sinclair had been very specific about what he wanted in a wife. But she knew that what he thought he wanted and what he needed were not the same thing at all. He needed a strong, independent, intelligent woman who wouldn't mind the isolation of the jungle or the hardships of such a life. He needed a woman who understood him, who could offer him the loving kindness he had never known as a child.

"Derek says Jason was scarred by life," Melanie said, as if she'd read Caroline's thoughts. "That's why he's hidden himself away in the wilds of Brazil for all these years. They were never close, not really. Jason grew up in a different world, a world of poverty. They lived on opposite sides of town. When his father died, Jason came to work for the company. He was only seventeen when his mother died and he left for Brazil. Fifteen years in the jungle."

Fifteen years, Caroline thought with a shudder, trying to imagine it. What would a man be like after fifteen years in the wild? She remembered reading accounts of men who had lived among the Indians of the American West twenty or thirty years ago and had become savages themselves. It seemed as if there was something primitive inside men, and whenever they were separated from civilization for too long, they reverted to a baser nature.

She was generalizing; she knew it. She could almost hear her father scolding her even from the grave. There were plenty of other accounts of men who had gone into the wilderness and tamed it, and that was obviously what Jason Sinclair had done. He had built a house, ordered books and other comforts from home, and now he wanted a wife. He hadn't lost the capacity to read and write. His letters had revealed a fiercely independent spirit, a dependable, hardworking man with the soul of a poet.

In short, Jason Sinclair was the absolute opposite of Wade Marshall, her first husband. He'd allowed life to rule his world, whereas Jason Sinclair obviously ruled life. Jason had decided on a course, set a goal and accomplished it. The obstacles he must have overcome would have crushed Wade.

All Jason needed was the right woman to bring him out of his shell of loneliness and self-imposed isolation. And Caroline knew that she was that woman.

Guilt squeezed her chest. The candid descriptions in Jason's letters of his childhood had been intended for Derek. But until she'd begun writing Derek's responses, Jason's letters had been dry and businesslike, without a hint of intimacy. It was as if something in her words had prompted him to confide in her—in Derek.

"Please don't let me upset you with my rambling," Melanie said, trying to sound lighthearted. "I suppose now is not the time to be telling you these things. I'm sure it's nothing to be alarmed about. I think it's terribly romantic. Falling in love through letters. . . ."

Unsure which of them Melanie was trying to convince, Caroline tried to focus on other things. Thinking back over the past year, she couldn't say exactly when she'd fallen in love with Jason Sinclair. His letters had spoken to her heart from the first one her employer, Derek Sinclair, had given her to read and answer.

At first, Derek had approved each response before she'd posted it, but as time passed and her skills in copying his handwriting increased, Derek's scrutiny had become less and less thorough. Eventually, Caroline became Derek's voice with his cousin. When the letter came from Jason requesting a wife, Derek was out of the country. Acting on Derek's behalf, and without his knowledge, she'd chosen the one woman who understood Jason better than anyone else—herself.

How well she understood the desire to shed the past and start over in a new place. Because she refused to live by the standards imposed upon women by New Orleans society, she'd been ostracized. She chose not to hide the fact that she was capable of using her mind for something other than picking the right color draperies for the sitting room. As a result, men looked at her with suspicion, as if she were a freak of nature.

Women distrusted her because she enjoyed the world of business, a world she shared with their husbands, a world entirely closed to them. Both men and women disliked her because she threatened the status quo. She'd been unwilling to compromise, to lower her standards in order to fit their mold, and so she'd been treated like a pariah.

Only Melanie had befriended her, and she'd repaid her kindness by entangling her in this desperate plot.

"I just wish I could have left you out of this," Caroline said sincerely. She picked up the envelope containing the other letter, the one to Derek, and gave it to Melanie. Her hand trembled slightly as she thought of what she was doing, what she had done. "Answering Jason Sinclair's request for a wife without so much as showing Derek the letter was shocking enough, but involving you. . . . He'll be furious."

"He'll get over it," Melanie assured her, her brown eyes dancing with mischief. "I'm glad to have helped. It was actually very exciting. How many women get the chance to be a groom in a wedding?"

Caroline laughed in spite of her doubts. "That was a stroke of genius."

Melanie shrugged dramatically. "Whoever said the proxy groom had to be a male?"

Caroline touched a finger to the writing on the letter she'd just finished. Satisfied that the ink was dry, she folded the paper quickly and slipped it inside an envelope before she lost her nerve.

Sealing the envelope, she stood and gathered her things, gazing one last time at the small wooden desk and chair that had been hers for the past year.

"You know, I think I'll actually miss this place," she said sincerely.

It was a shame most women were never allowed a glimpse into the exciting, dynamic world of business.

Here at the Sinclair Coffee Company, she'd felt needed, competent. And there was a certain satisfaction that came from earning one's own way.

"And I shall miss you." Melanie smiled a sweet, melancholy smile.

The two women embraced, and when they drew apart, Caroline's eyes brimmed with tears. "And I you. I—I've never had a friend like you before." Caroline laughed. "I've never had a friend at all, not really."

"I am your friend always," Melanie assured her, her tone solemn, her expression serious. "Remember that."

Caroline nodded, unable to speak past the emotion that clogged her throat, trembling as a shiver of apprehension crawled up her back. Was she doing the right thing? She prayed God she wouldn't regret this decision a few months from now.

Straightening her shirtwaist, she followed Melanie to the door, where she stopped, glancing around the familiar dark lobby.

She might miss the vigorous world of the Sinclair Coffee Company, but she would be glad to leave New Orleans behind, glad to escape the strictures of a society into which she had never fit, a society that had always tried to crush her independence.

Bolstering her courage, Caroline walked through the front door and into the noisy bustle of Tchoupitoulas Street for the last time.

1

Caroline stood on the pier, watching uneasily as the mail boat rounded a bend in the river and disappeared from view. She dabbed her face with a damp handkerchief and gazed around, unease threatening to become genuine fear at the vast wildness of the jungle. A screech she now recognized as a macaw pierced the other sounds, sending an army of goose flesh up her arm.

At least he could have sent someone to meet me.

The jungle sweltered with tropical heat, even though the sun had begun to set in the western sky. A fragile breeze set the foliage at the tops of the tall trees in motion. She longed for its soothing touch to chase away the heat and the incessant gnats that hovered around her unprotected face. But the air at her level remained unaffected.

Unbuttoning the top few buttons of her bodice, Caroline dabbed at her moist throat, glancing at the dirty white sack the boat's pilot had dropped on the dock. Logically, she knew that if the inhabitants of this isolated, remote wilderness didn't know when to expect the mail boat, they certainly couldn't know when she would arrive. Still, the boat's captain had blown the whistle several times as they'd approached the pier. Surely someone must have heard. How long would she have to wait before someone realized she was here?

A feeling of unreality gripped her. During all the preparations, Brazil had seemed a world away, a vague dream. All she'd been able to think of was escaping the dull emptiness of her life in New Orleans and grasping at what might be her last chance at happiness. Now, as she stood on the very threshold of a new life in a savage wilderness awaiting a man she'd never laid eyes on, her heart grew faint.

A loud splash at the edge of the river startled her, and she gazed up to see a *cayman* slither slowly into the water, disappearing beneath a mantle of red and gold water lilies. They were smaller than the alligators in Louisiana, but here in the Amazon there were no cities bustling with people where the creatures wouldn't dare venture. This was their domain, and she was the intruder.

Fifteen years in the wild.

What would he be like after being cut off from civilization for so long? As she'd read his letters, she'd formed a mental image of Jason Sinclair as a polished, refined gentleman planter. But her long journey west from the mouth of the Amazon had opened her eyes to the primitive conditions he'd lived under. The towns where they'd stopped along the way could hardly be called towns at all, with the exception of Manaus, which had stood out in this boundless wilderness like a ruby in a pig's ear.

The few homes she'd seen along the way had been raised Indian huts. Most of them barely passed as dwellings. Some didn't even have walls but were just wooden frames with thatched roofs.

And the heat and the insects! She'd thought they were bad in New Orleans, but they were nothing compared to what she'd experienced here. Somewhere between the Amazon and the Rio Branco, she'd stopped wearing a corset—until today. Today she wanted to look her best, but the torturous garment had quickly become soaked with perspiration. The cloying fabric caused her skin to itch miserably.

Movement at the edge of the jungle caught her attention. A figure emerged from the rich verdure, moving toward her with the casual grace and strength of a jaguar. Her mouth went dry and she began to tremble with anticipation. Was this man walking toward her with long, sure strides her husband?

The closer he came, the larger and more commanding he appeared and the smaller and more vulnerable she felt. Tan breeches hugged muscled thighs, disappearing into black knee-high boots. She caught a glimpse of broad, muscled chest as he shrugged into a white shirt and worked at fastening the buttons.

The sultry air vibrated with male power as he drew near. He brought to mind the animals she'd seen at the circus—restrained for the moment, but always there was the sense of wildness just below the surface.